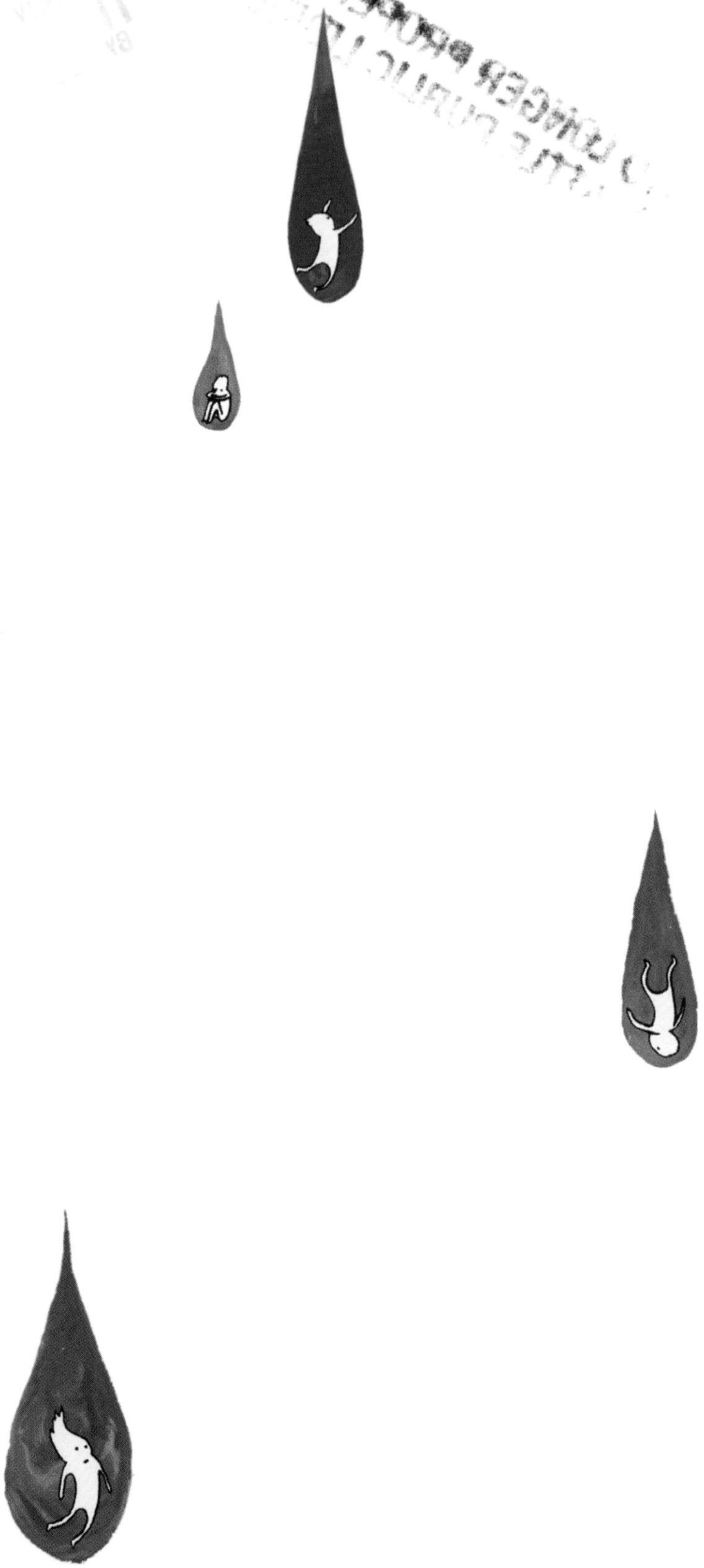

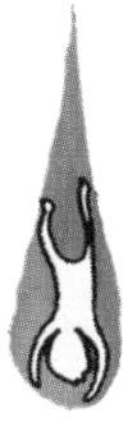

12

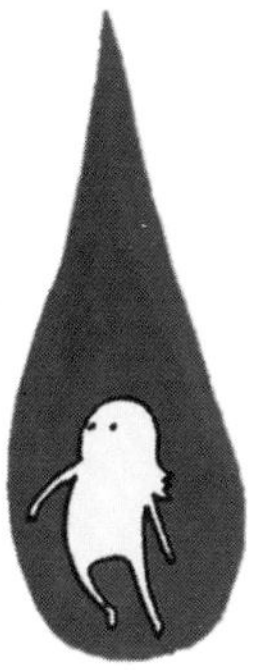

manix abrera

FOR YOU, DEAR READER,
WHERE INFINITE STORIES
ABOUND. ☻

manix

For Ablaze

Managing Editor
Rich Young

Editor
Kevin Ketner

Designers
Rodolfo Muraguchi
Cinthia Takeda Caetano

Publisher's Cataloging-in-Publication data

Names: Abrera, Manix, author.
Title: Manix Abrera's 12 / Manix Abrera.
Description: Portland, OR: Ablaze, 2022.
Identifiers: ISBN 978-1-68497-000-1
Subjects: LCSH Short stories, Philippines—Comic books, strips, etc. | Graphic novels. |
BISAC COMICS & GRAPHIC NOVELS / General
Classification: LCC PN6790.P5.A37 2022 | DDC 741.5—dc23

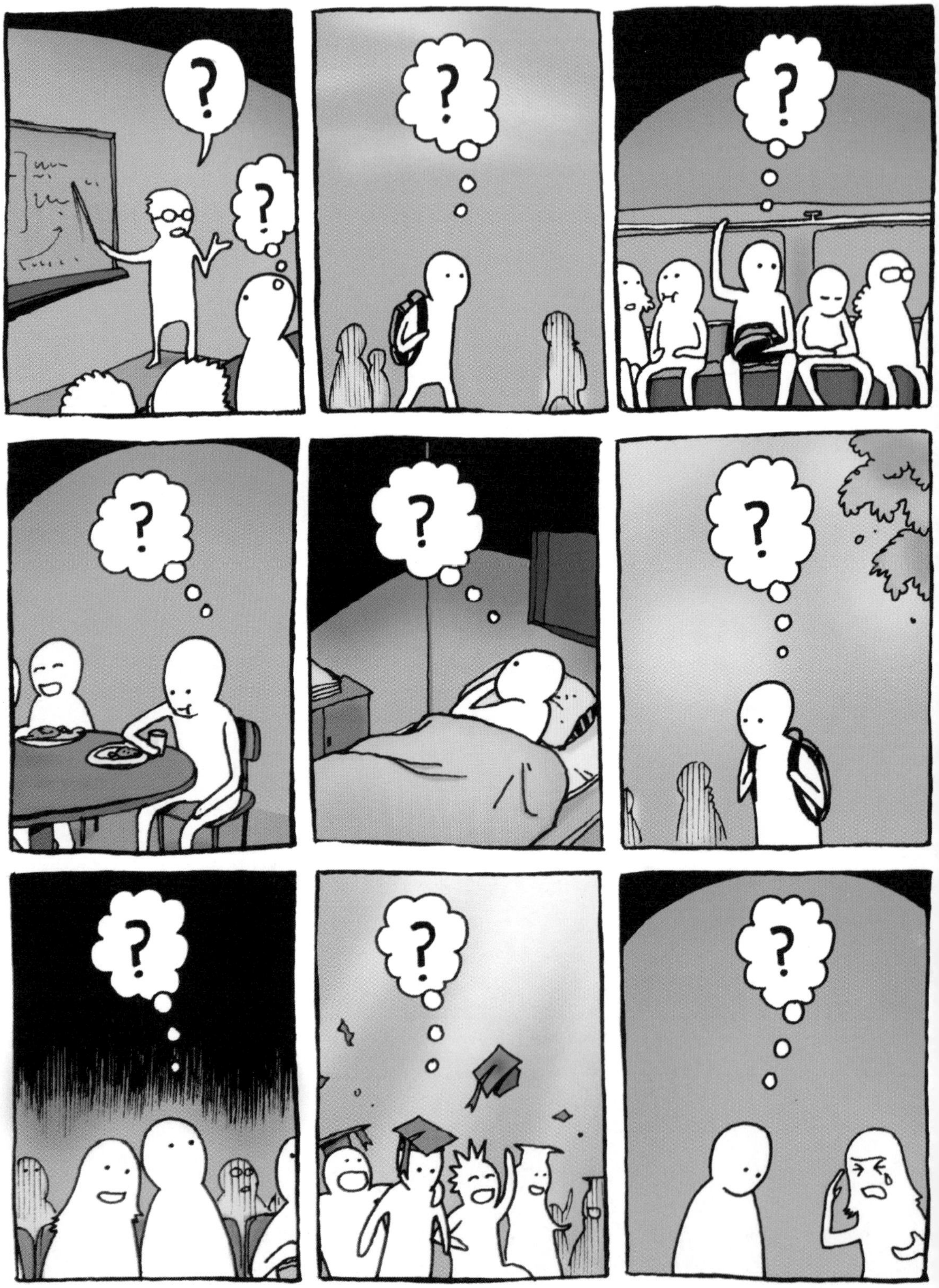
?
?
?
?
?
?
?
?
?
?

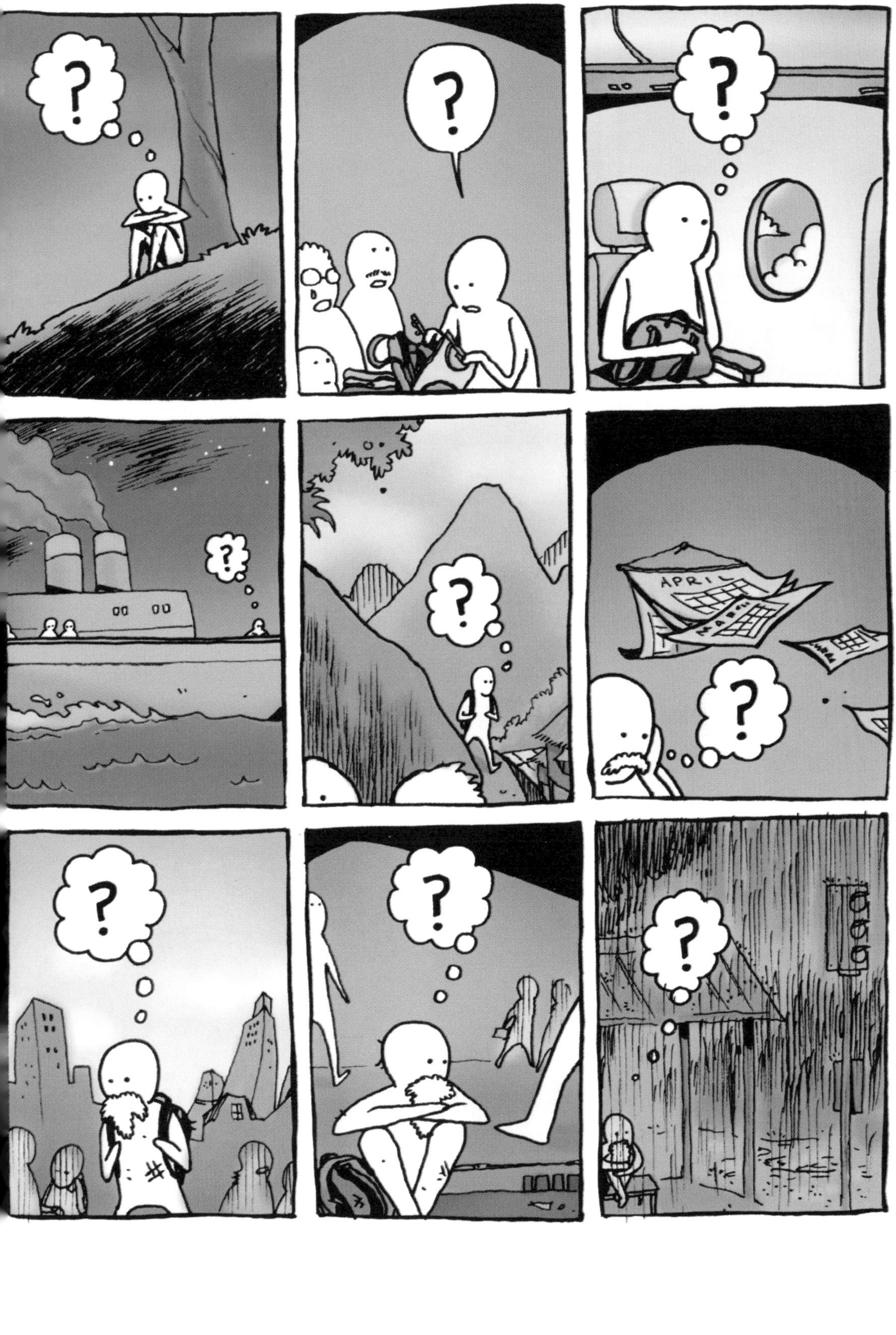
?
?
?
?
?
APRIL
?
?
?
?

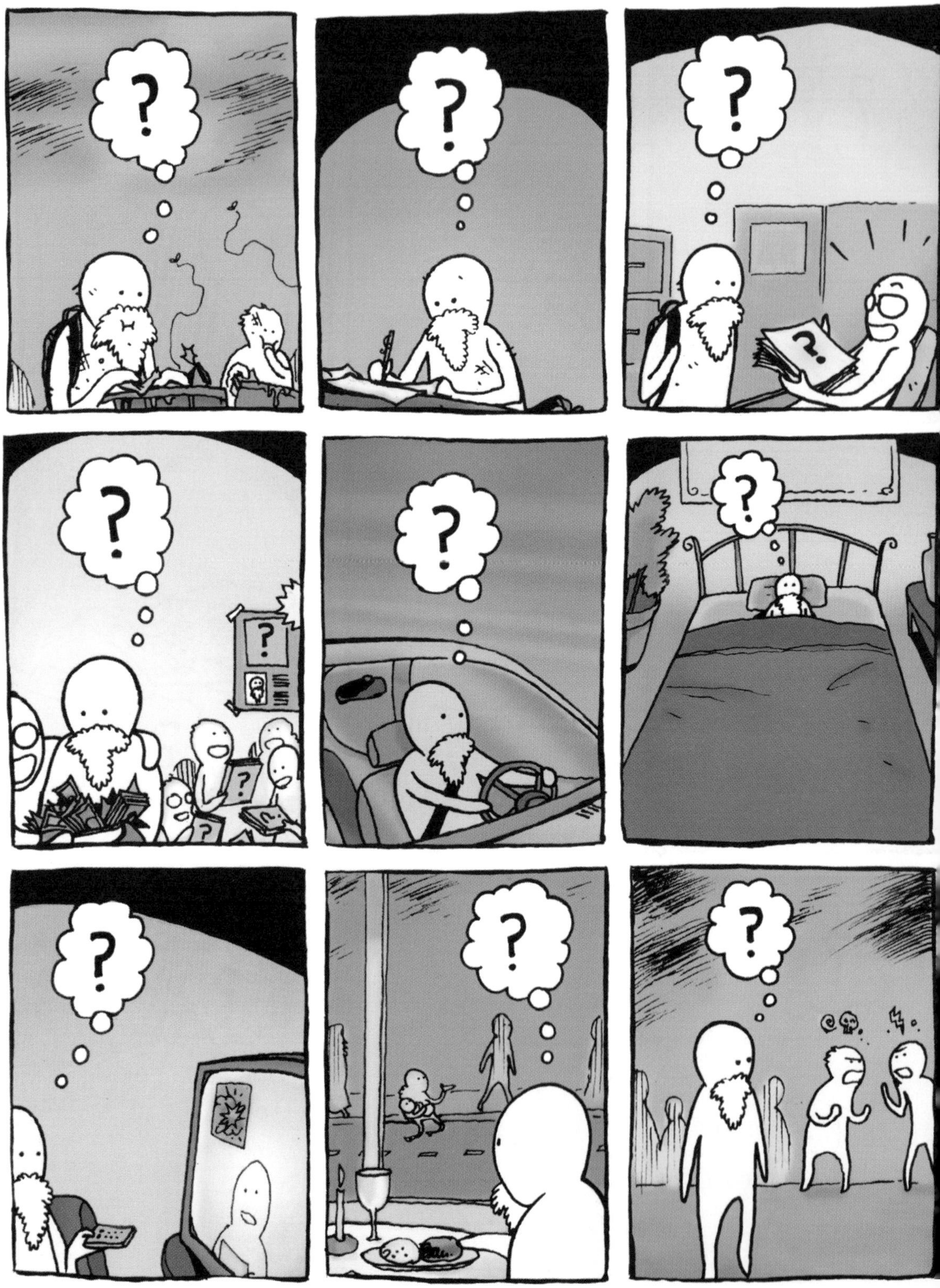
?
?
?
?
?
?
?
?
?

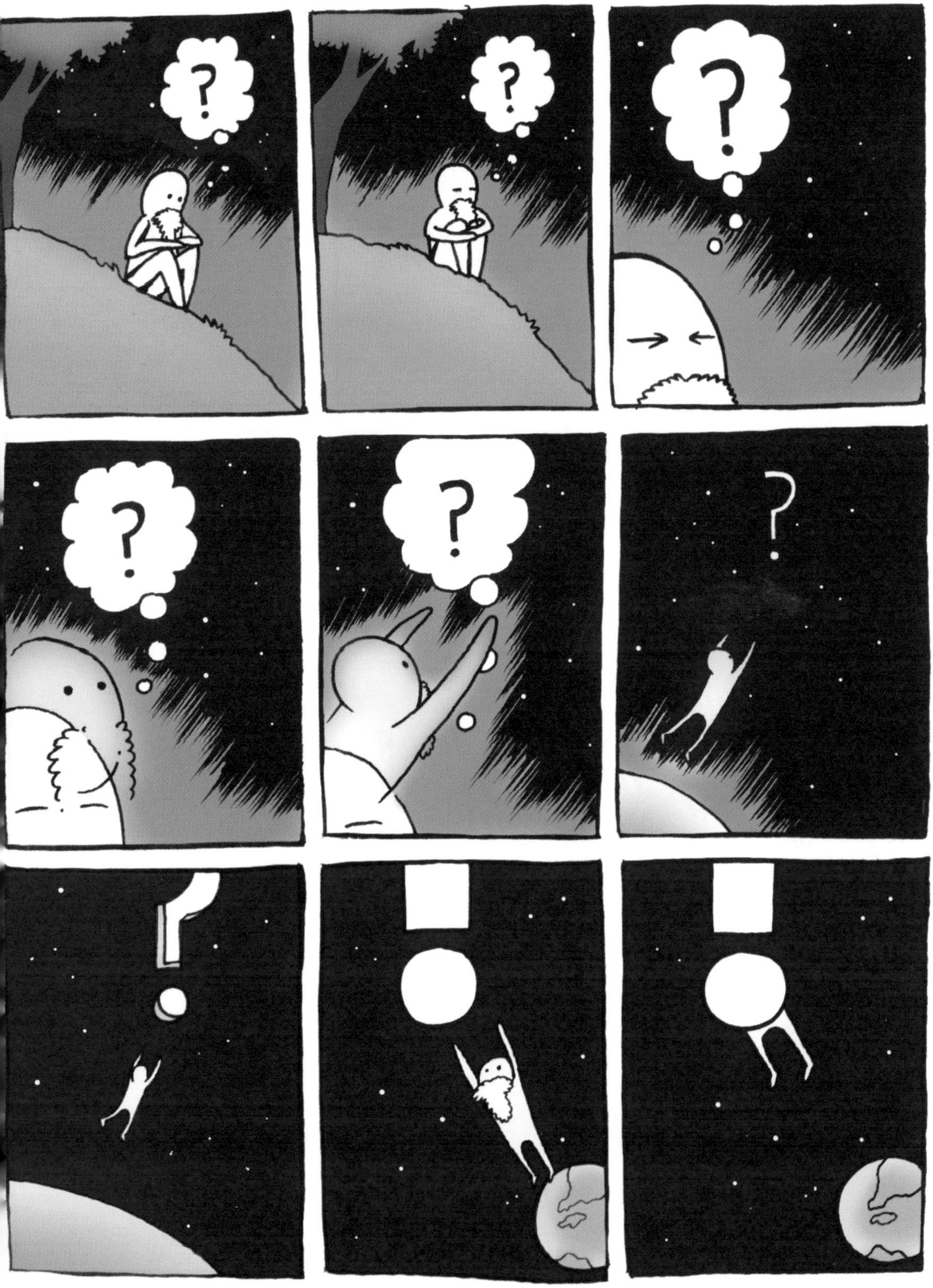

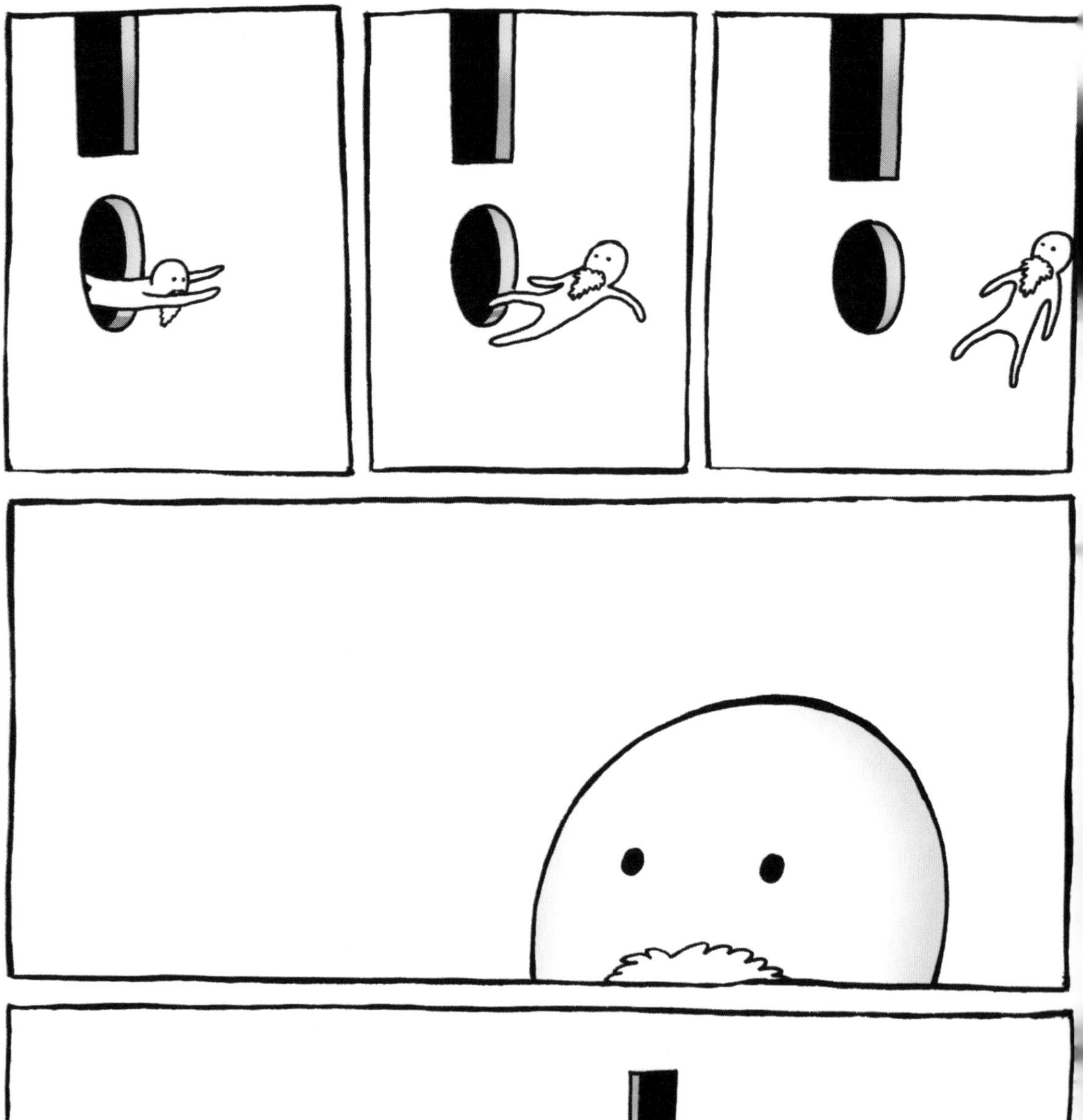

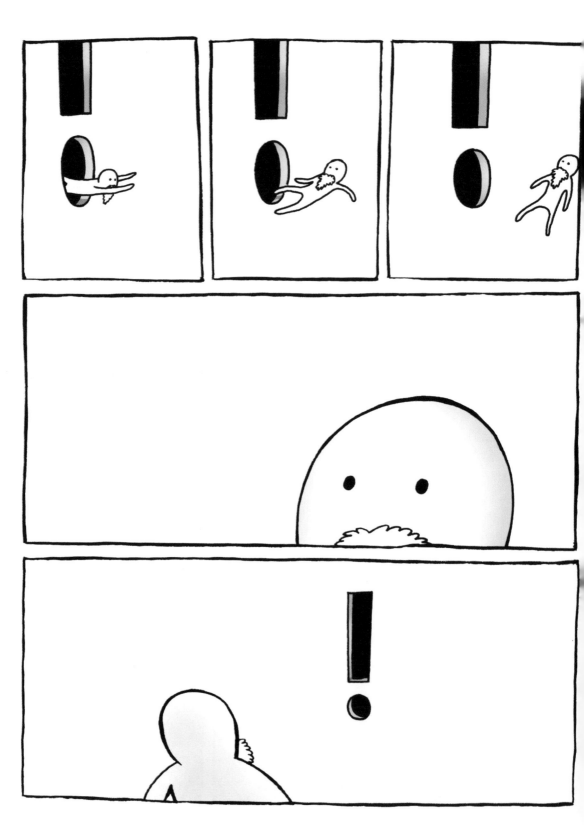

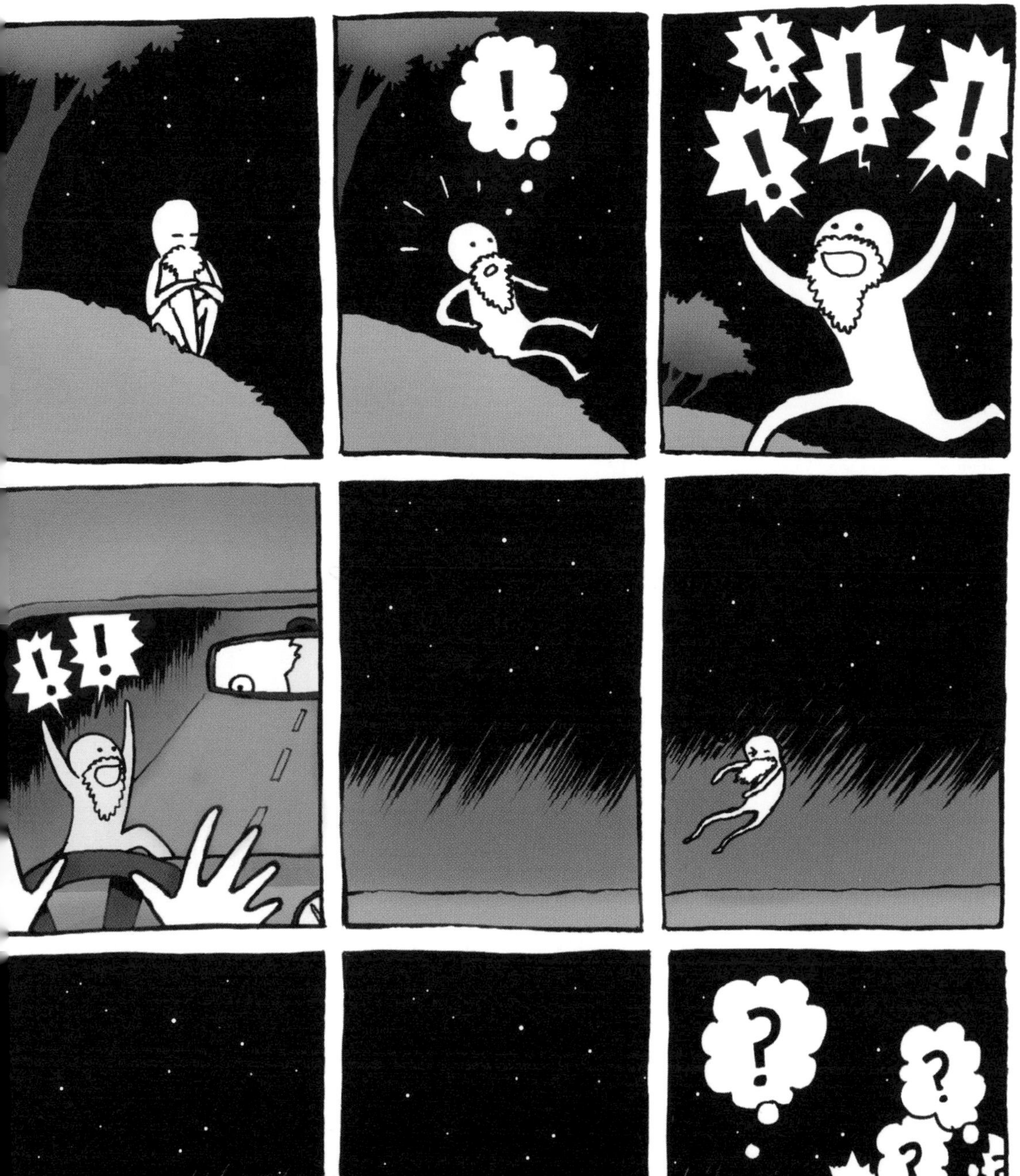
!
!
!
!
!
!
!
?
?
?
?

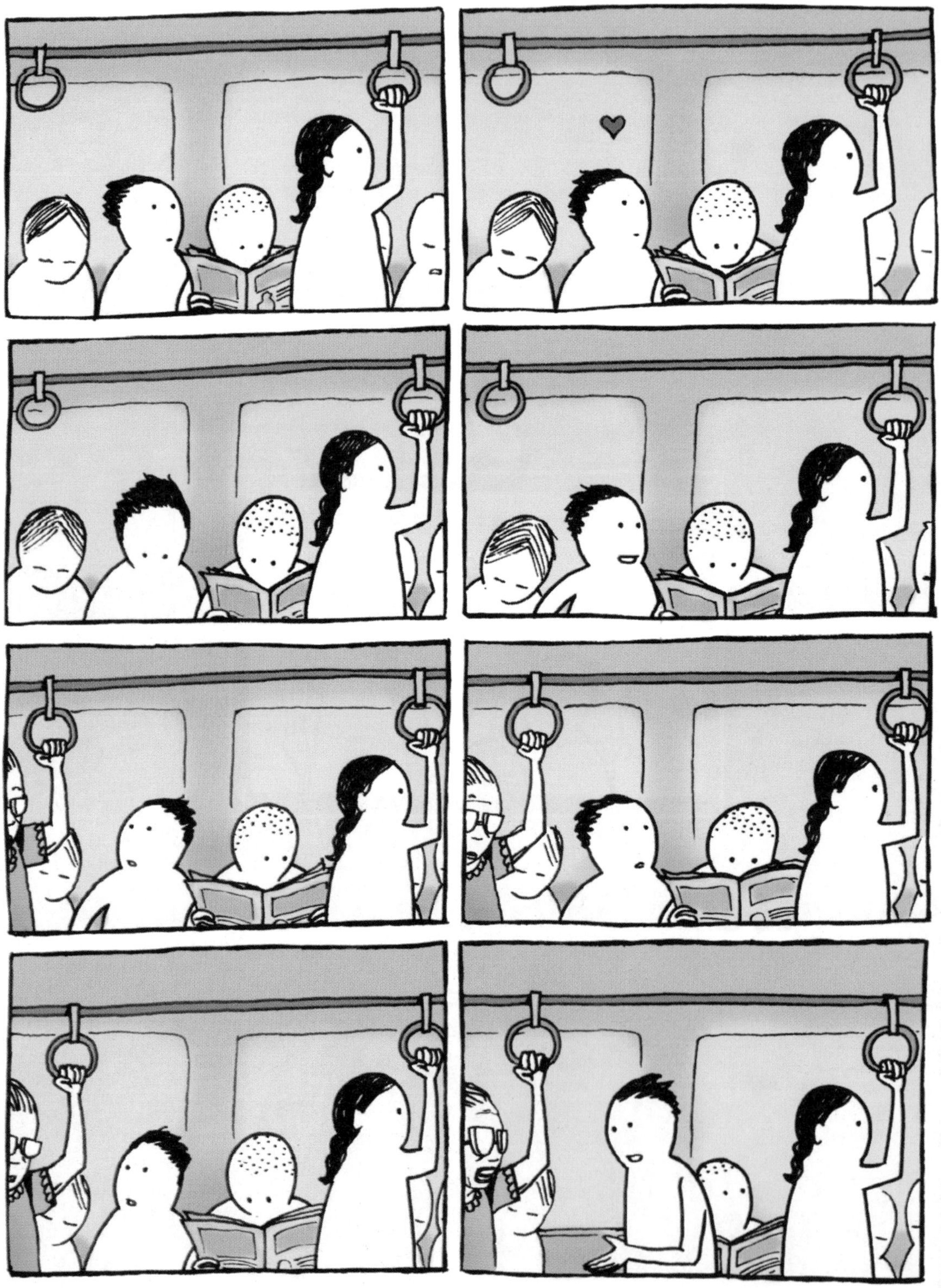

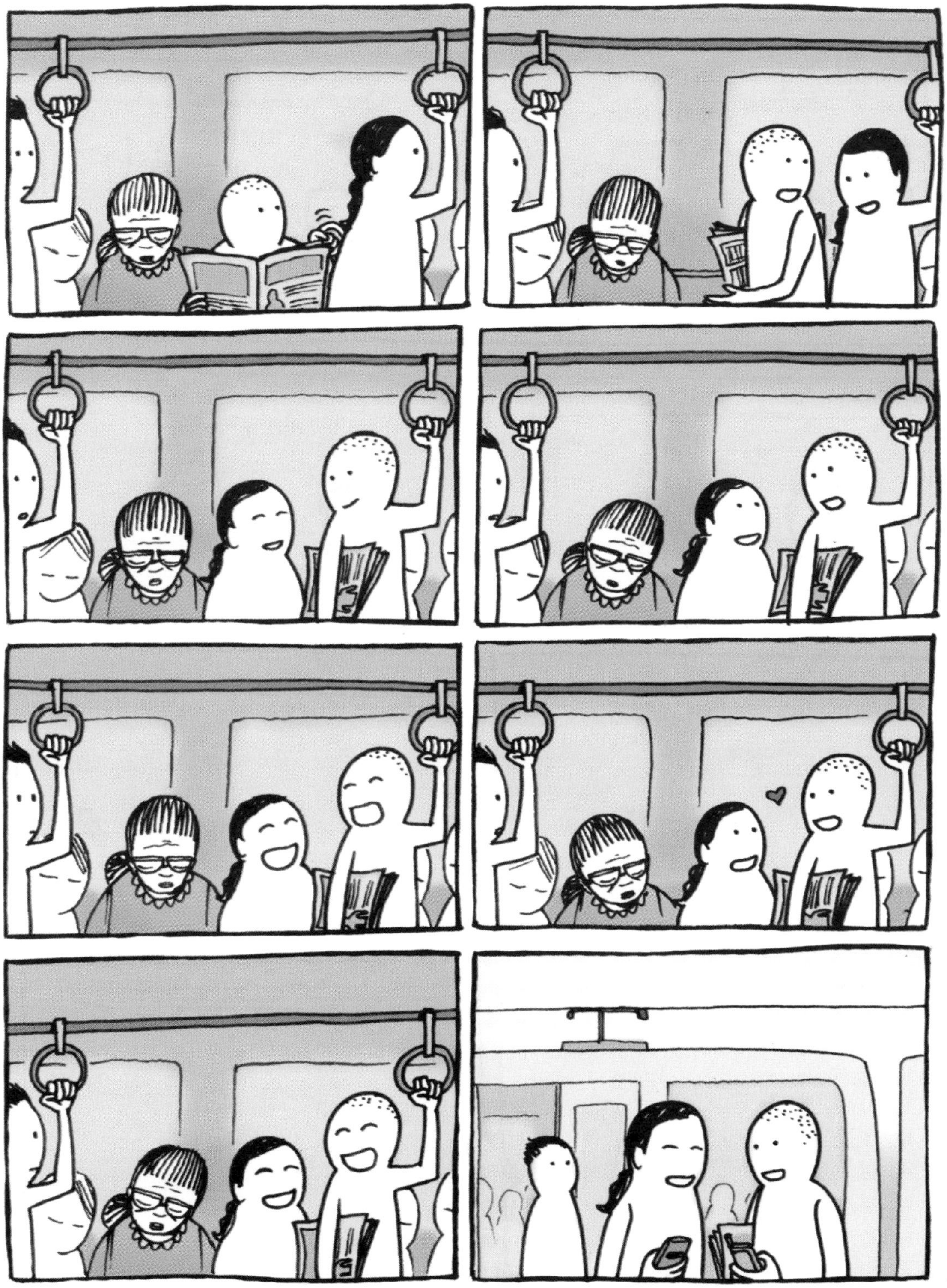

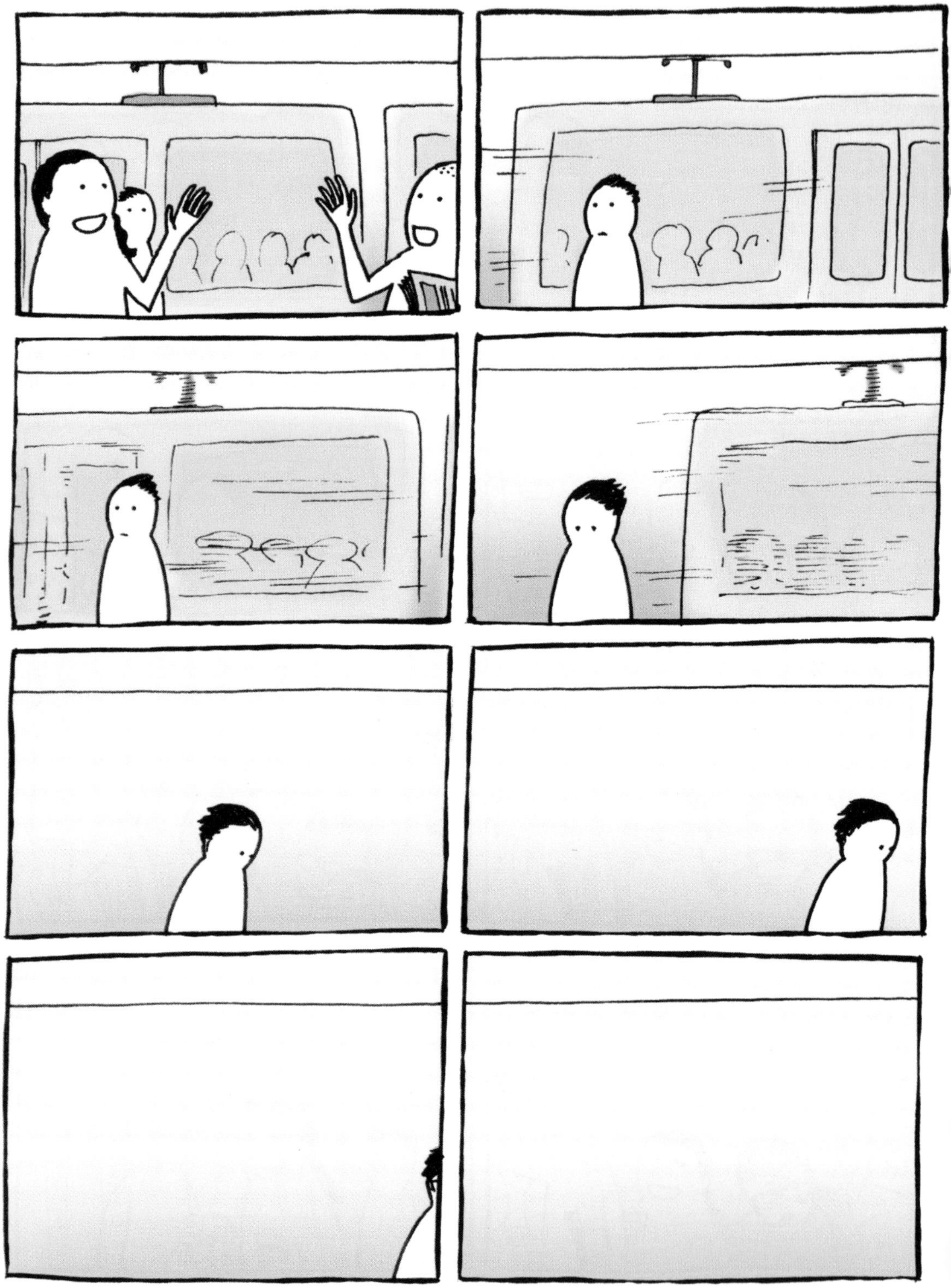

3

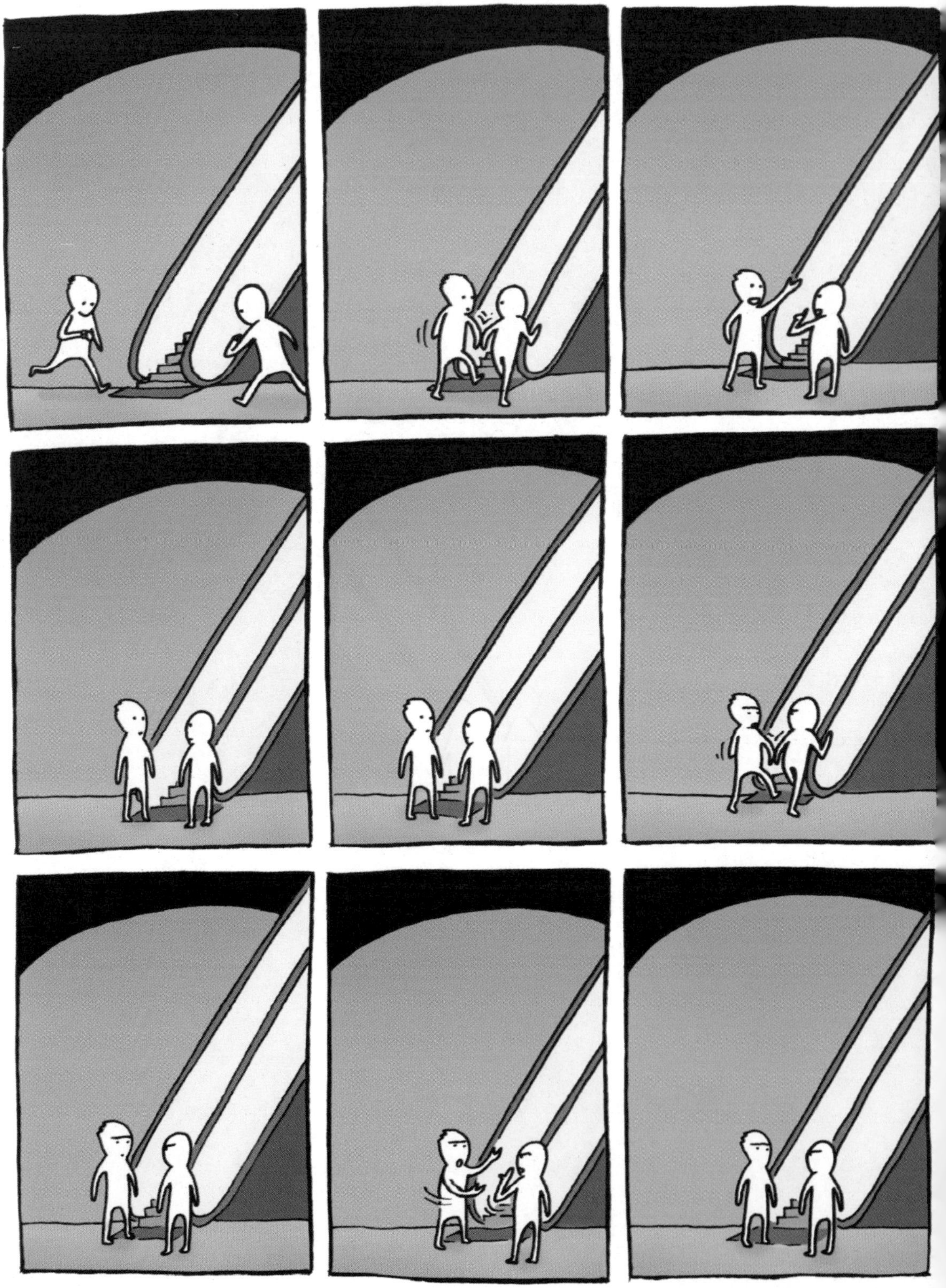

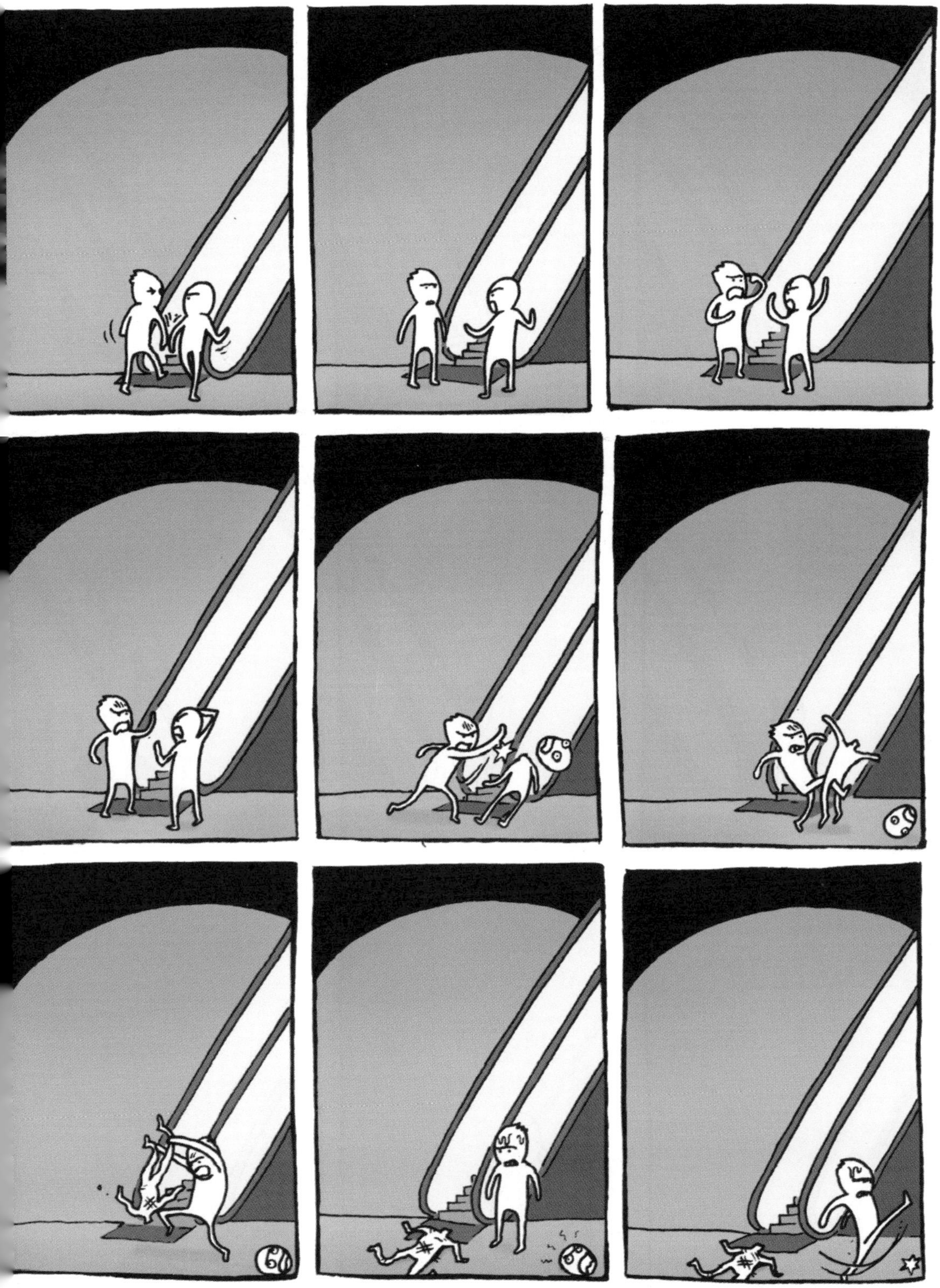

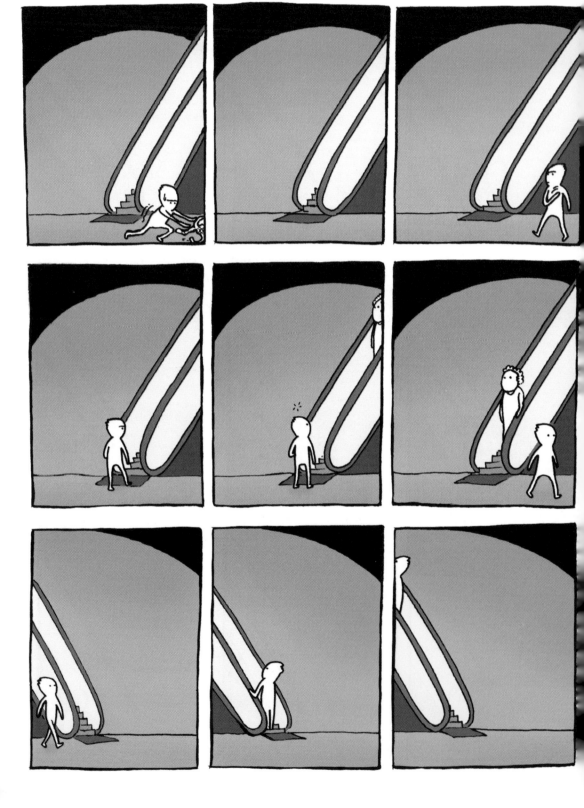

4

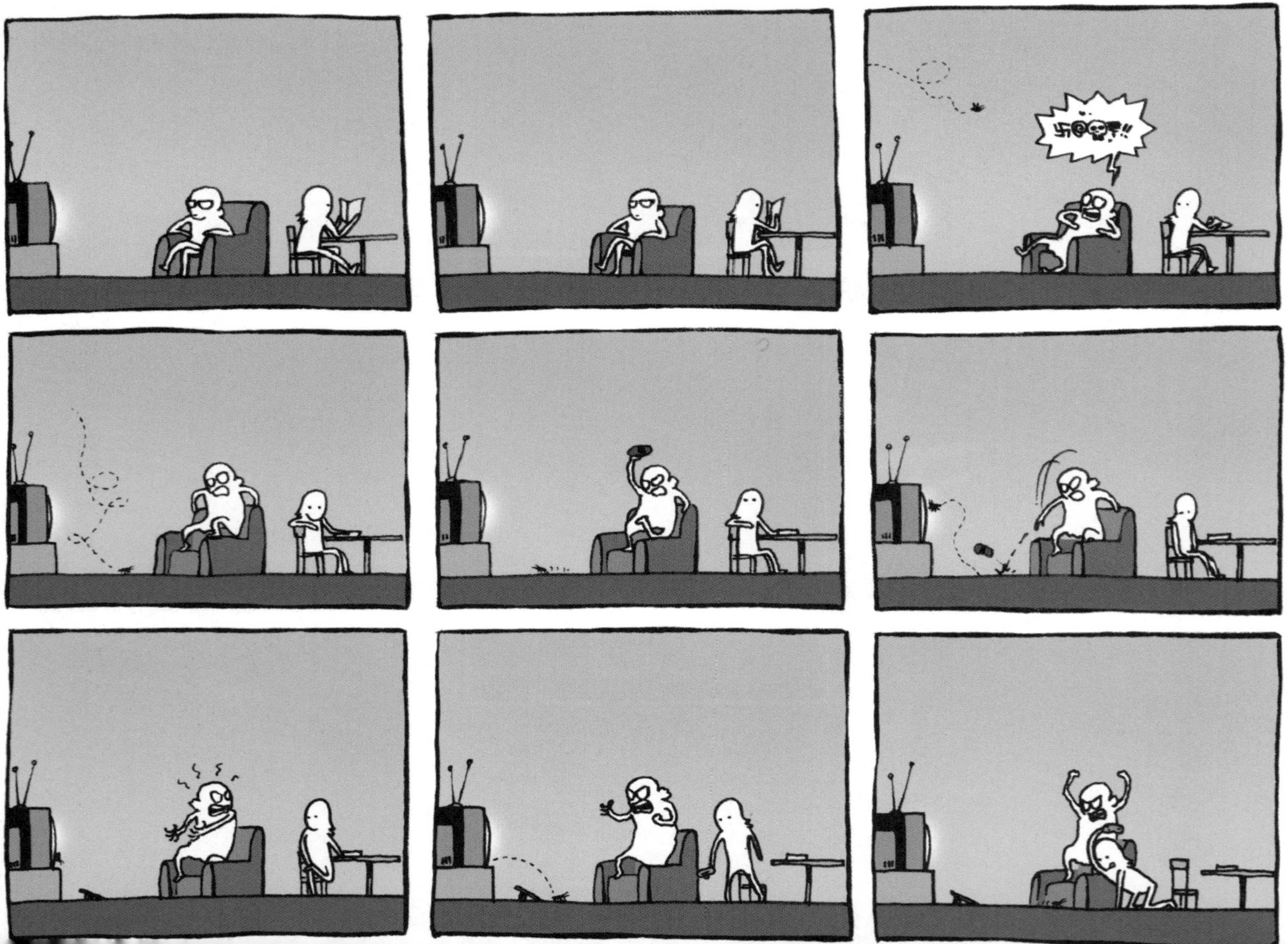

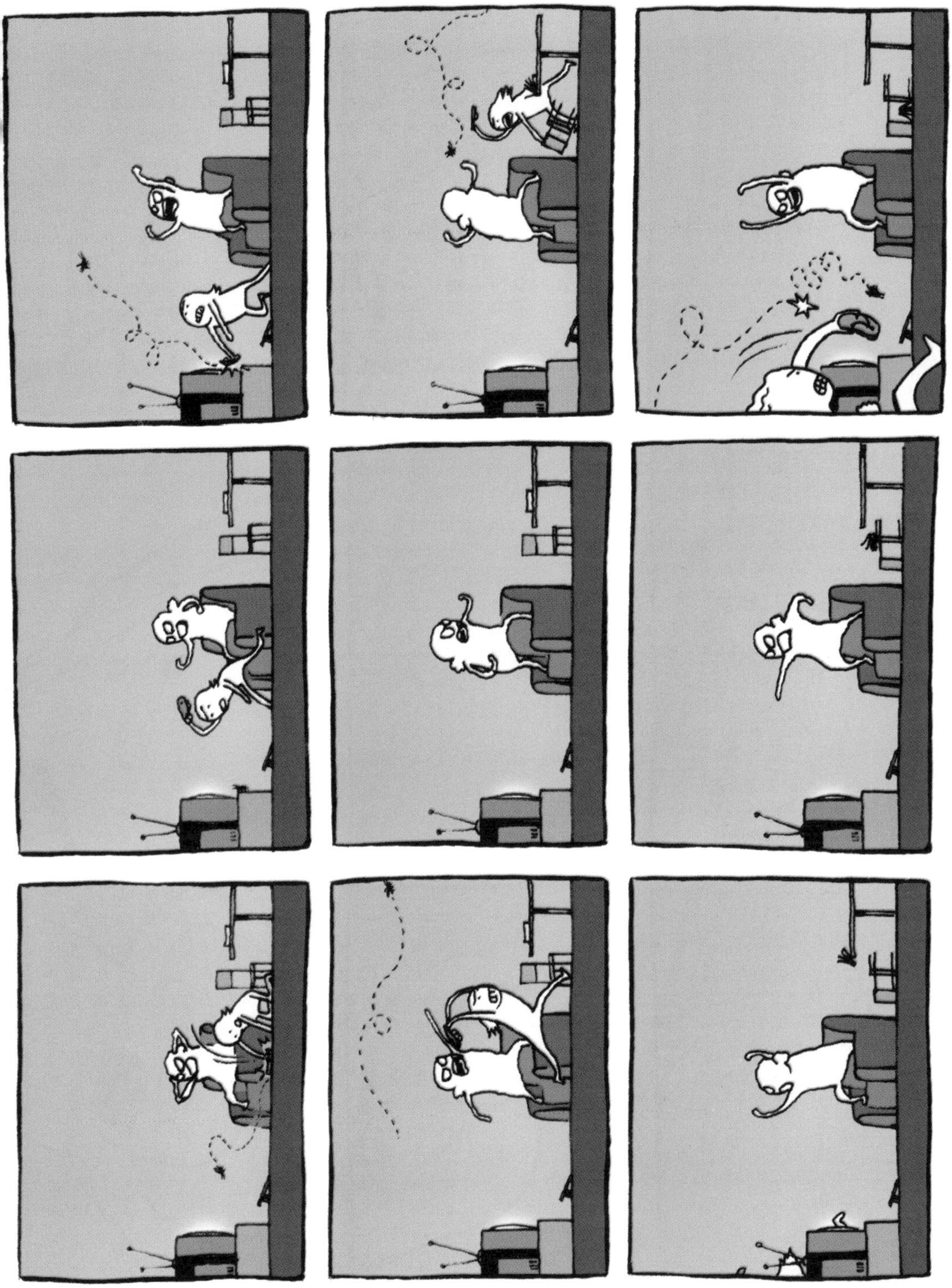

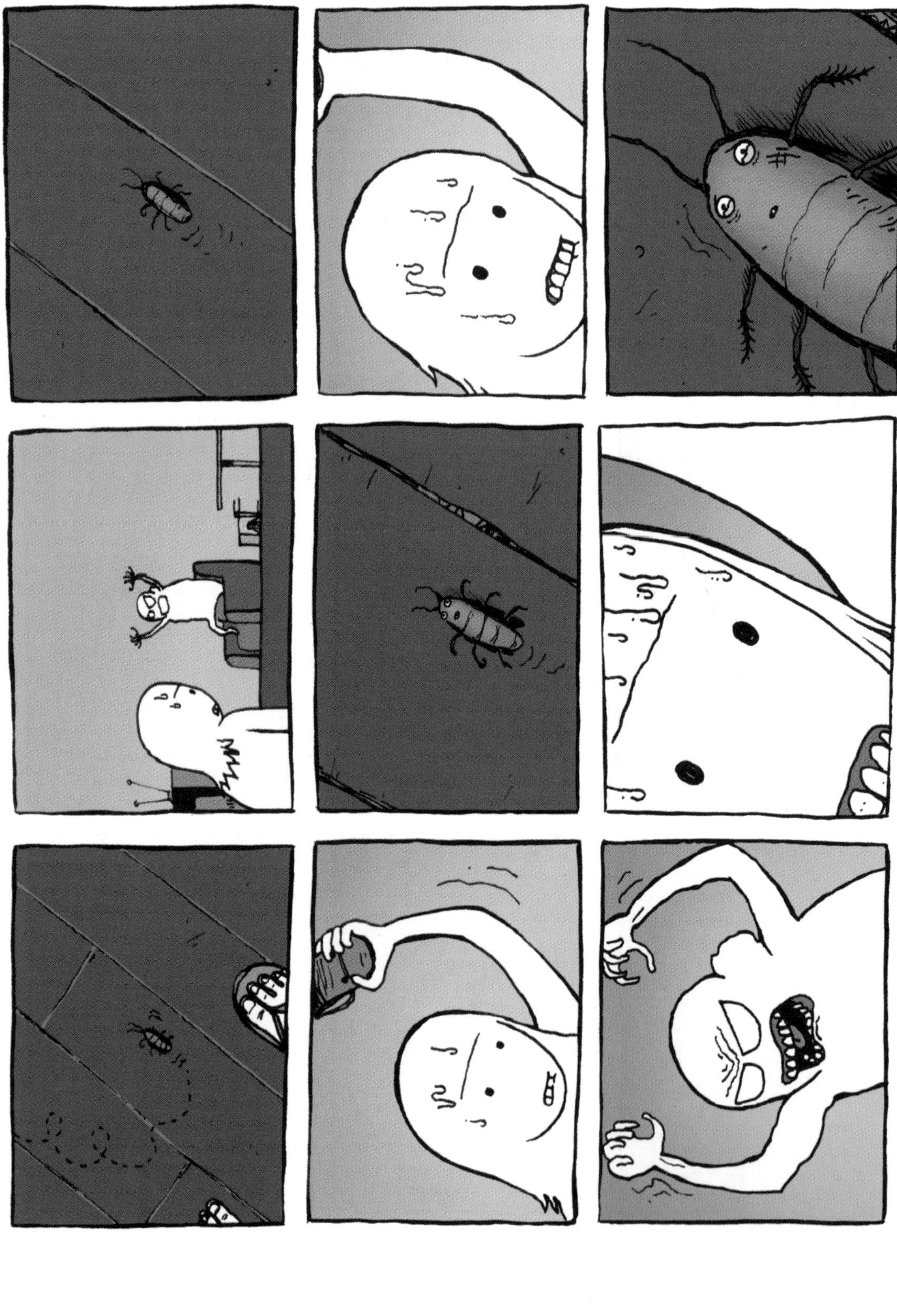

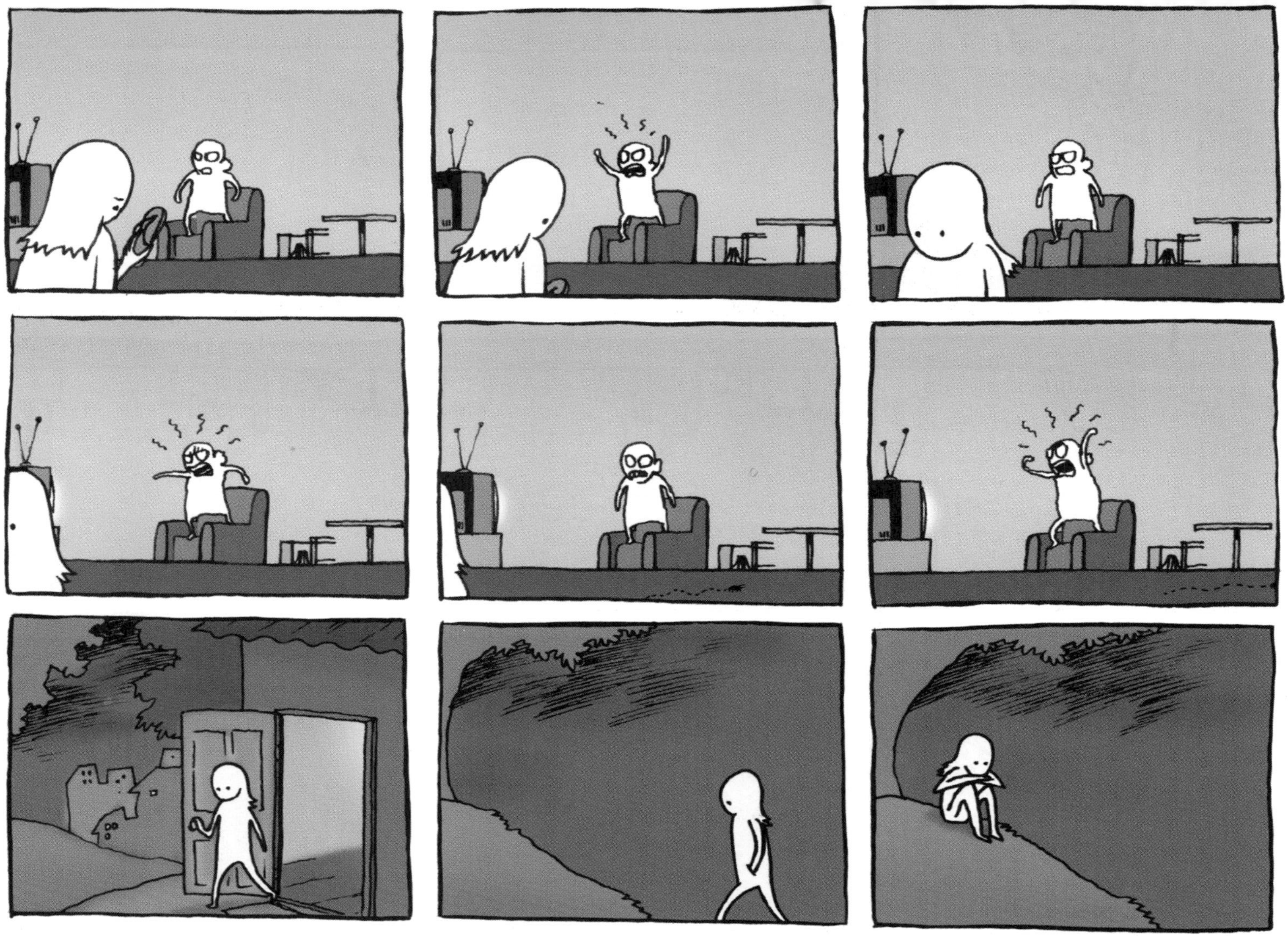

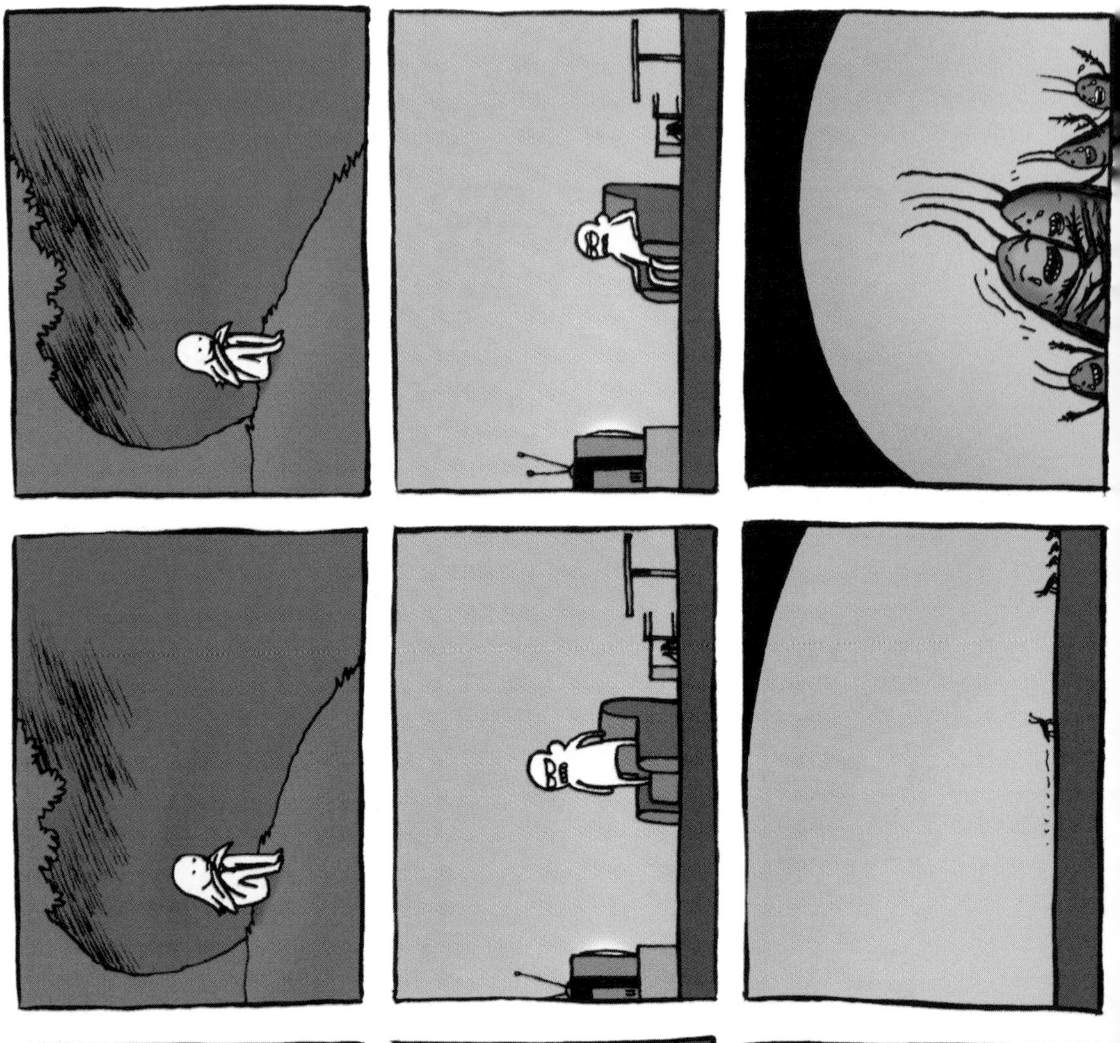

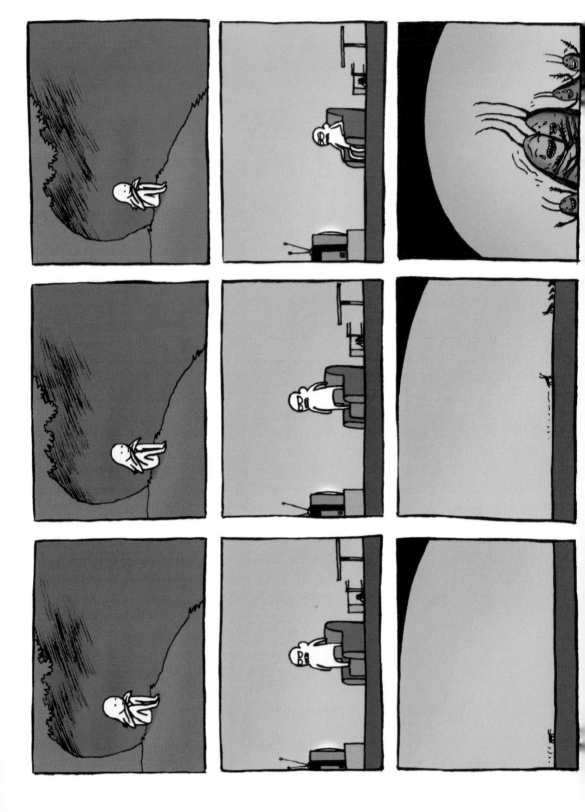

5

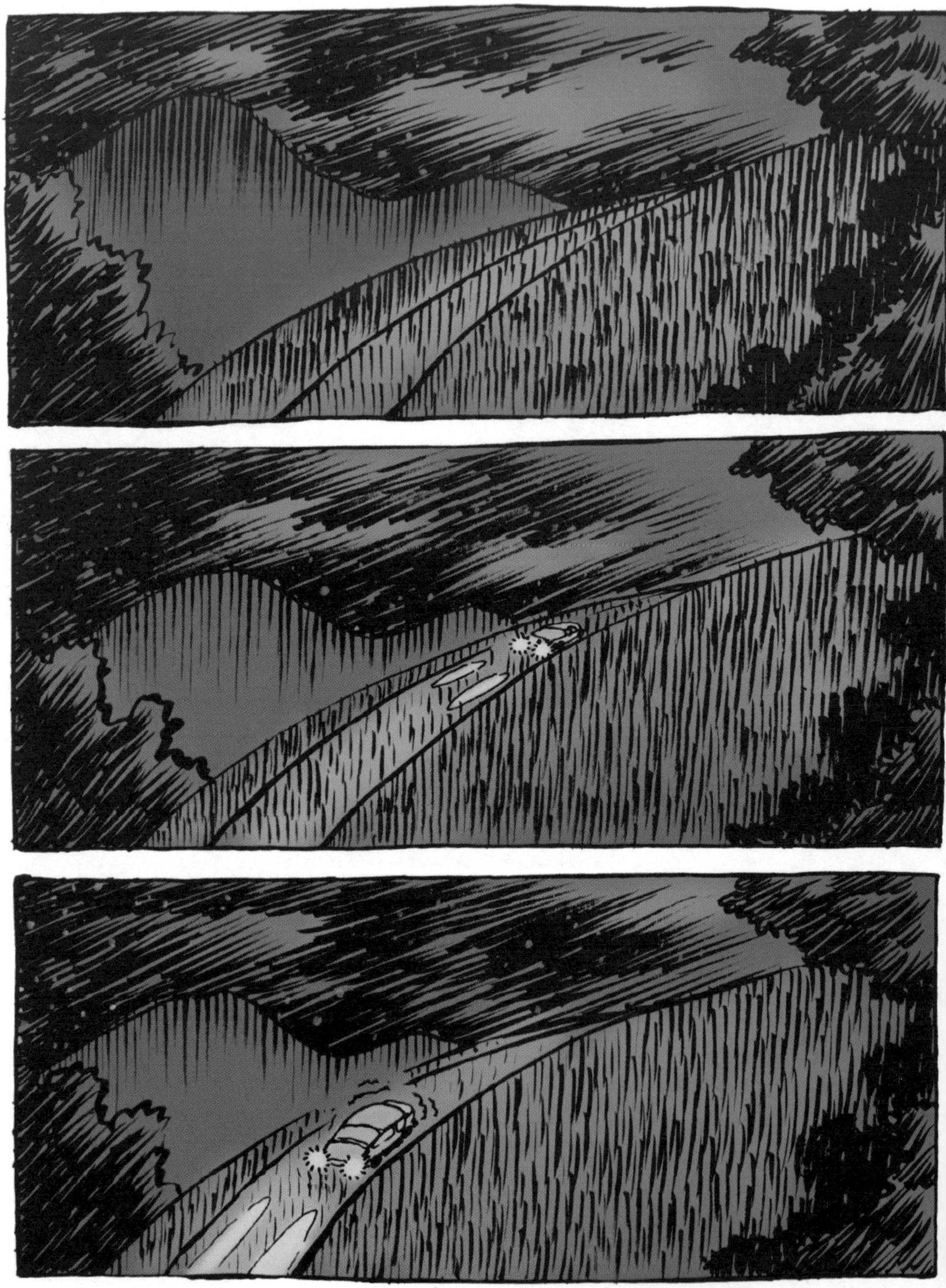

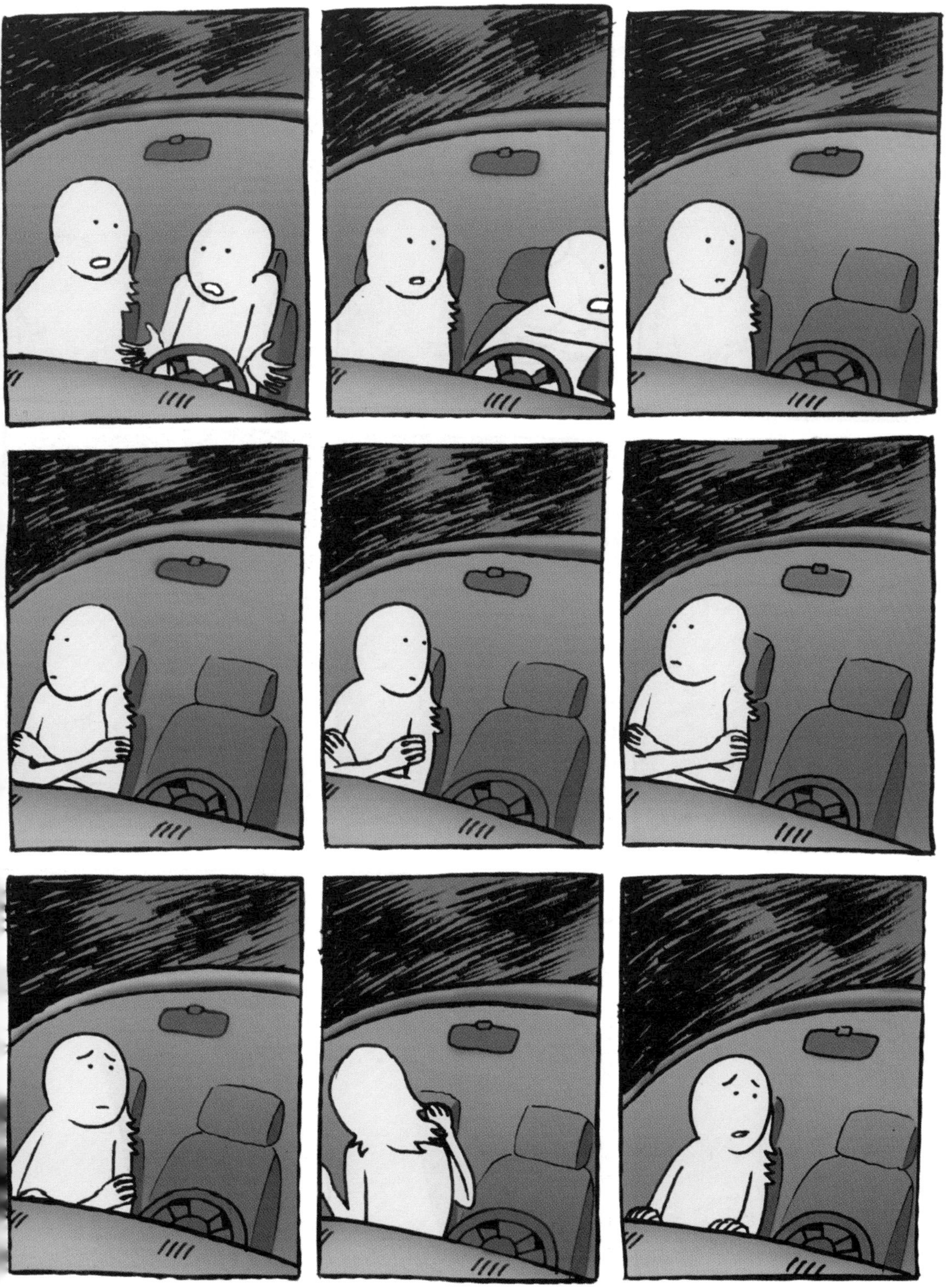

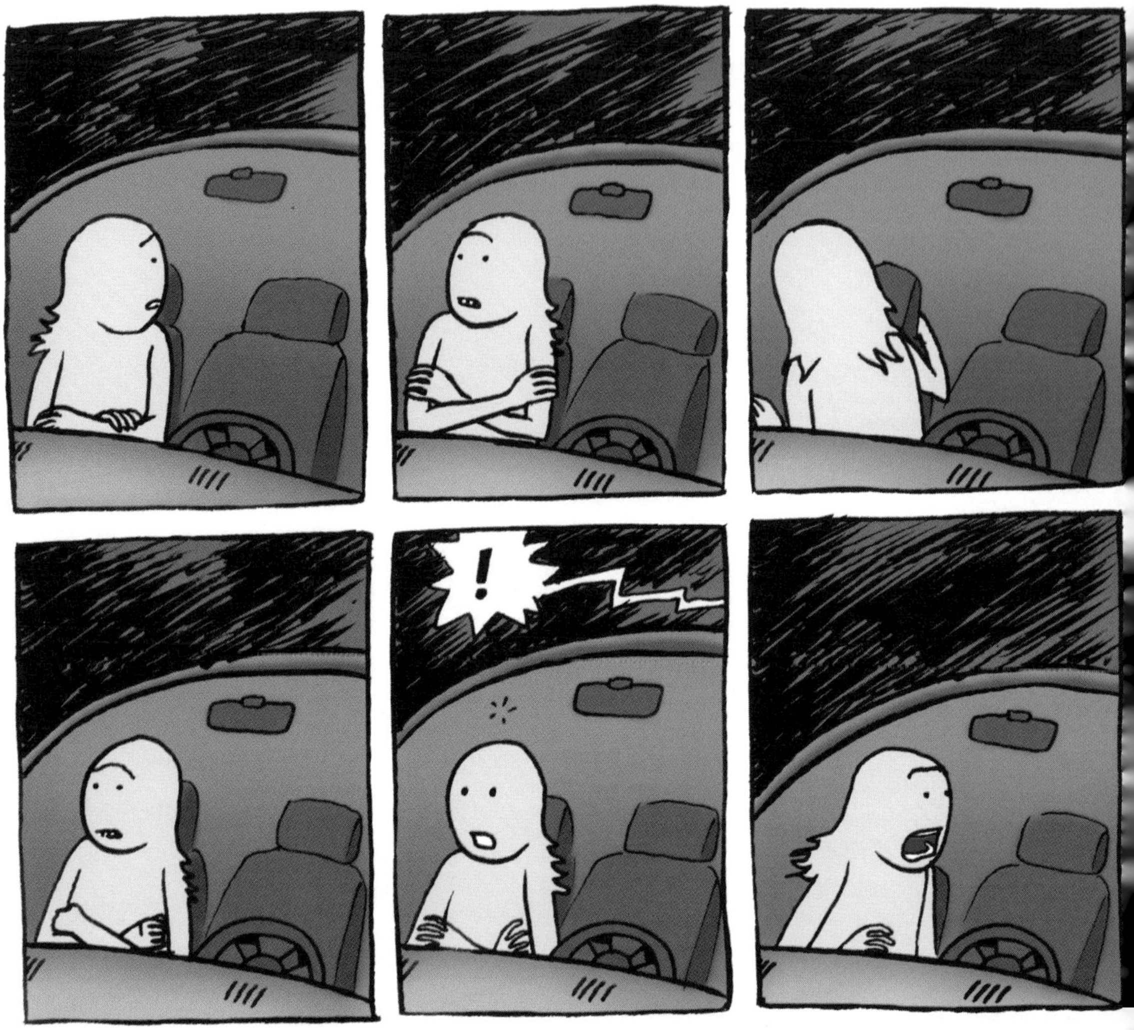
!

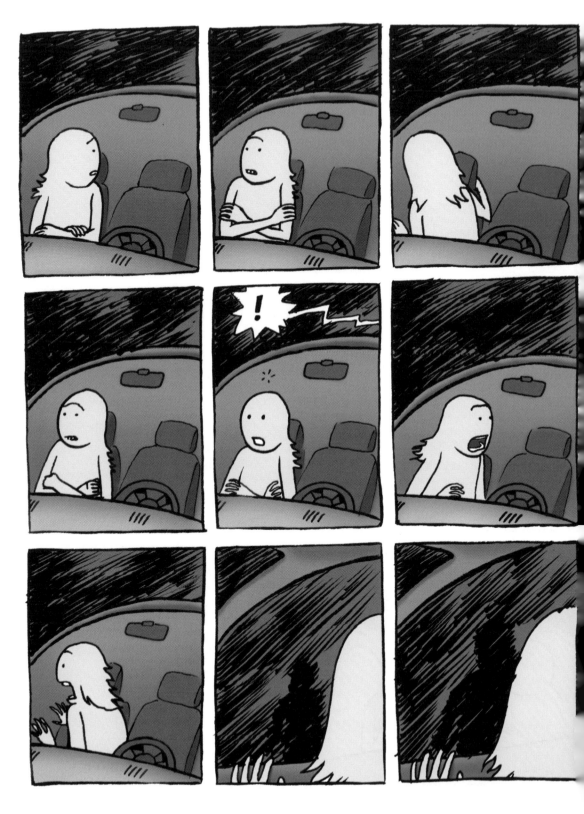

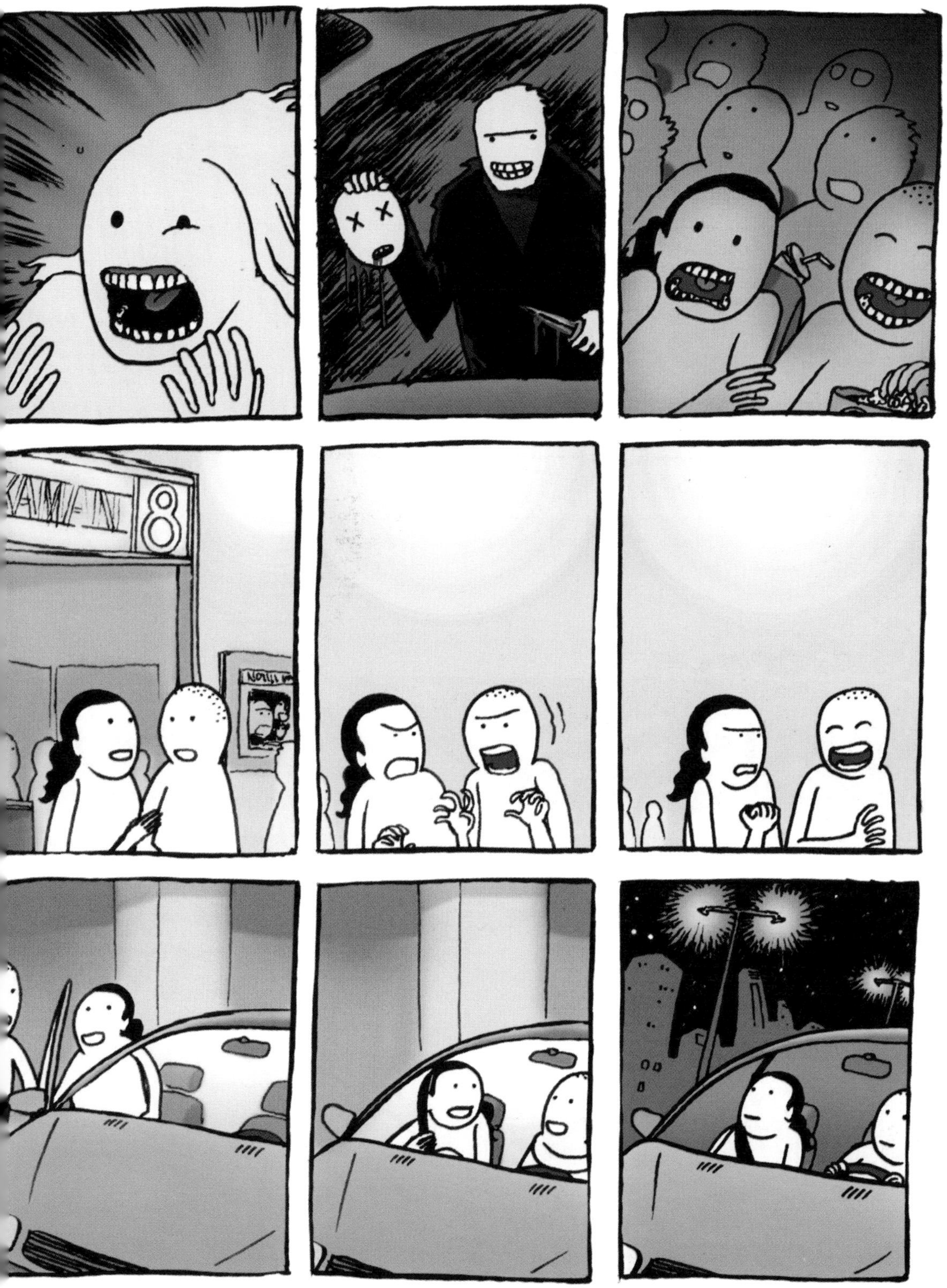

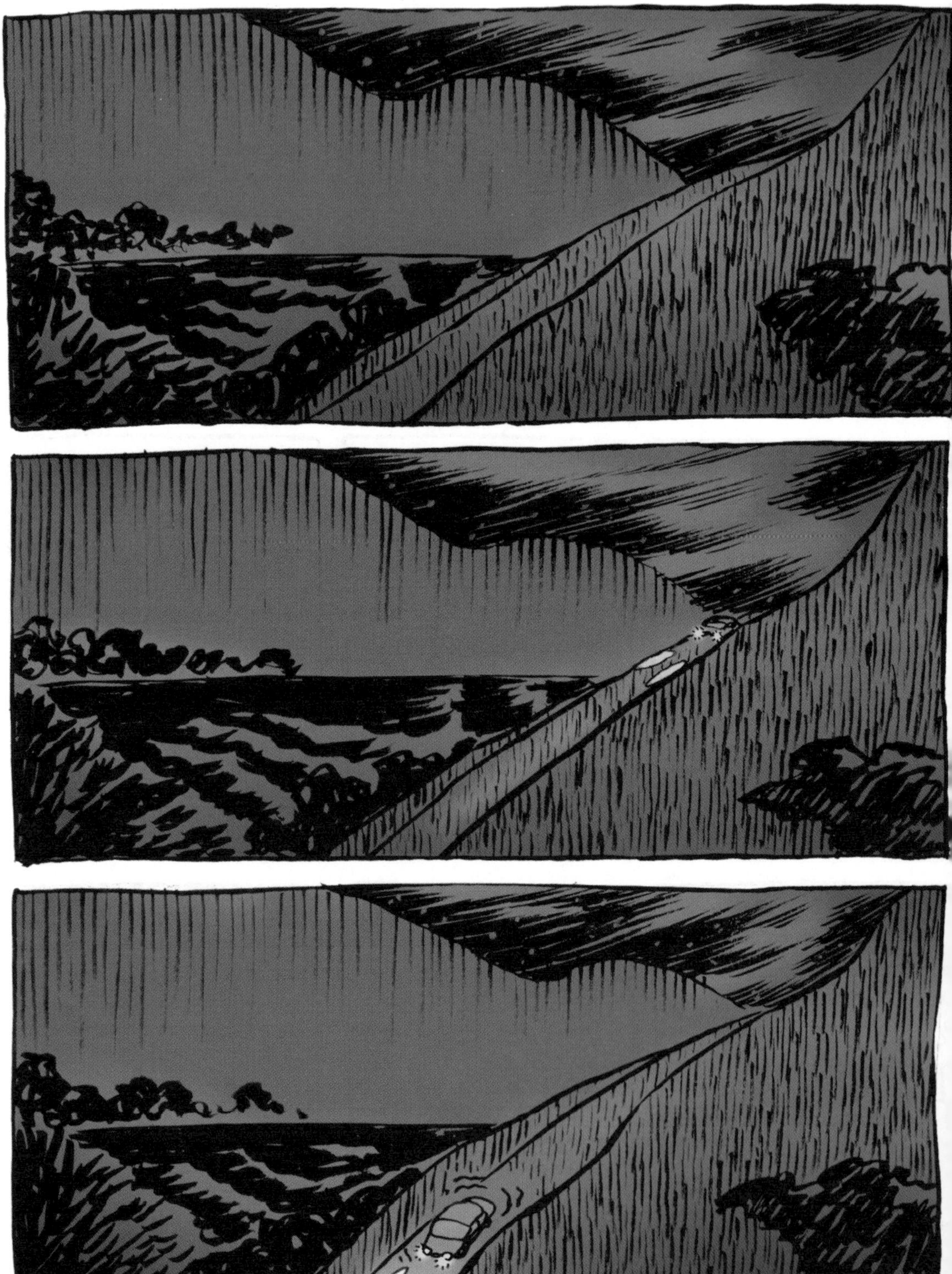

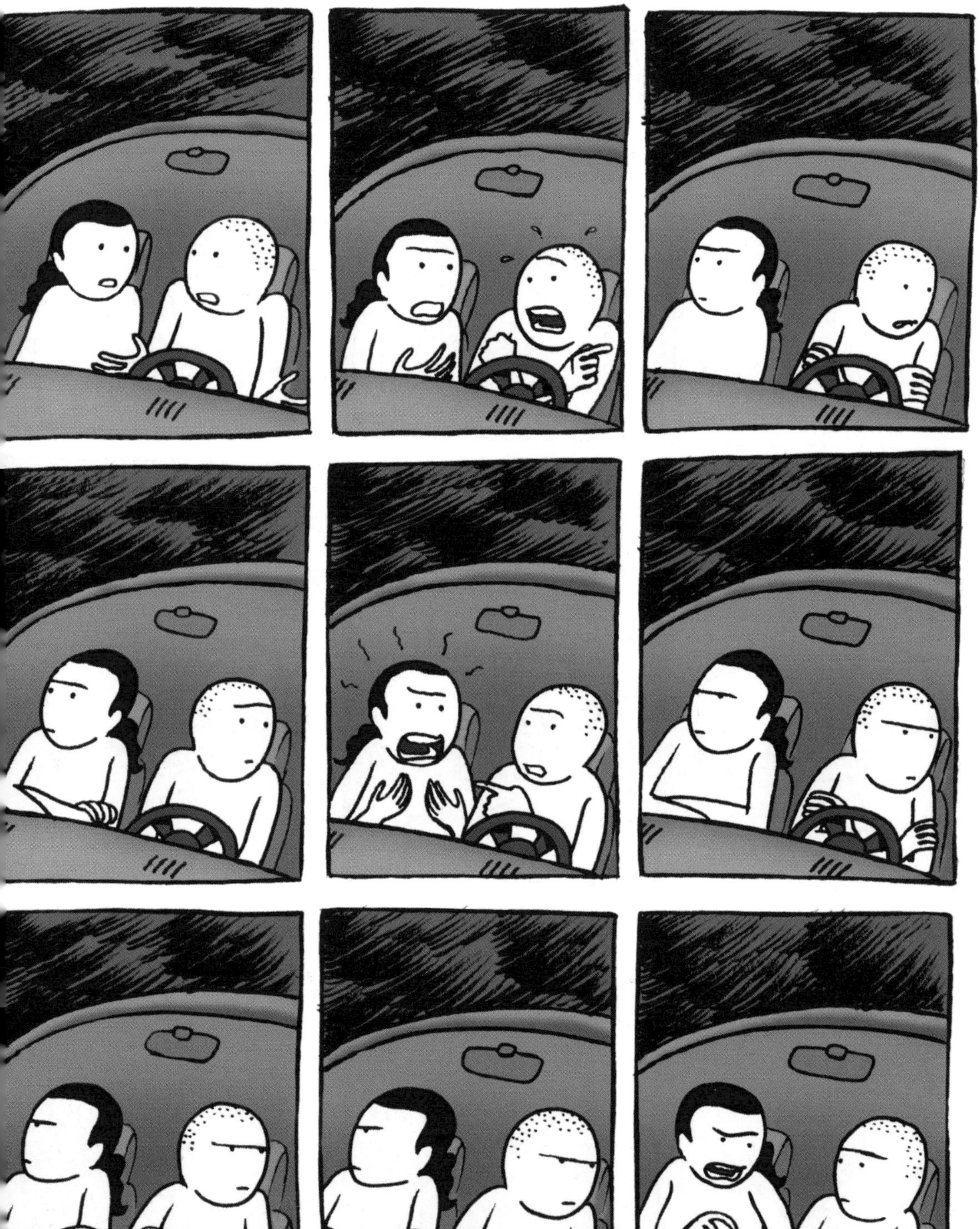

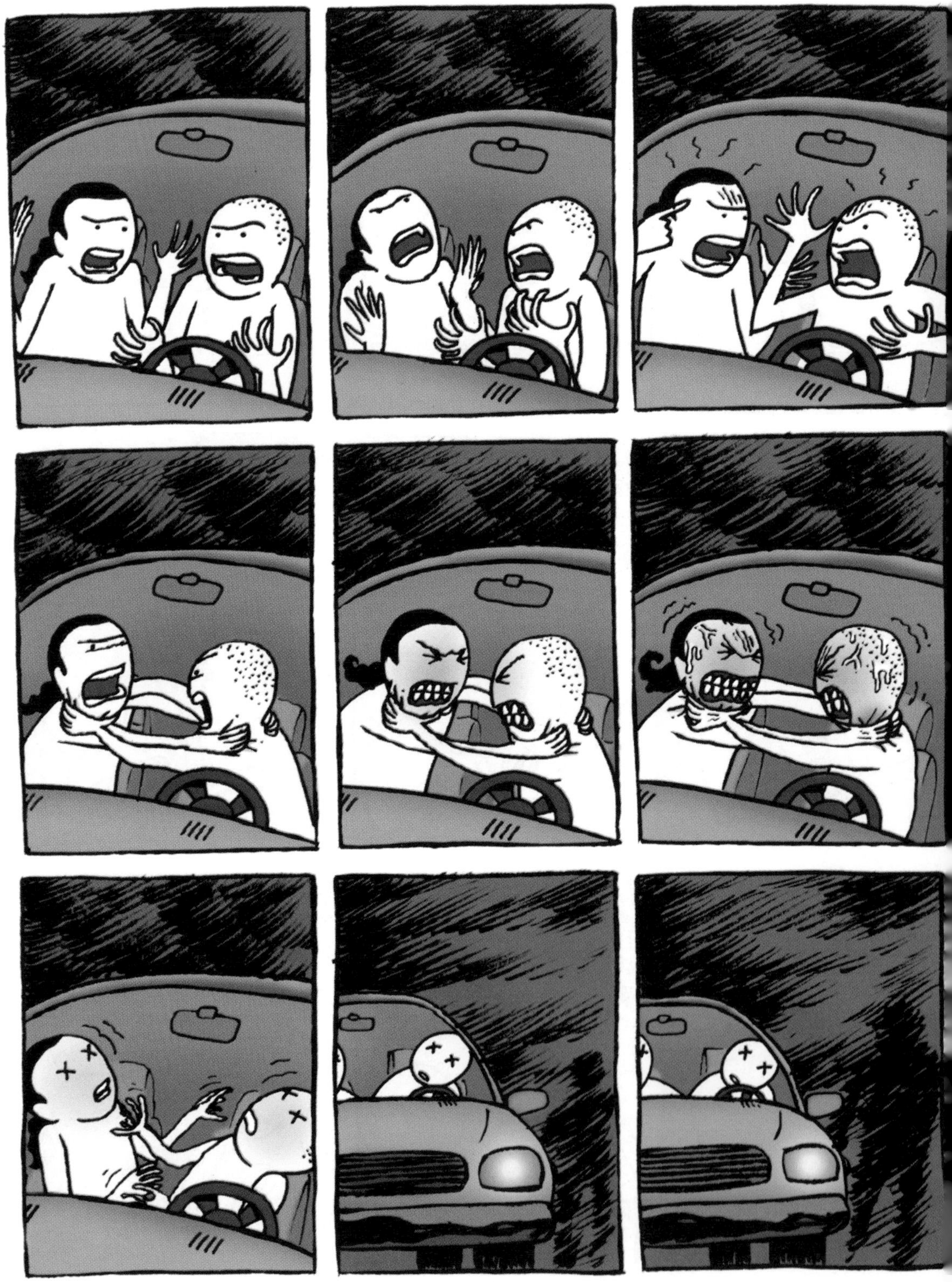

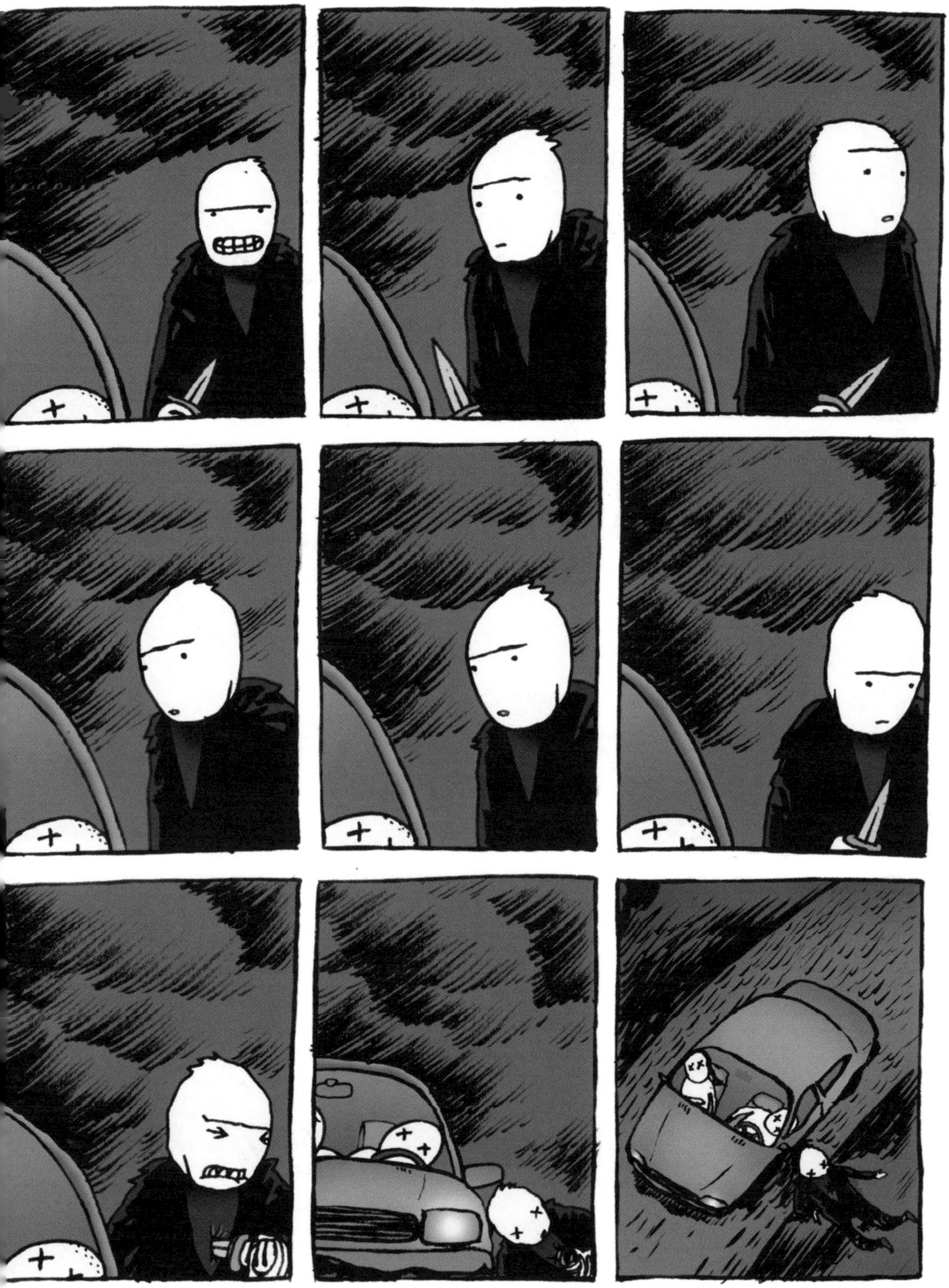

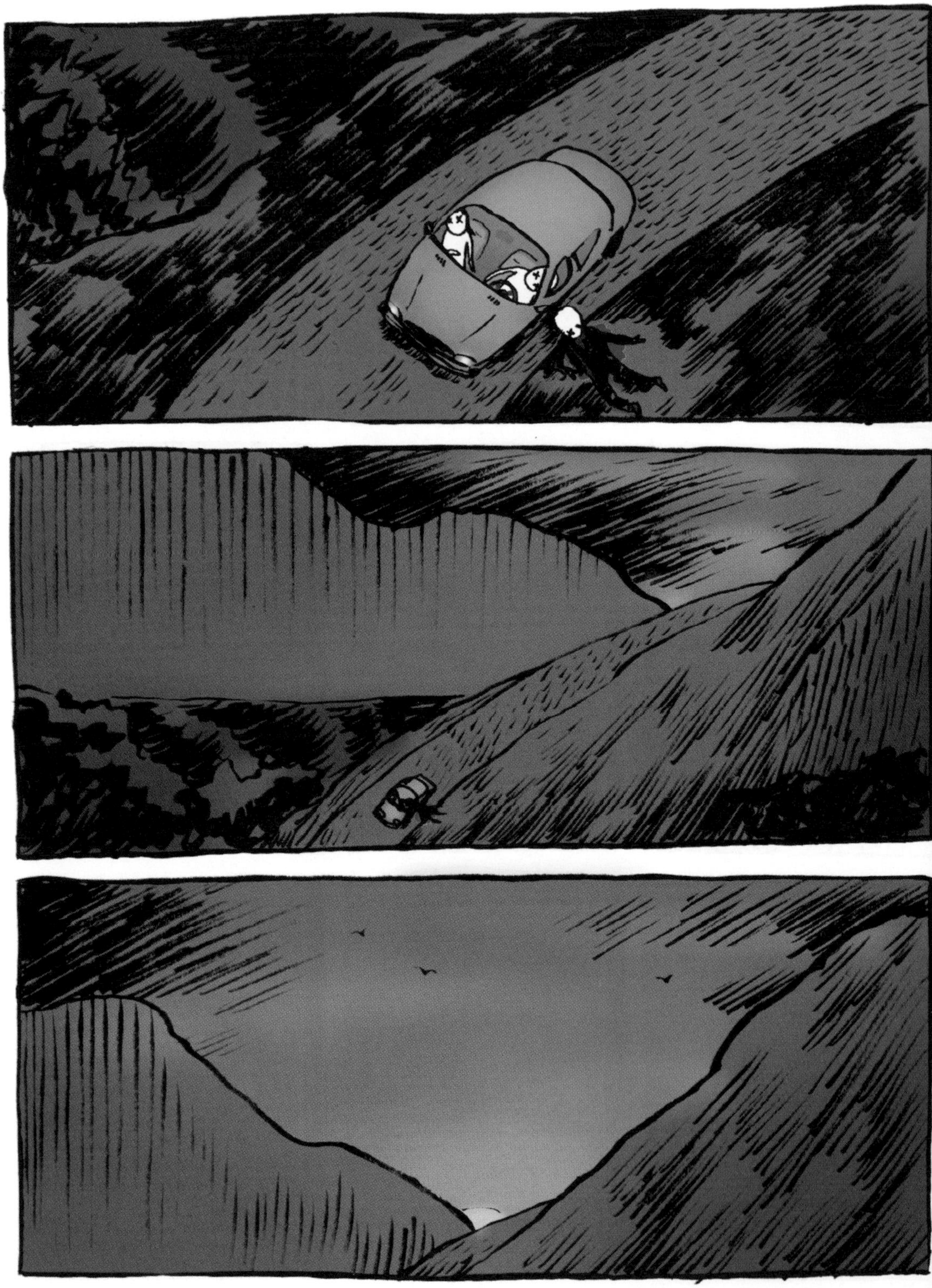

6

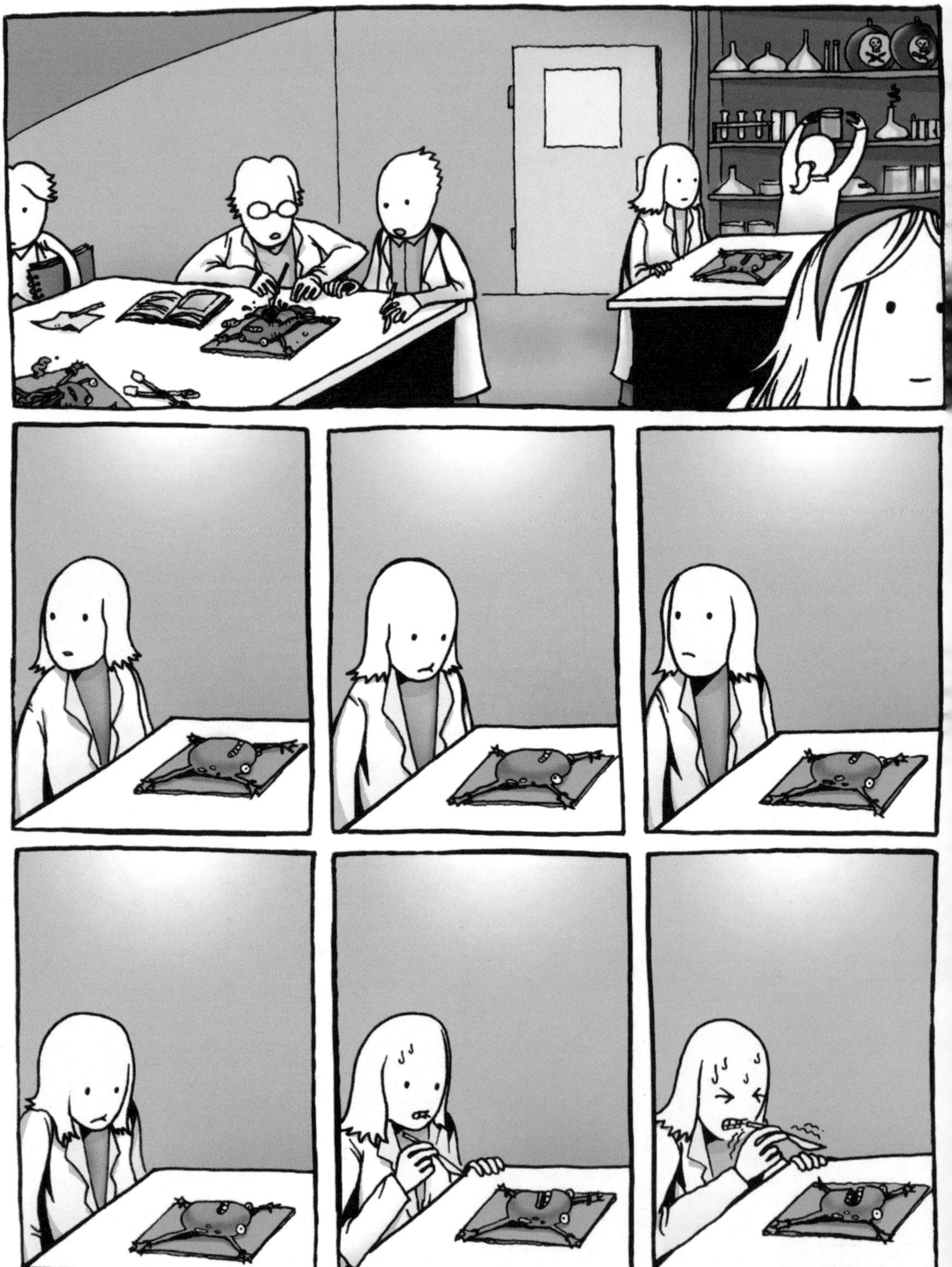

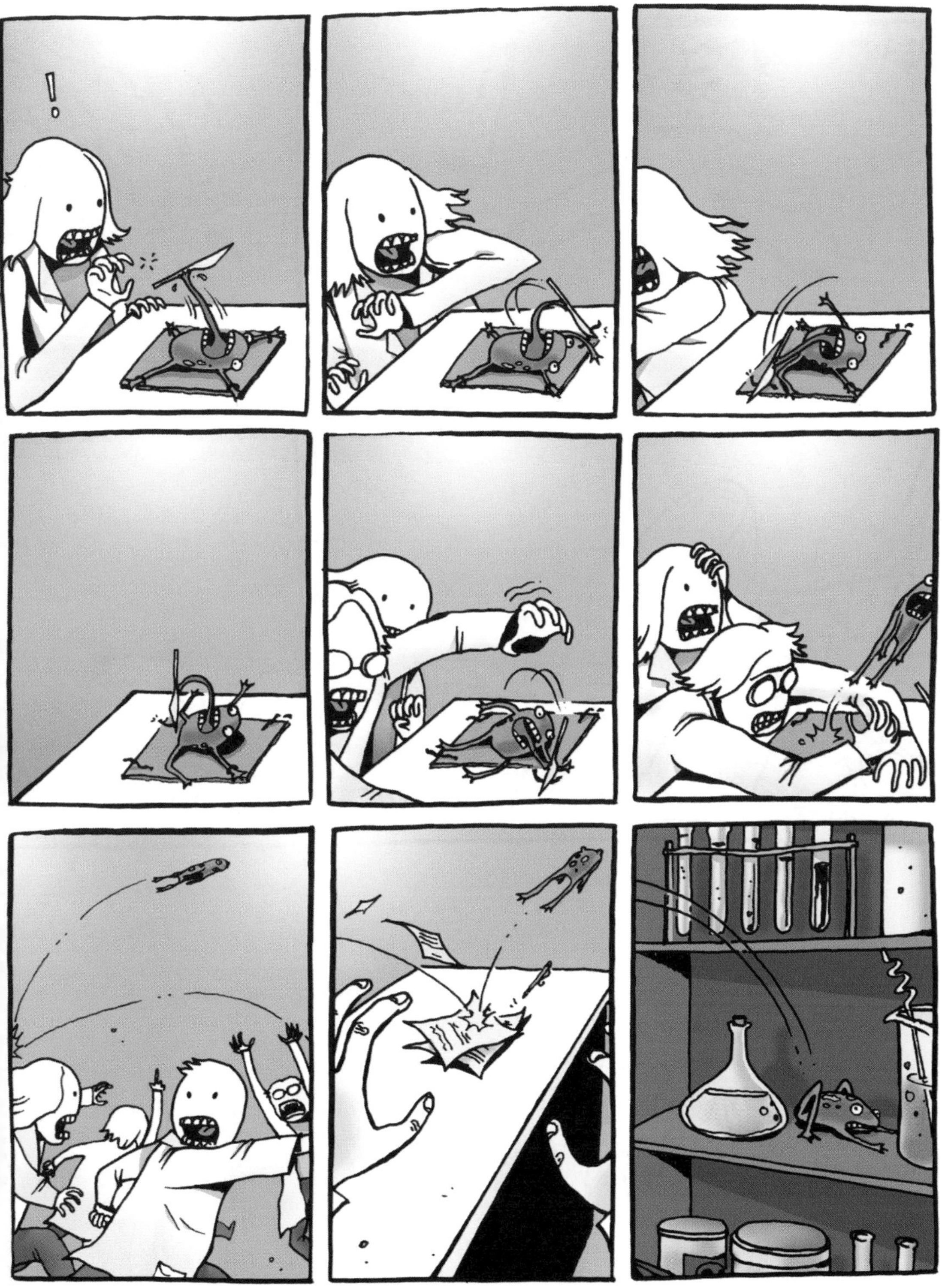
!

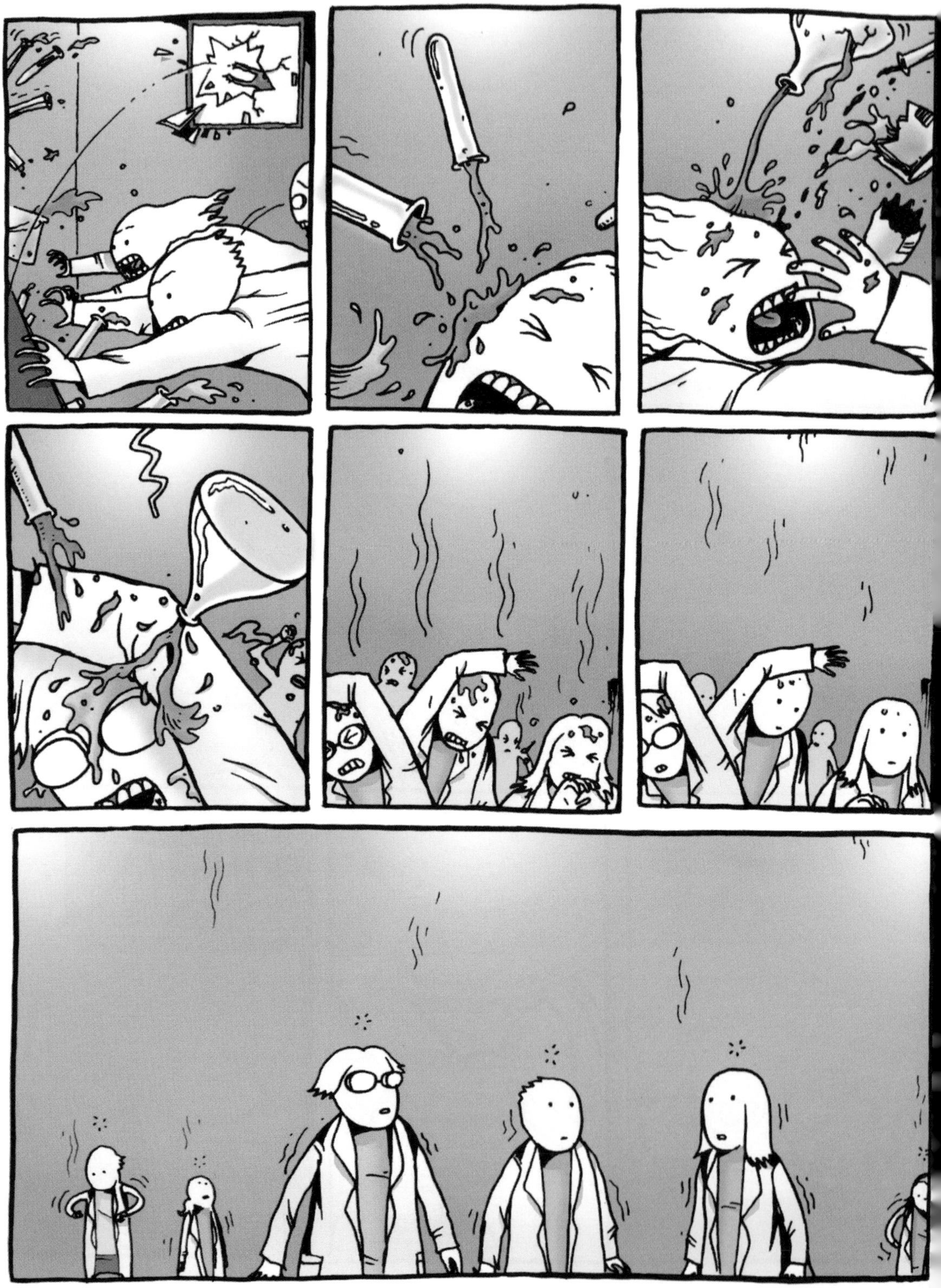

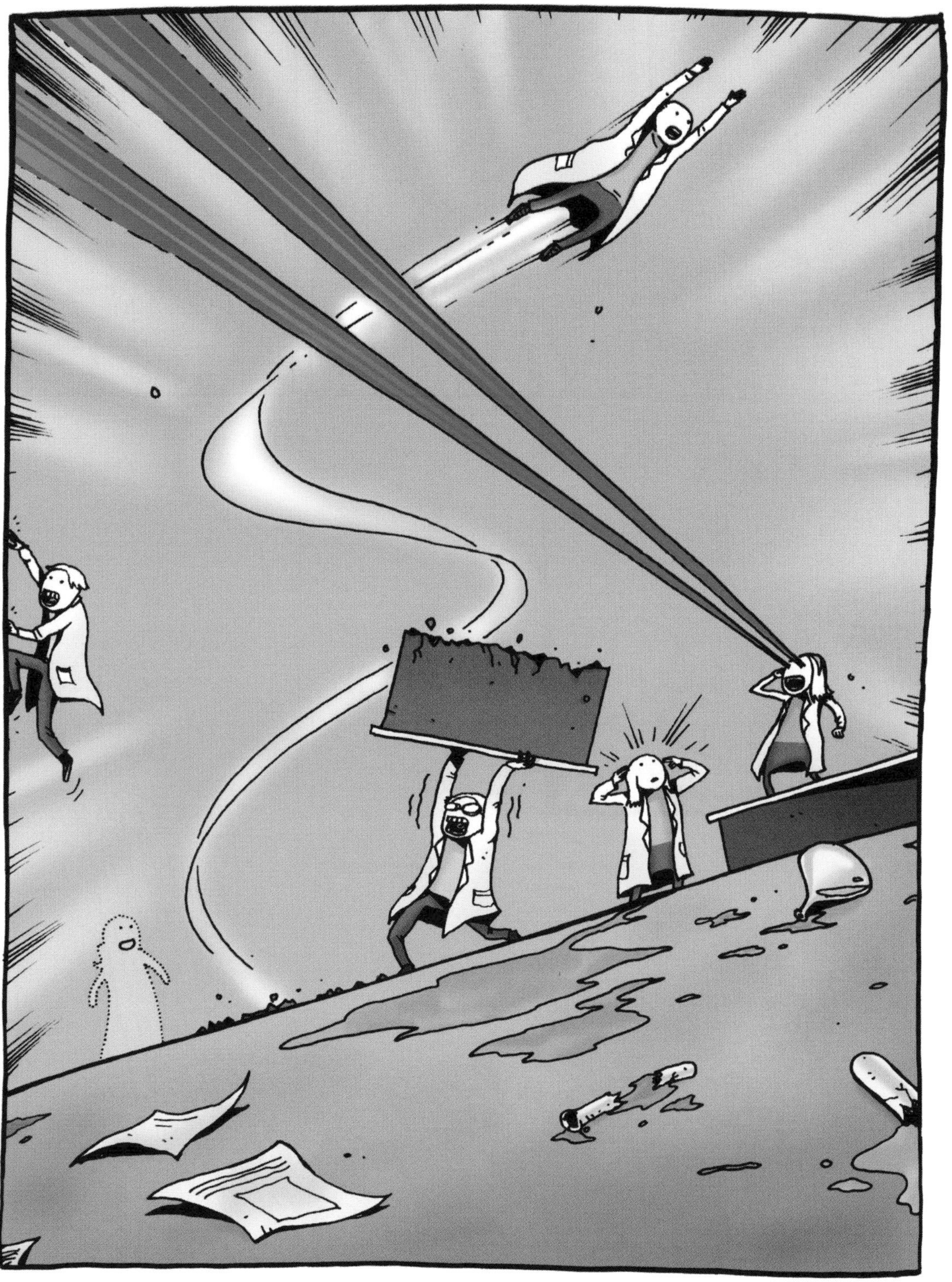

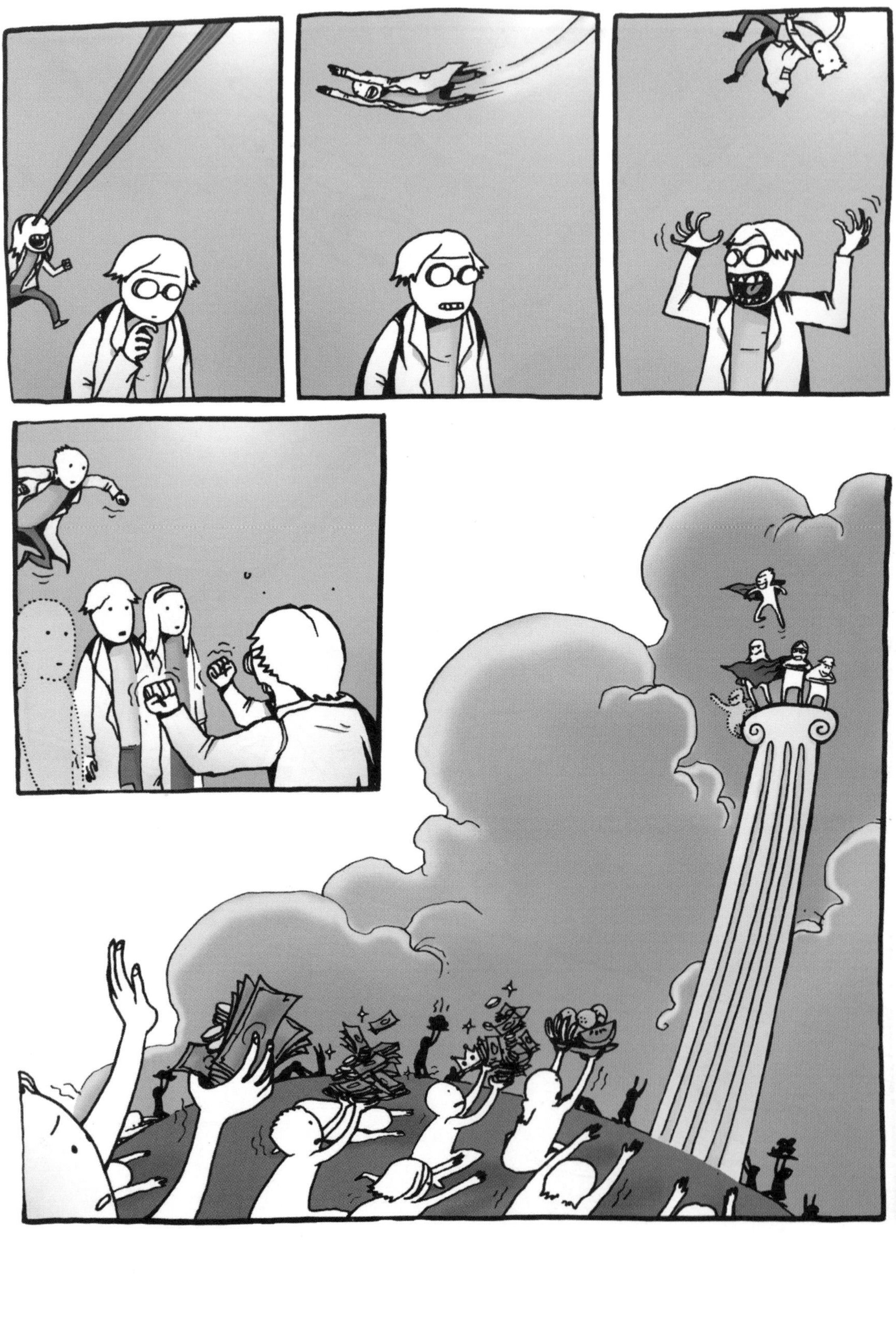

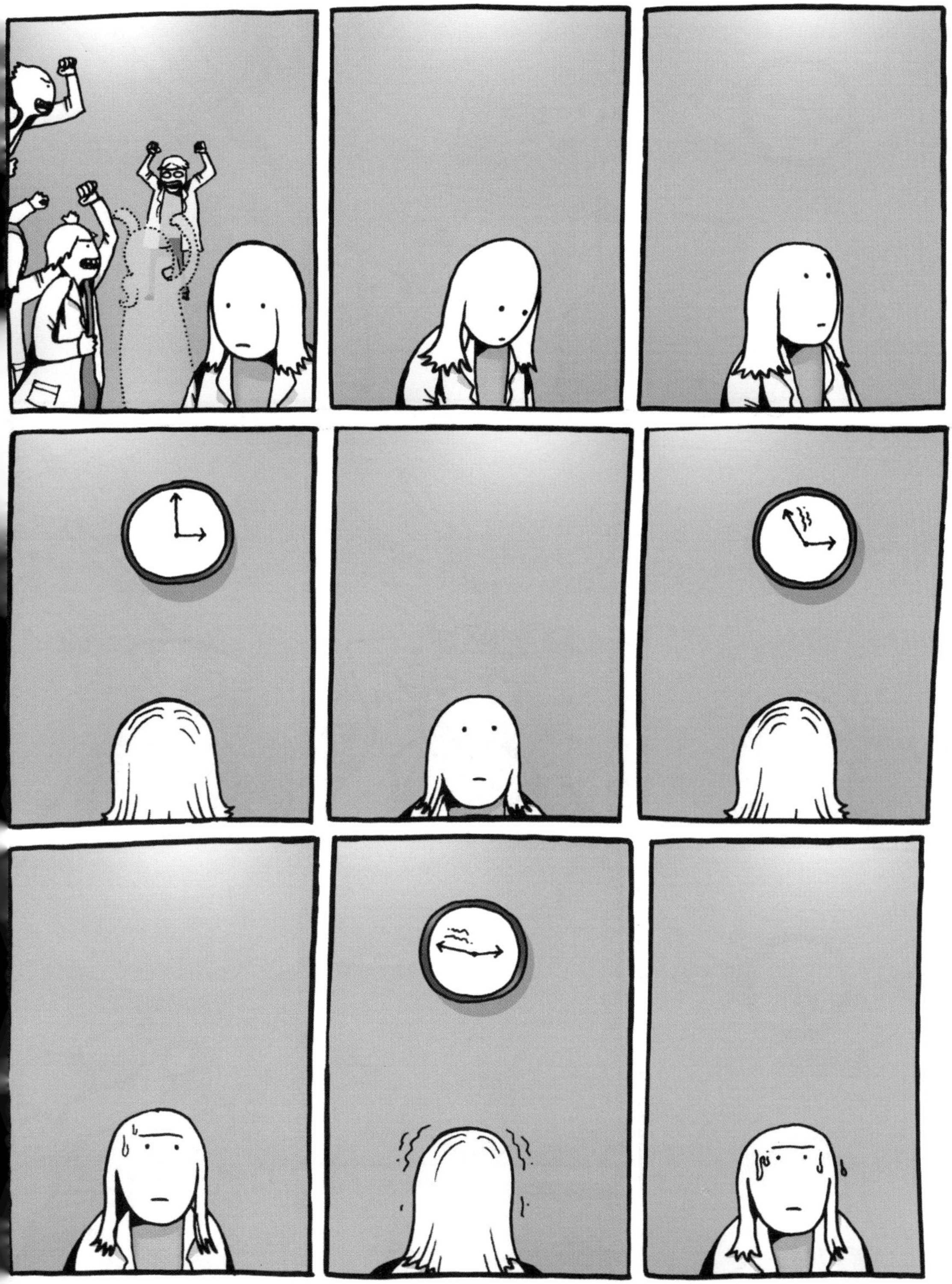

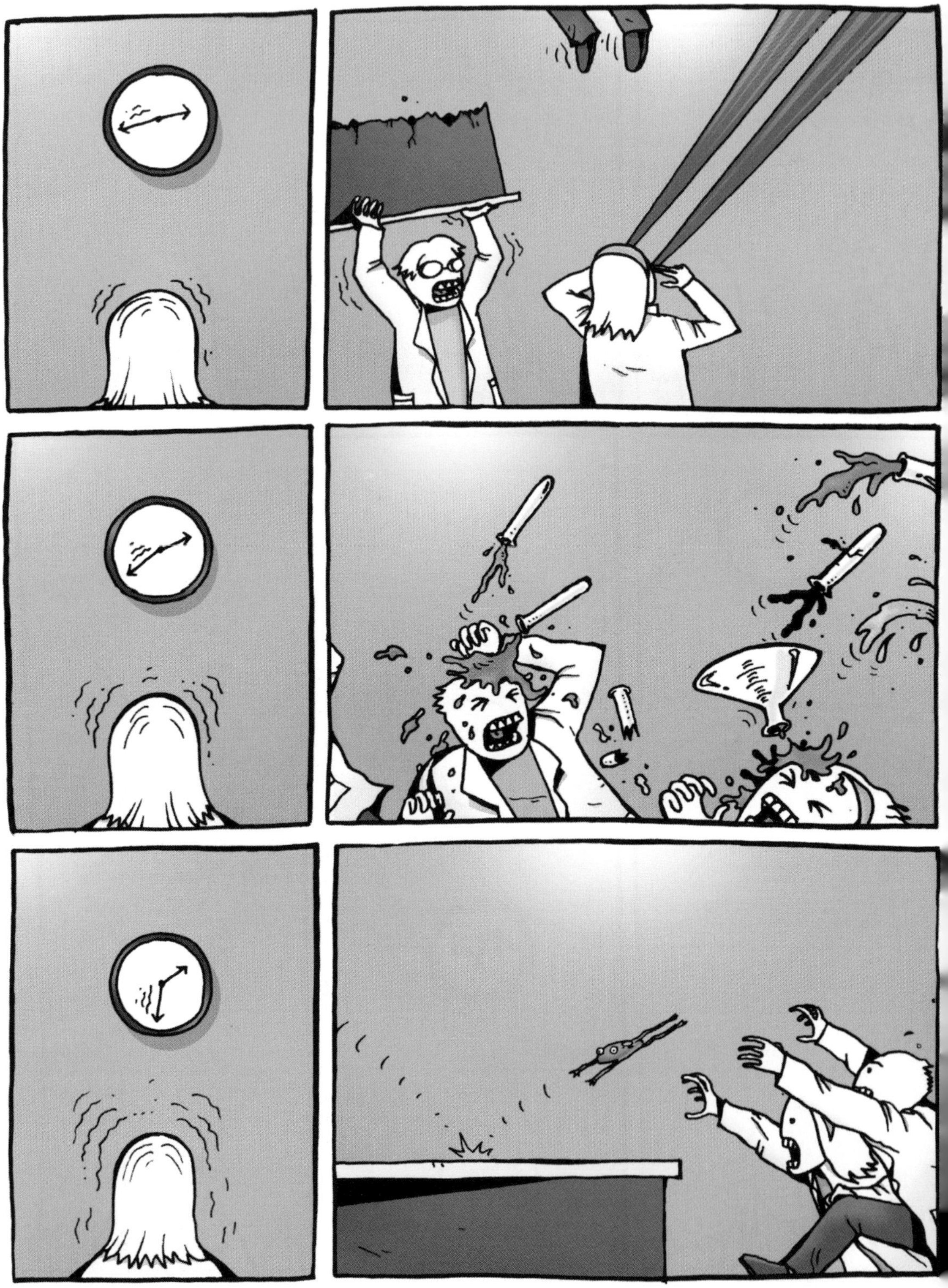

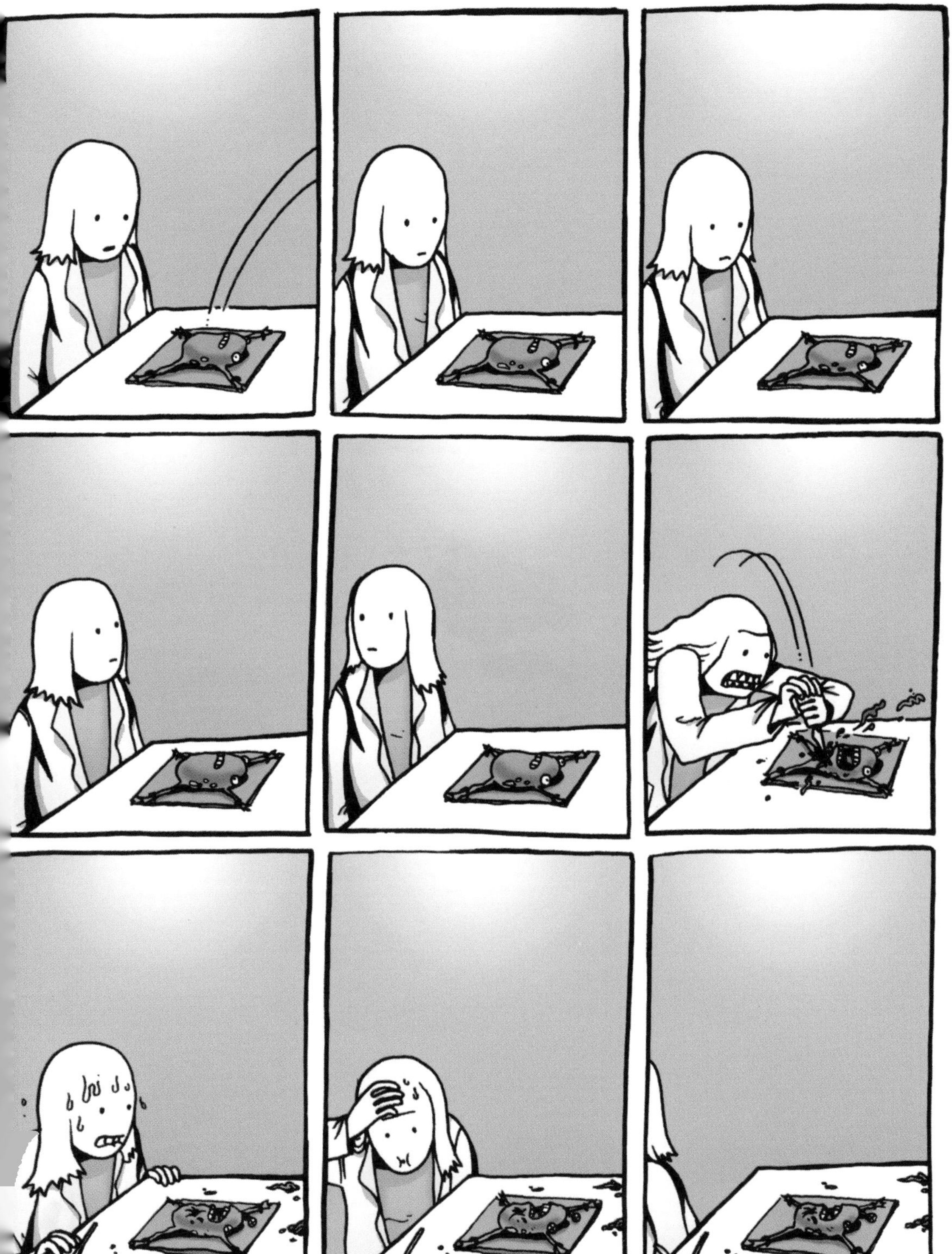

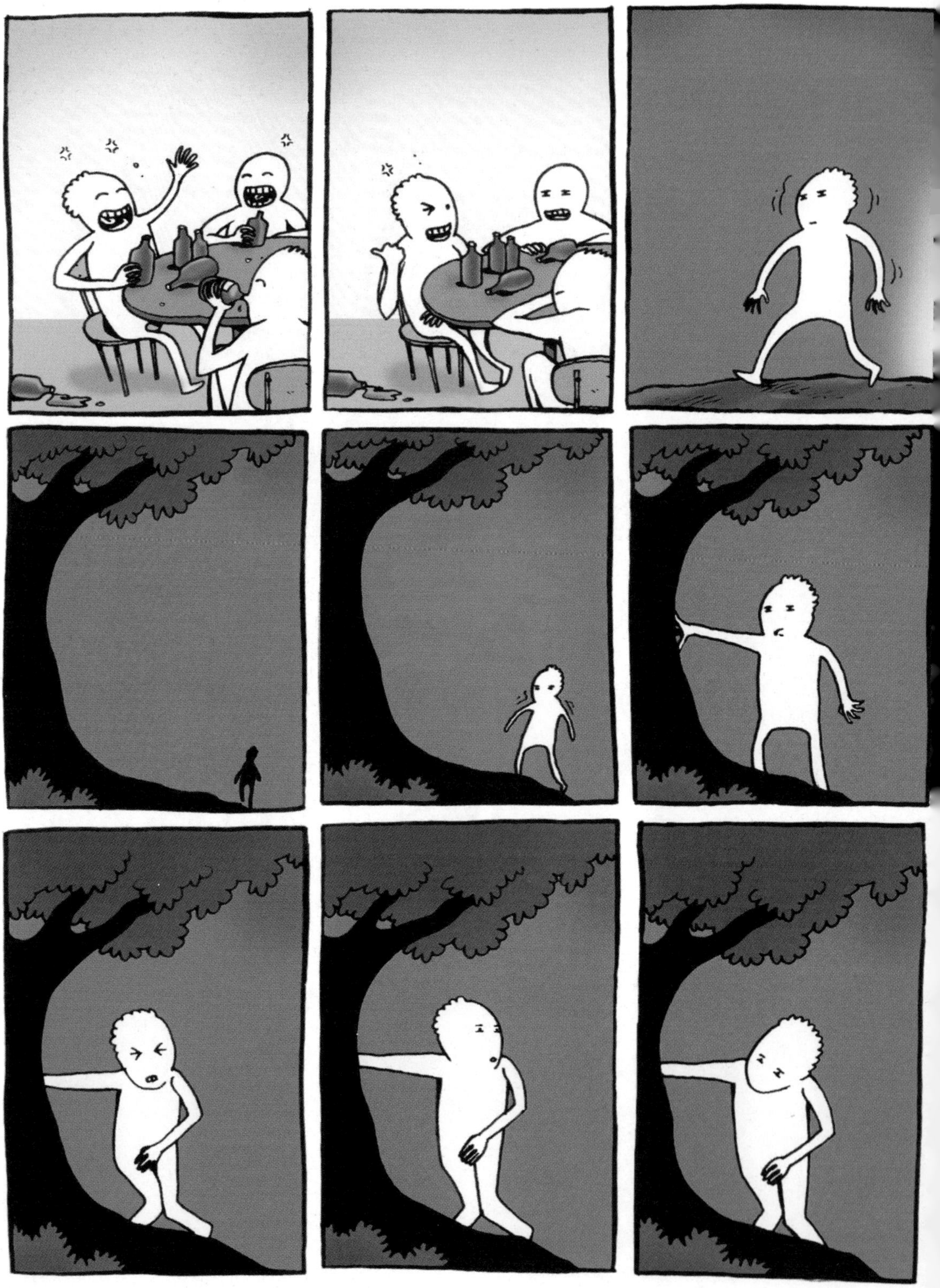

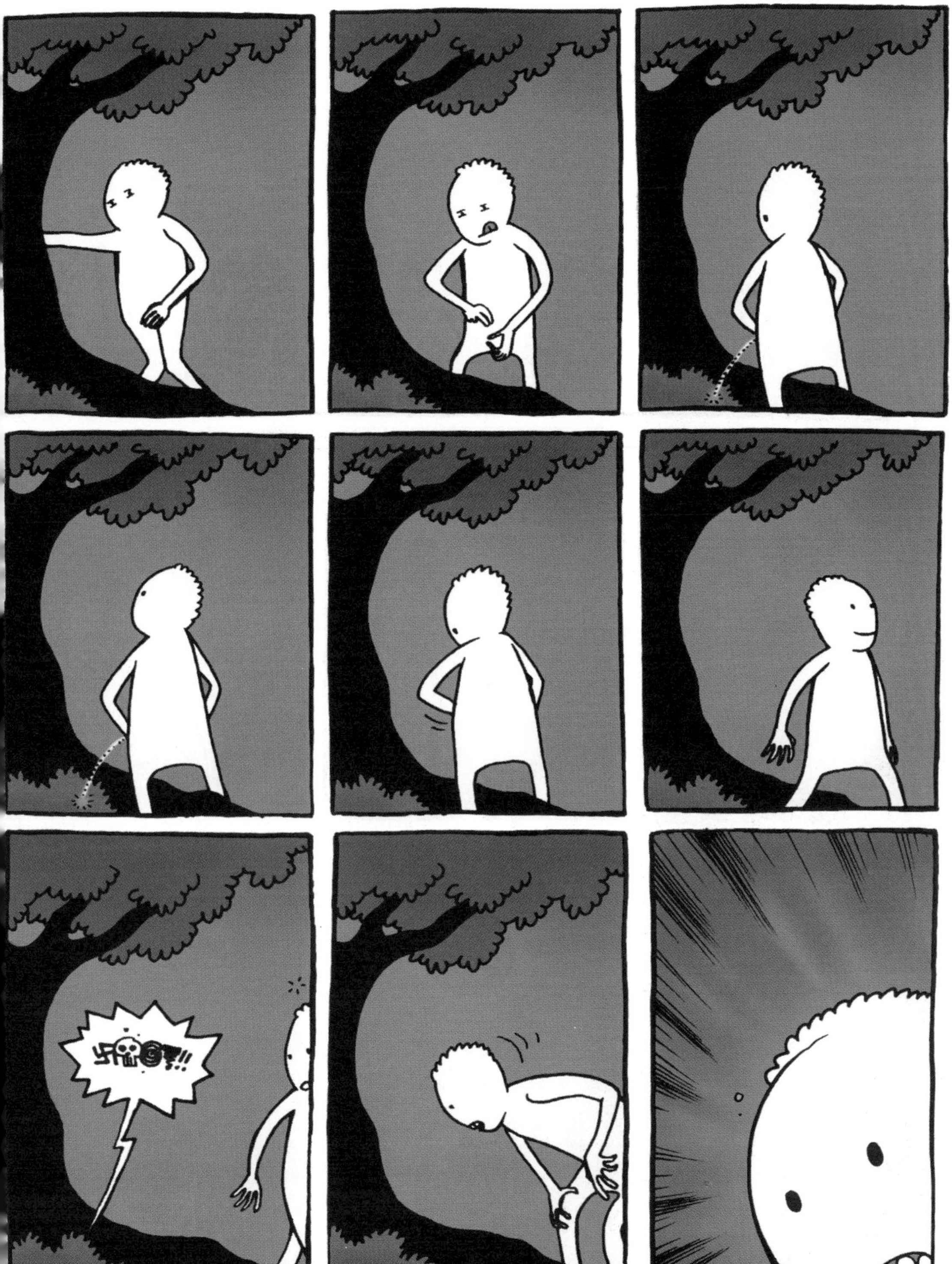

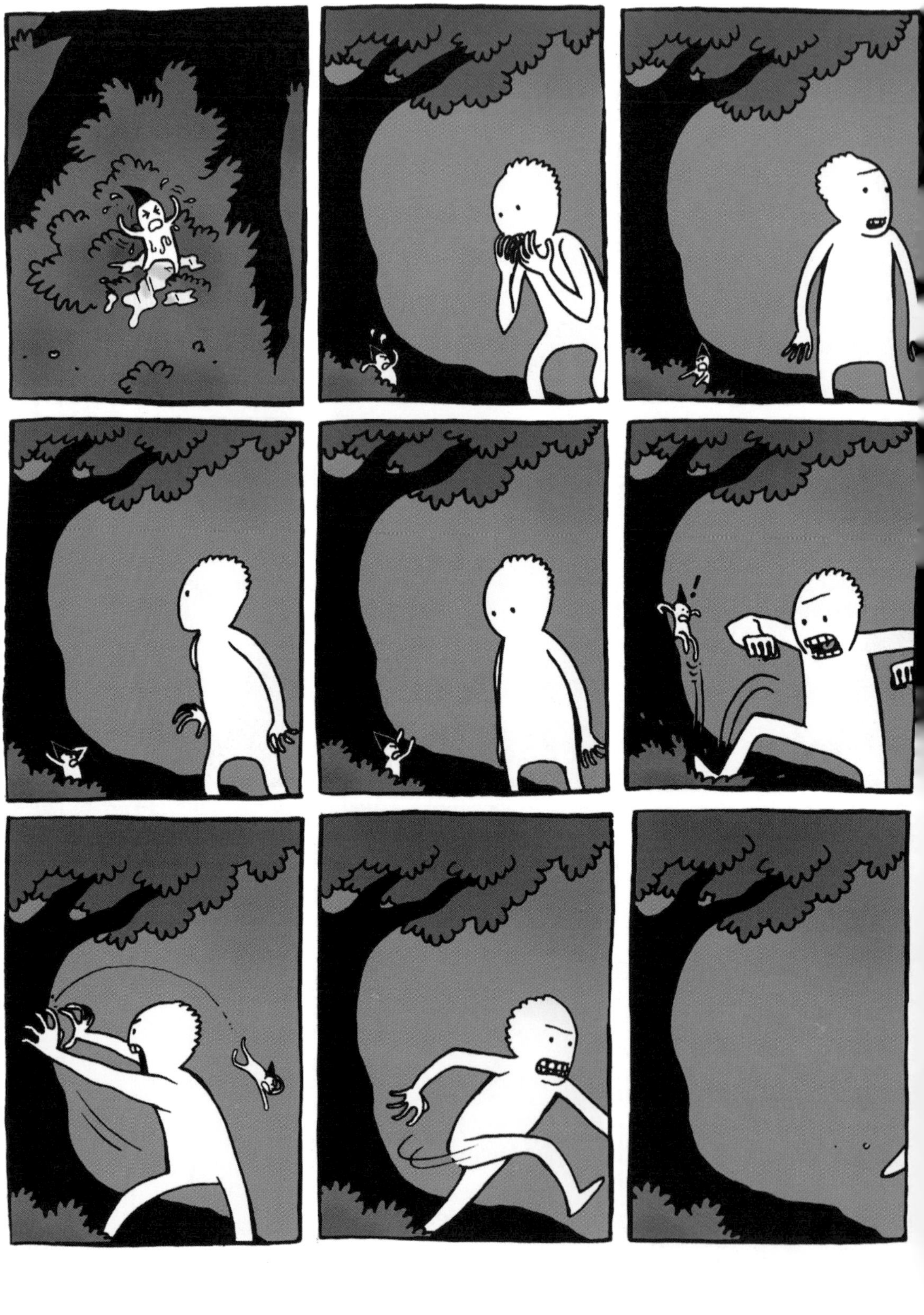

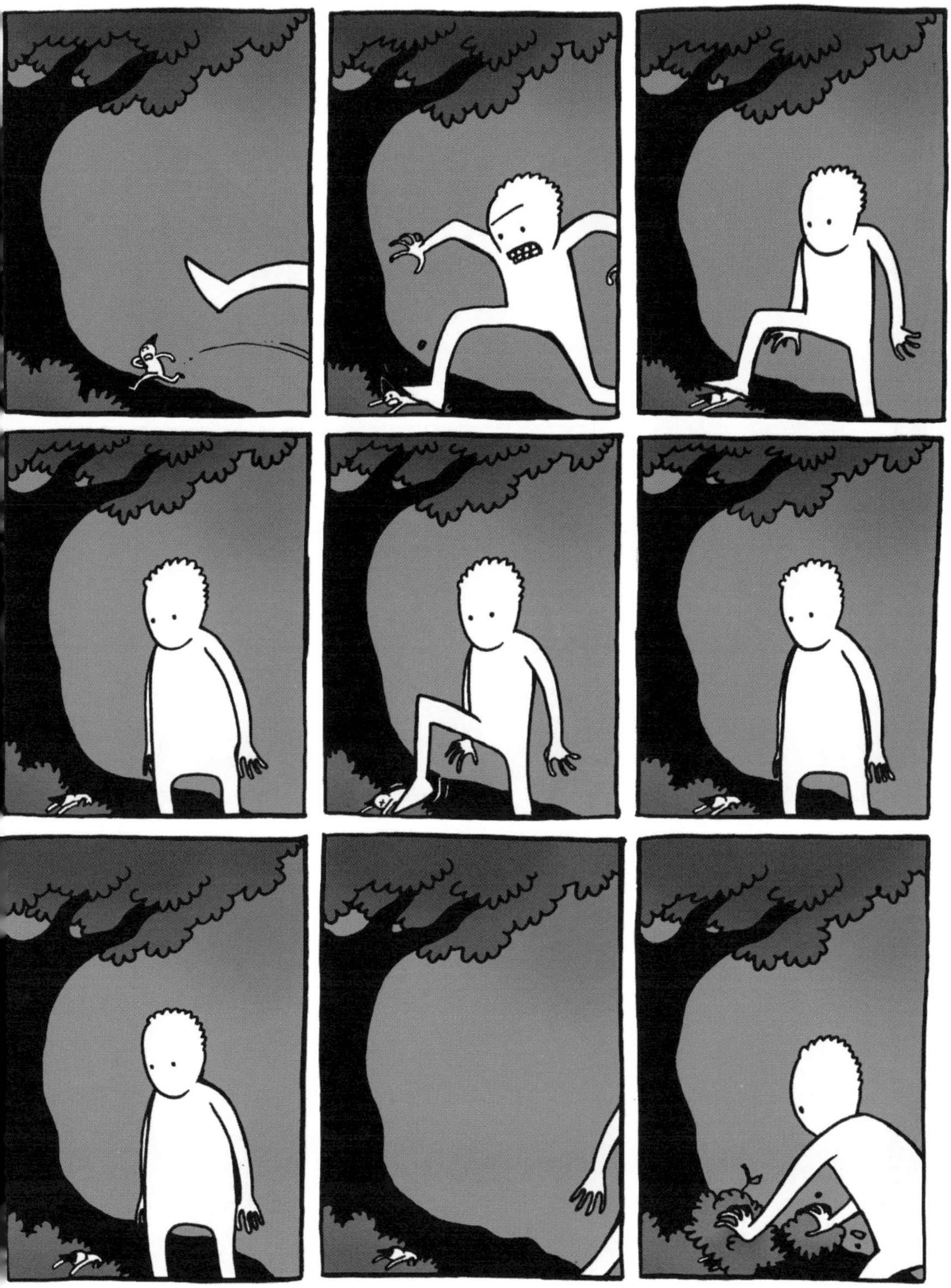

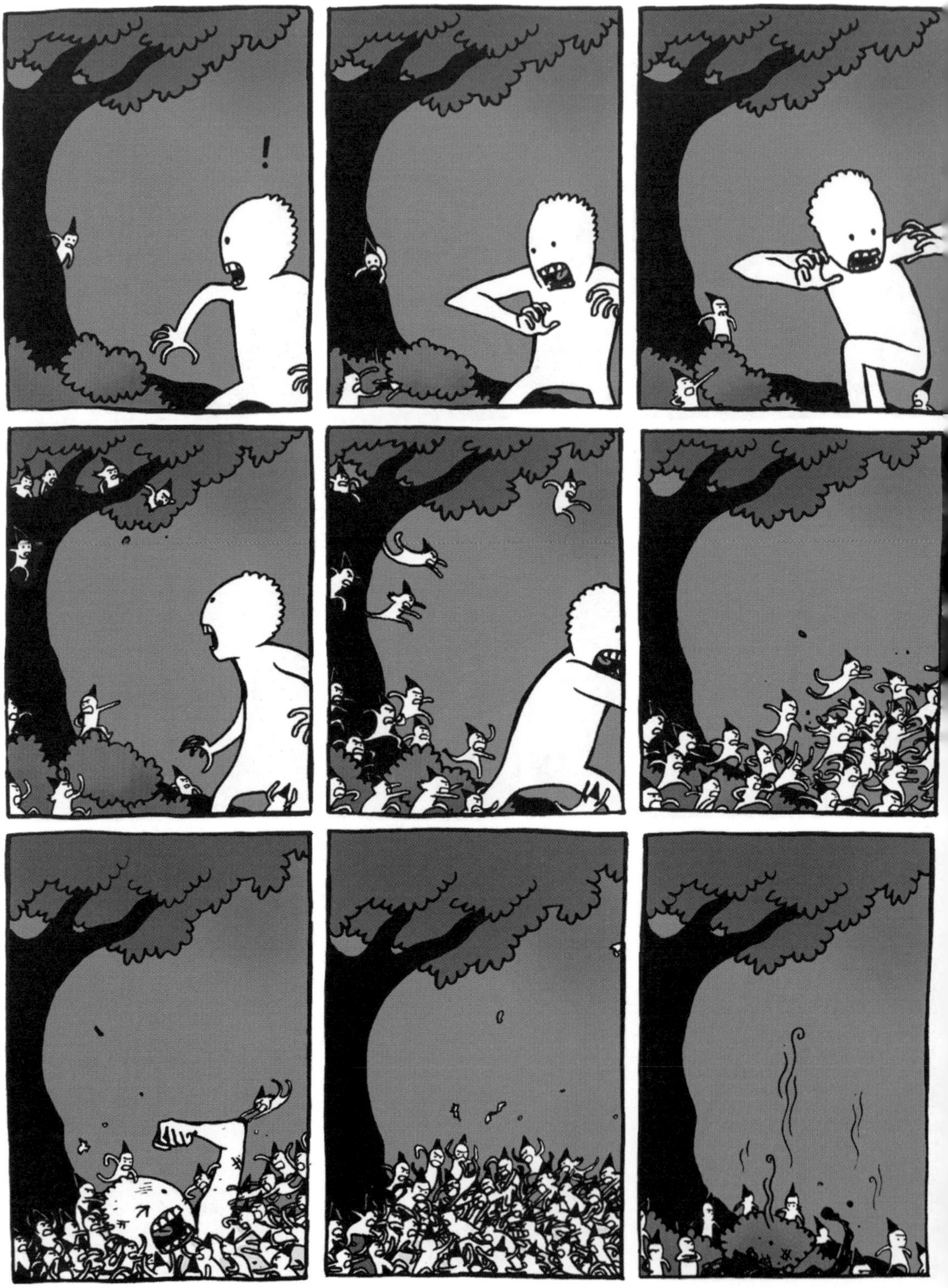
!

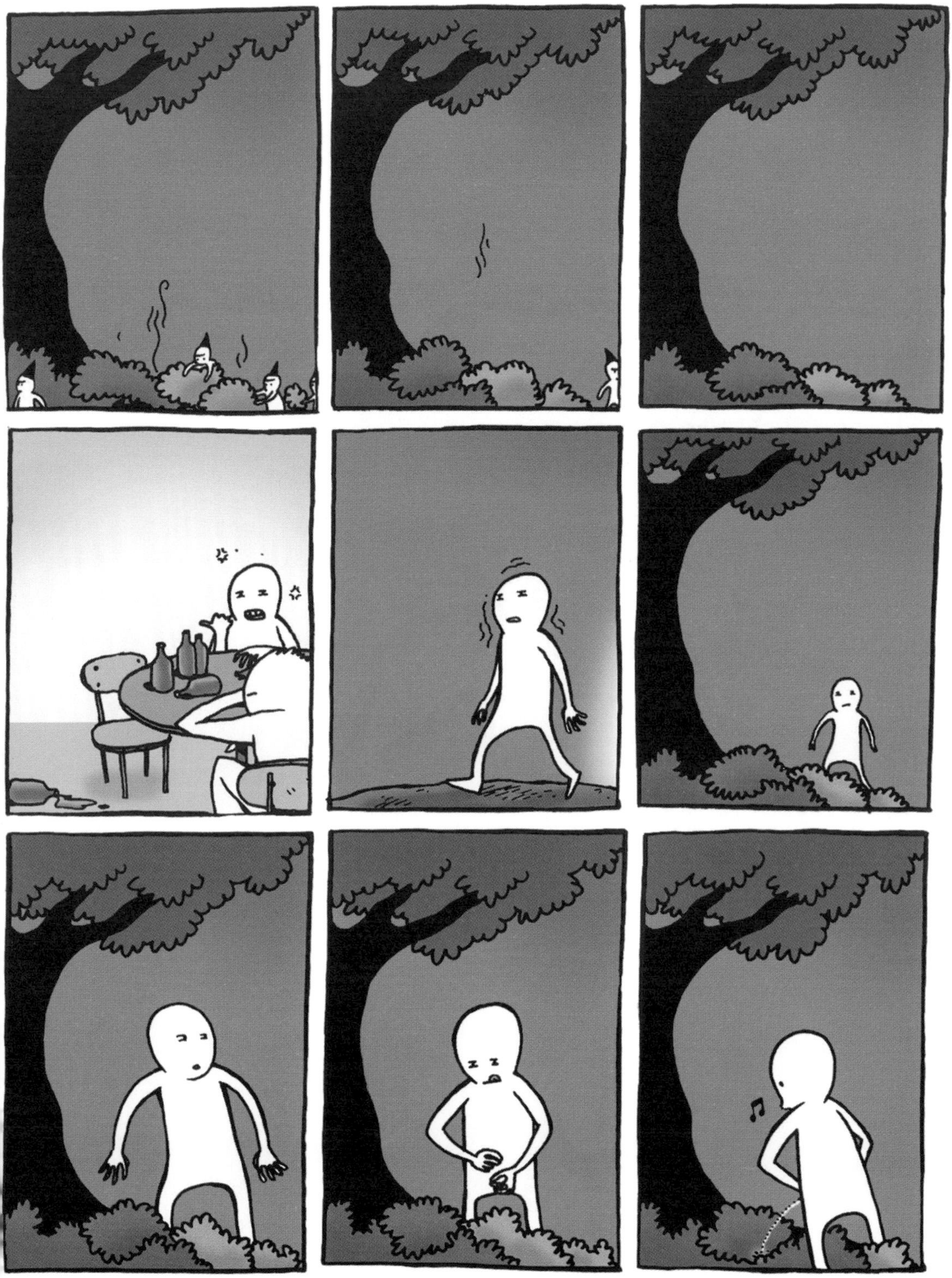

8

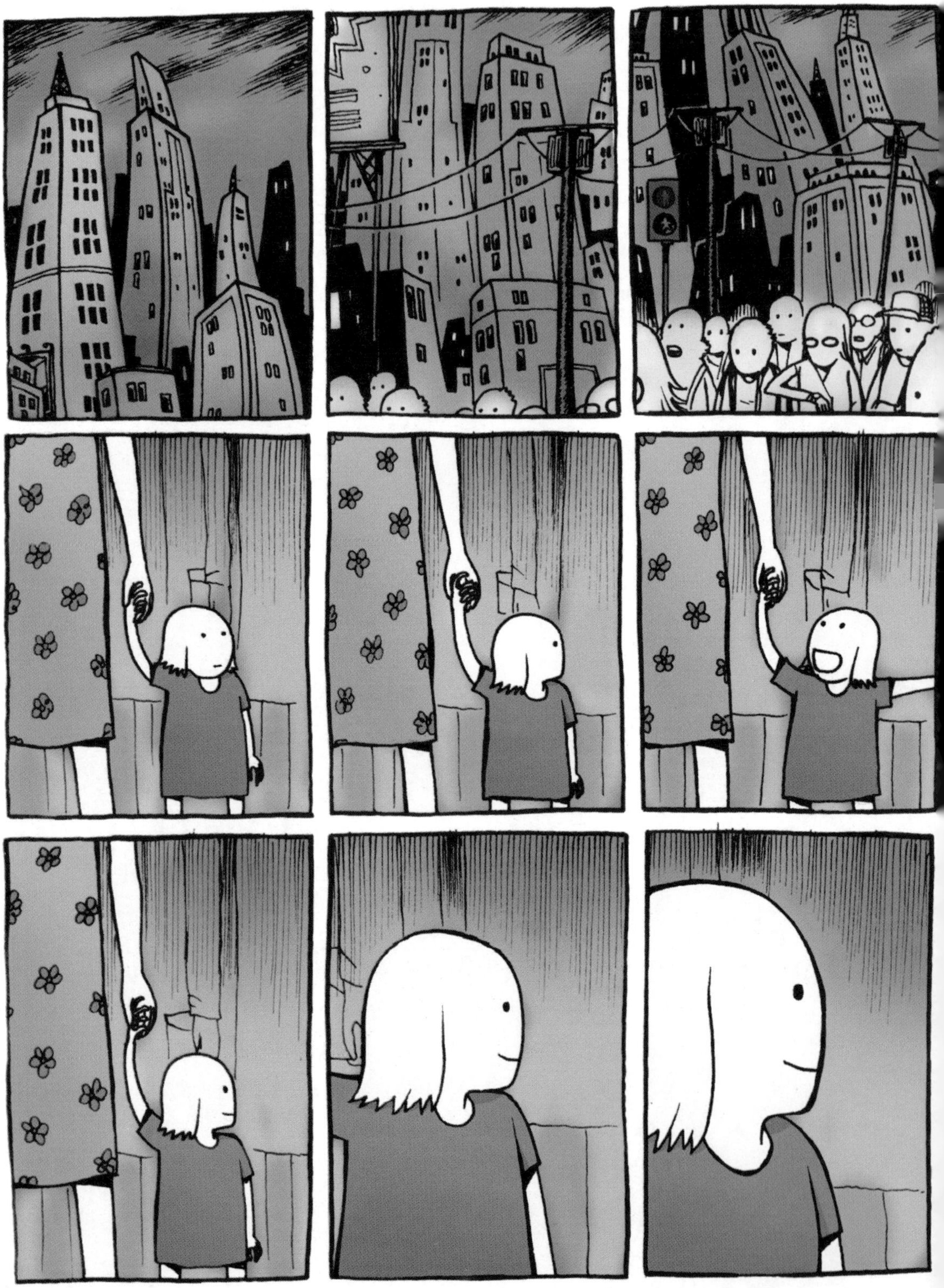

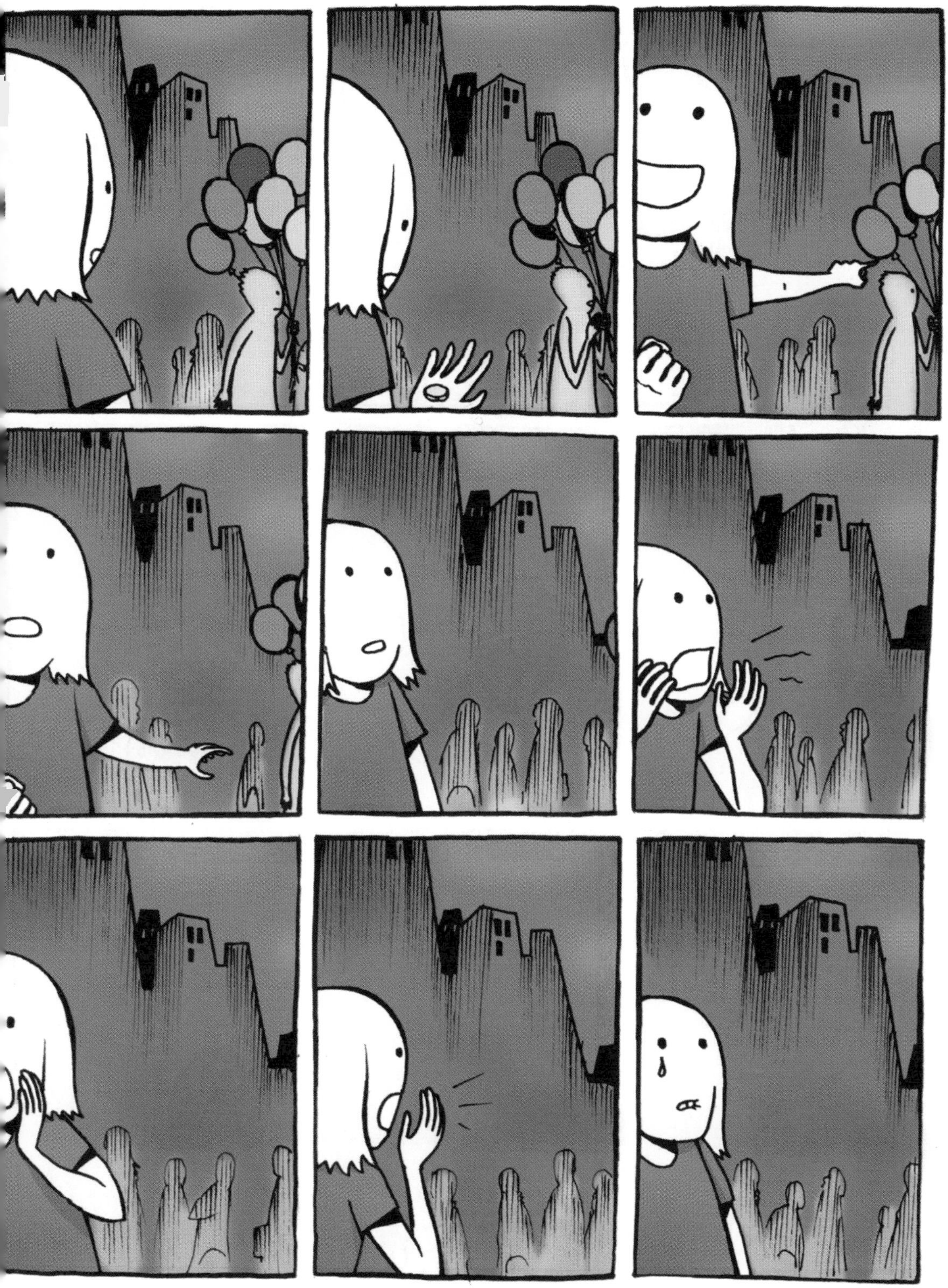

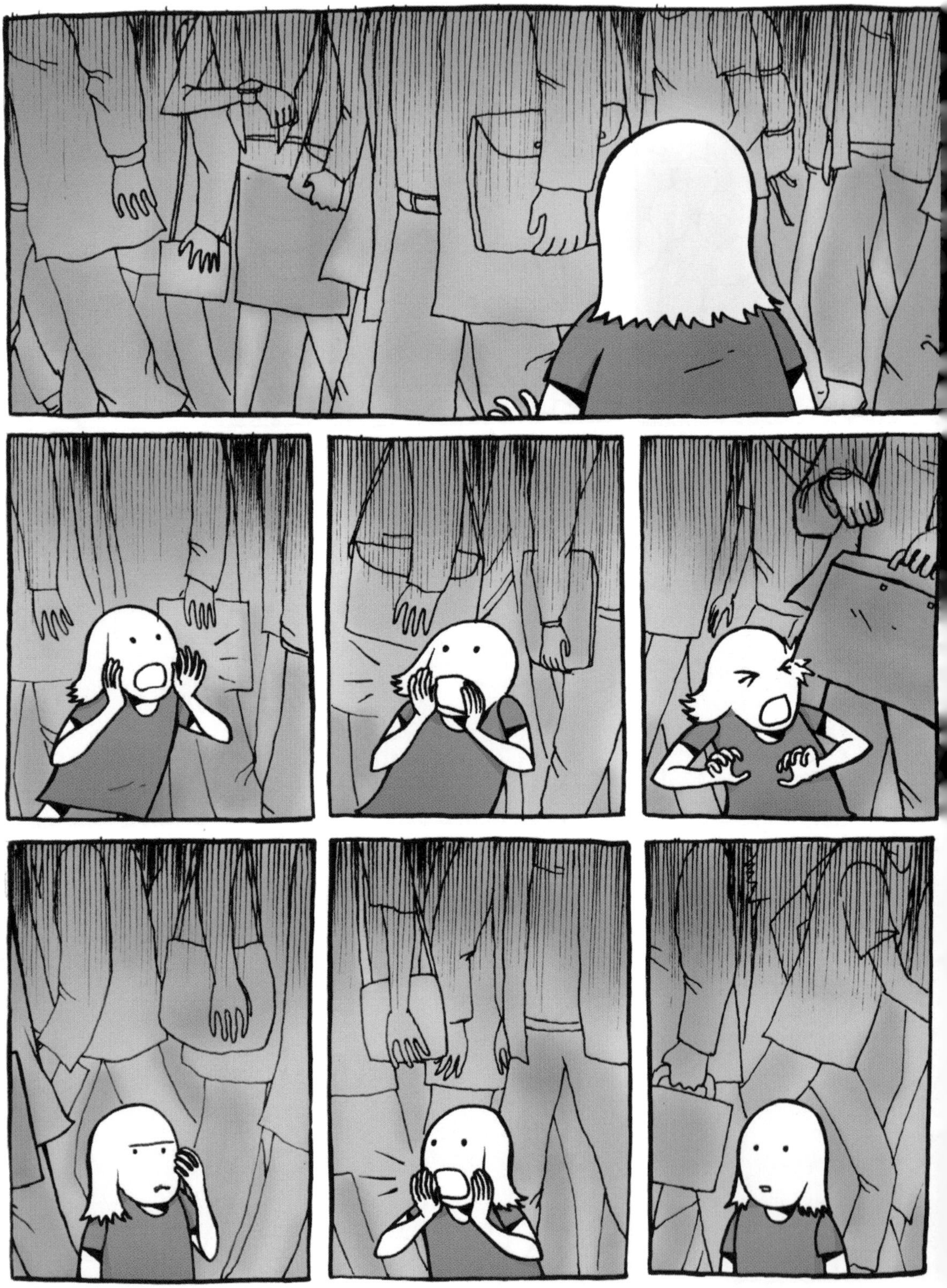

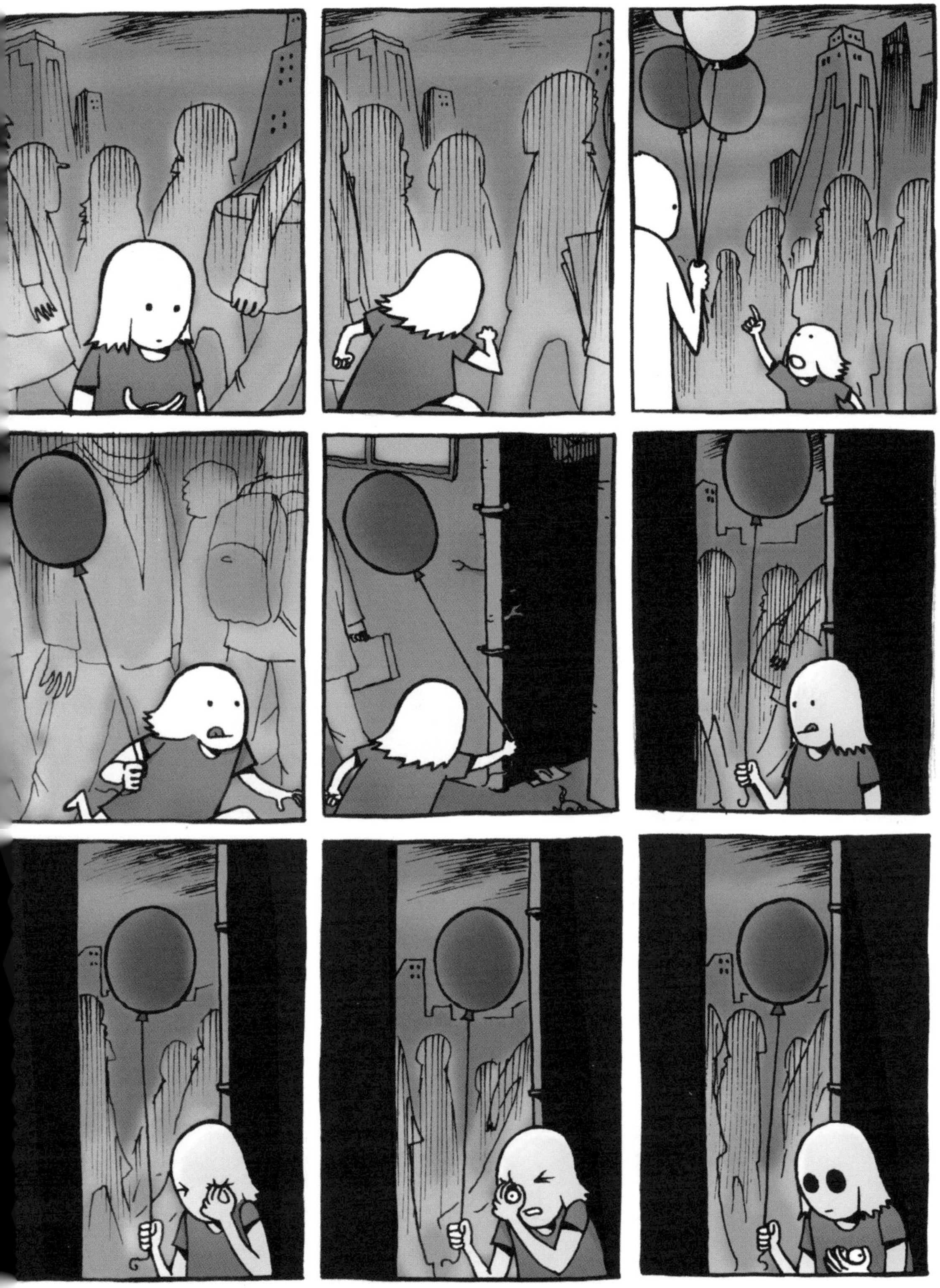

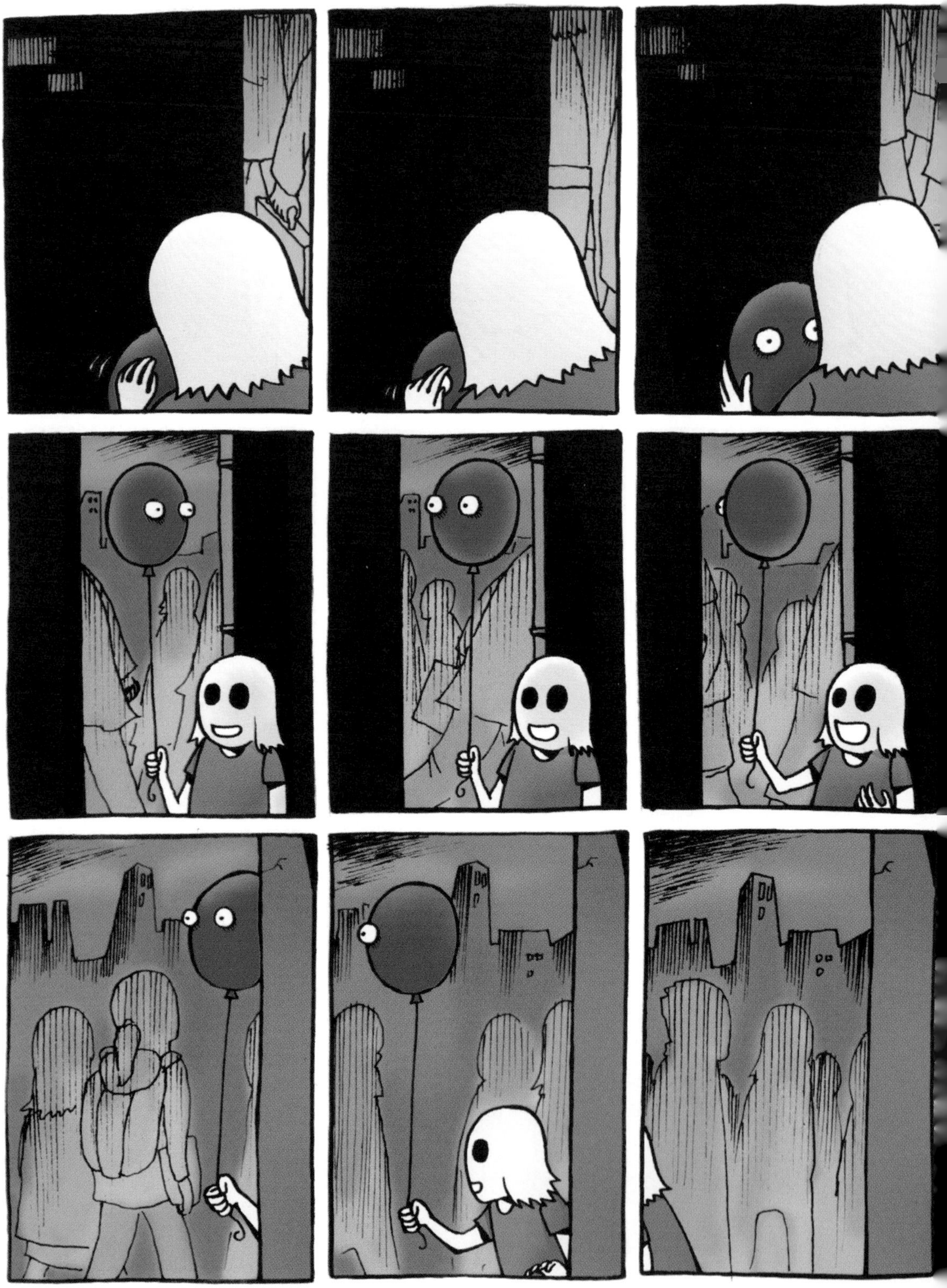

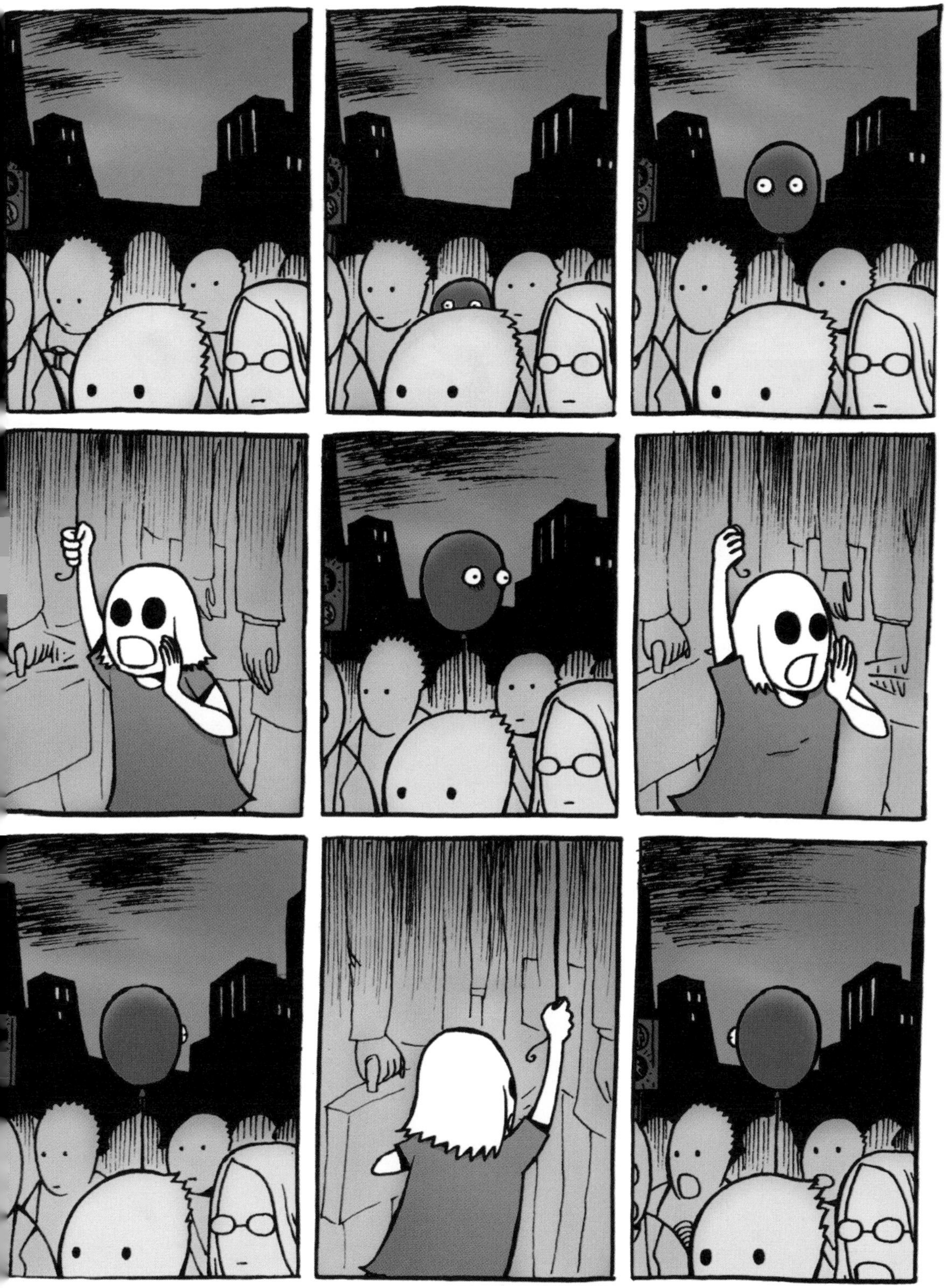

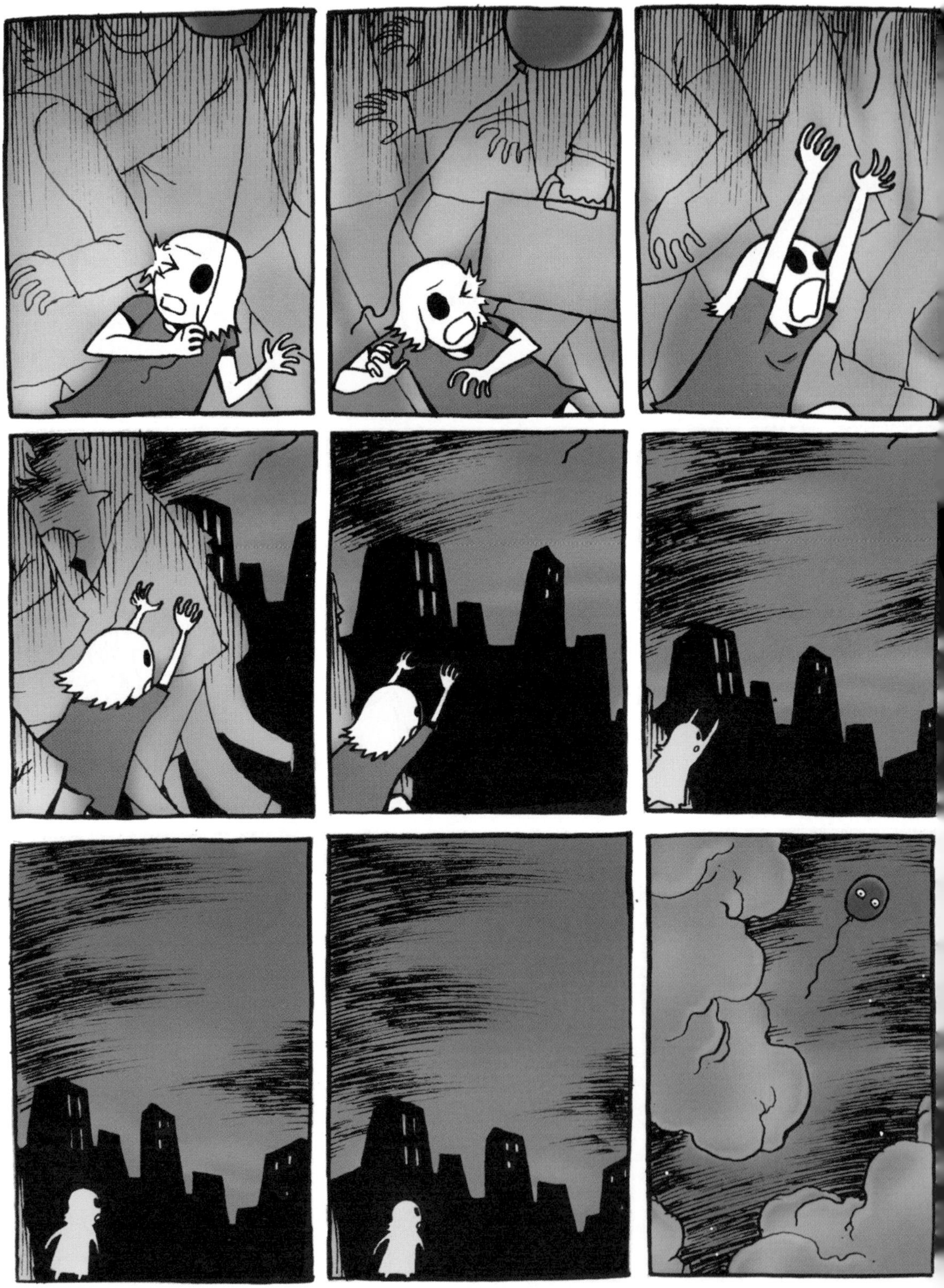

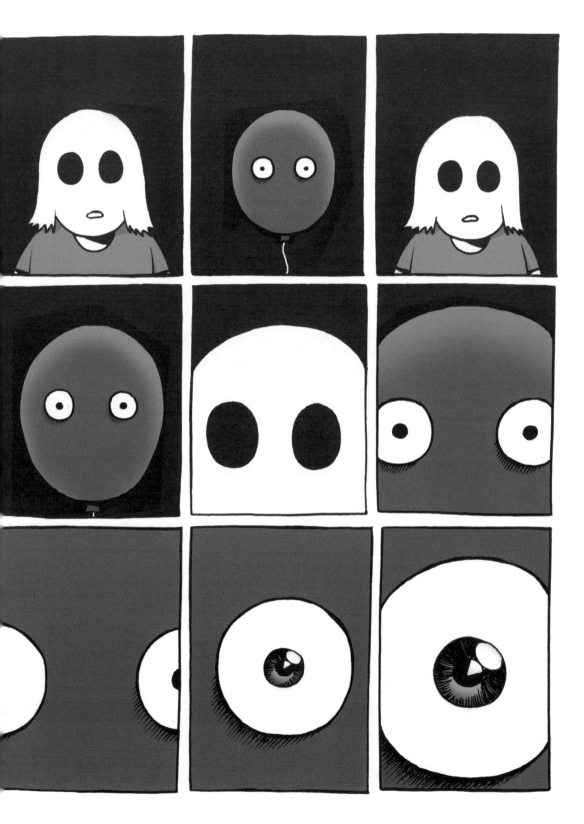

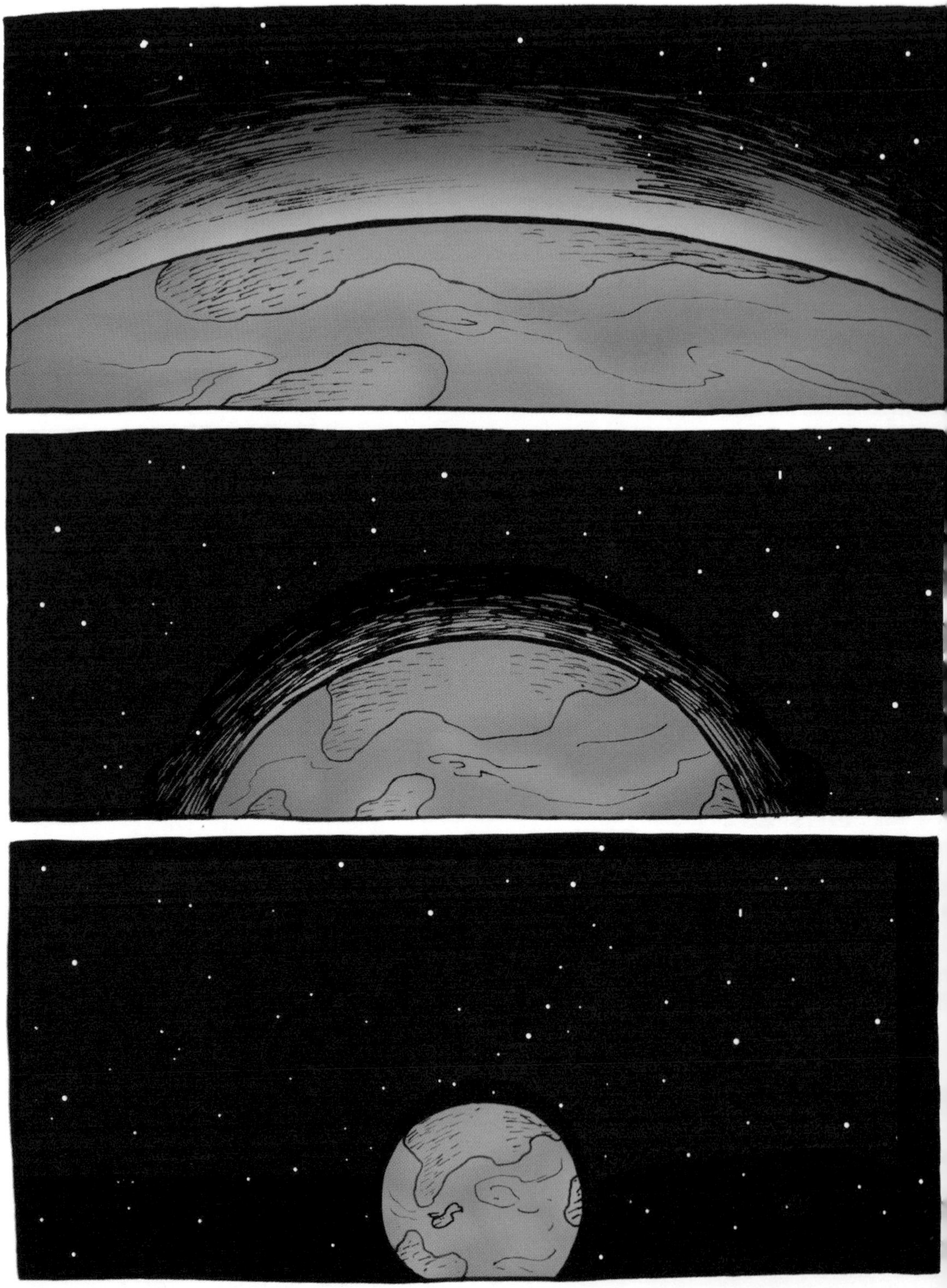

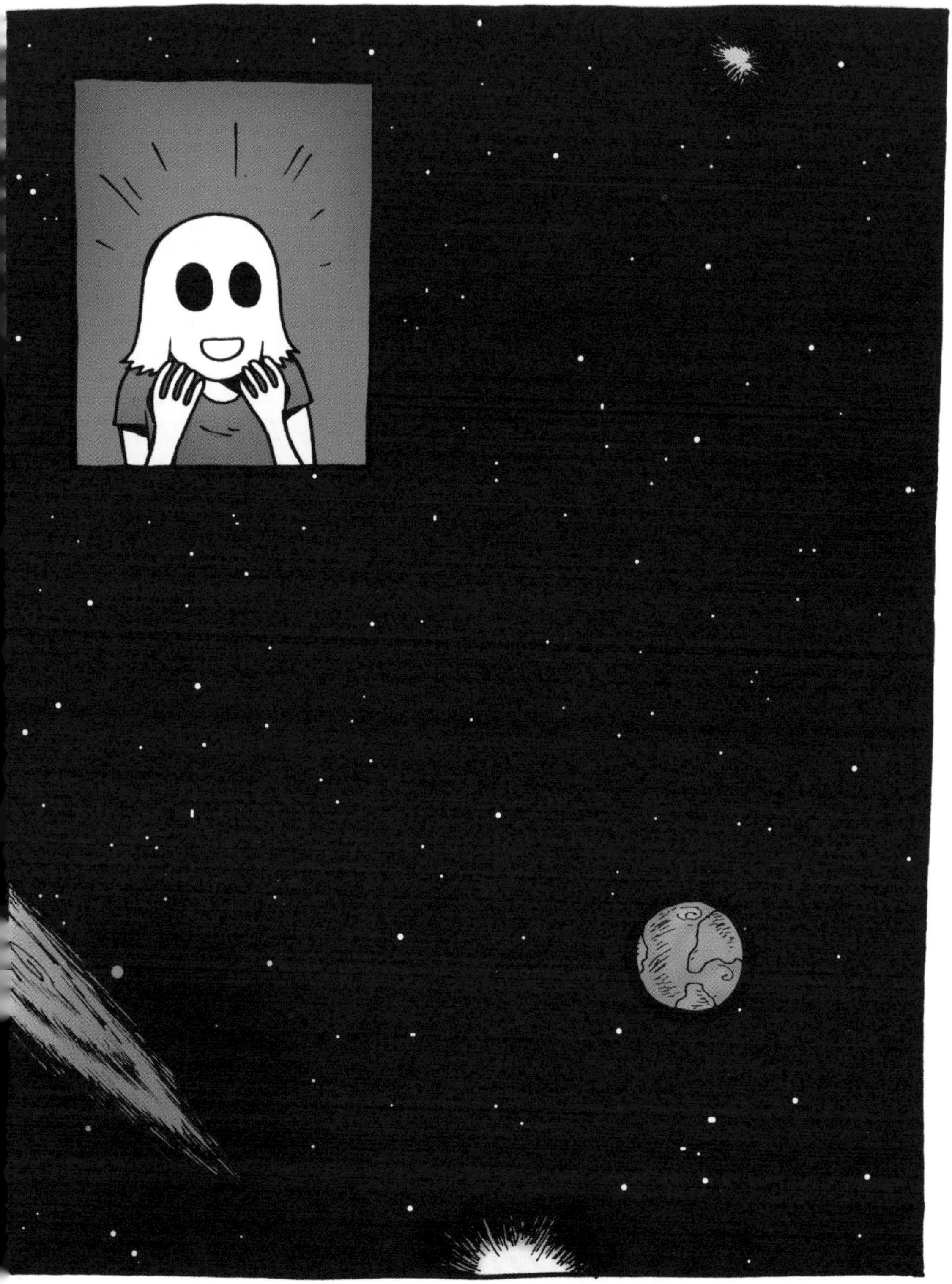

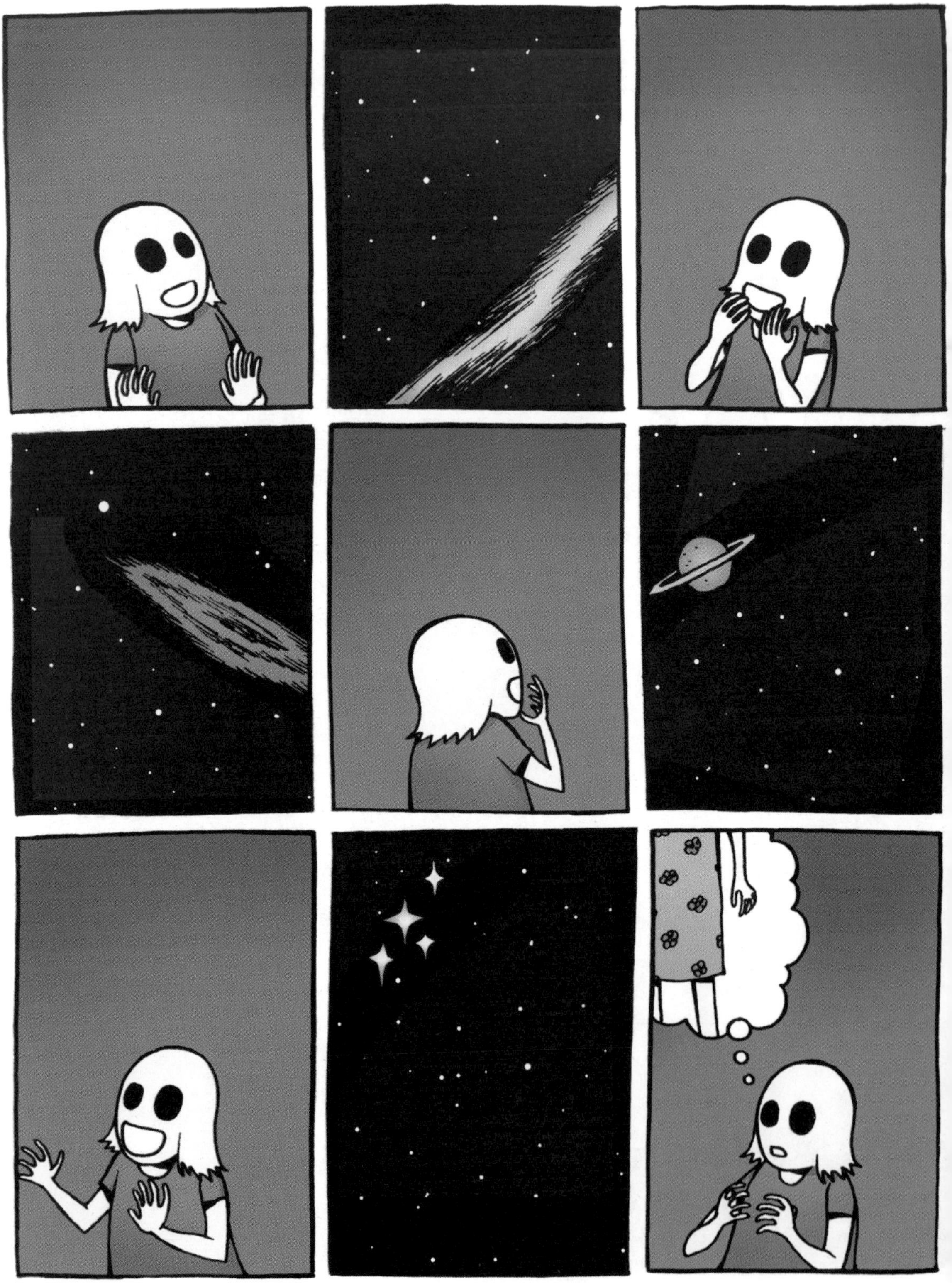

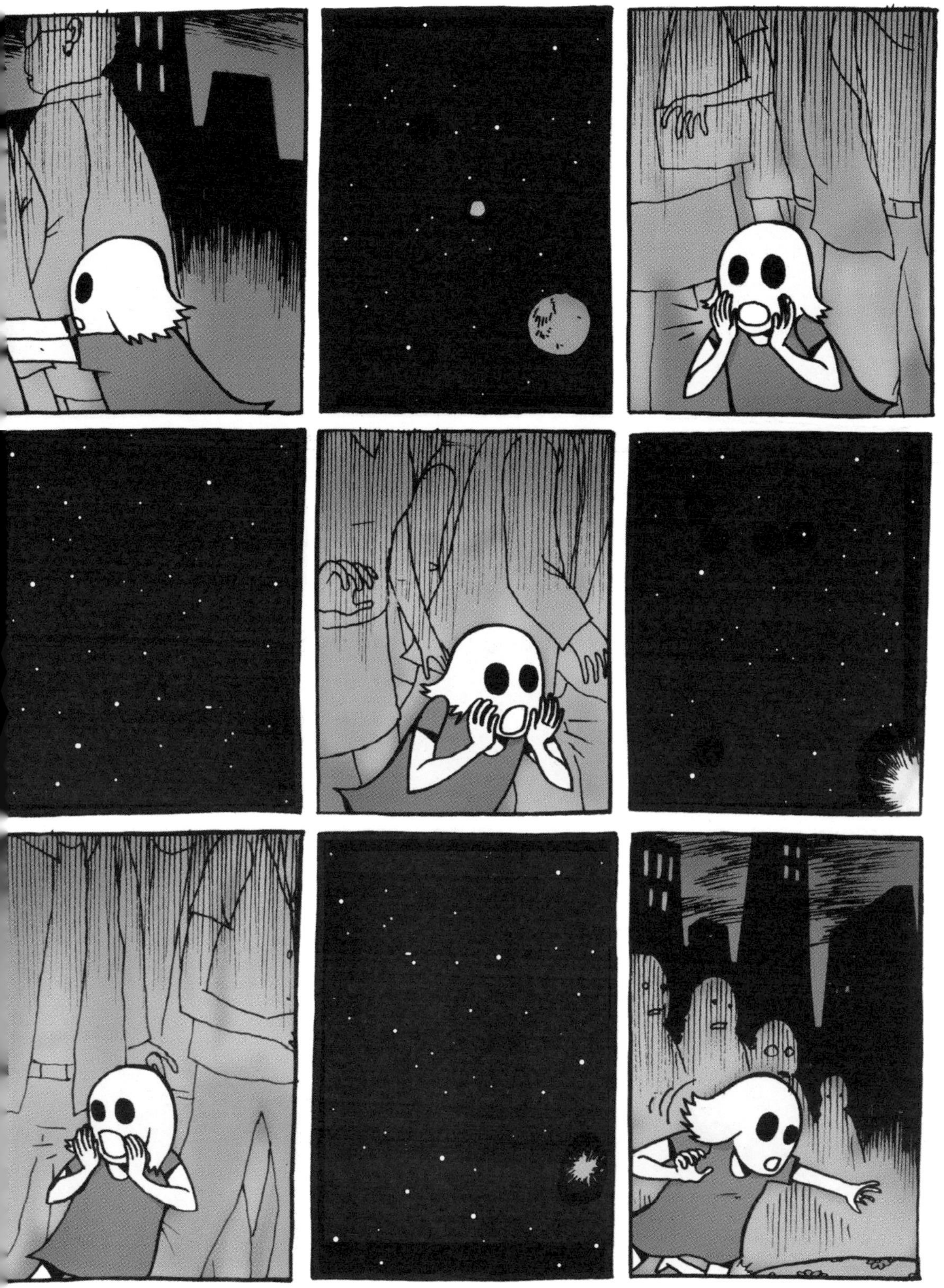

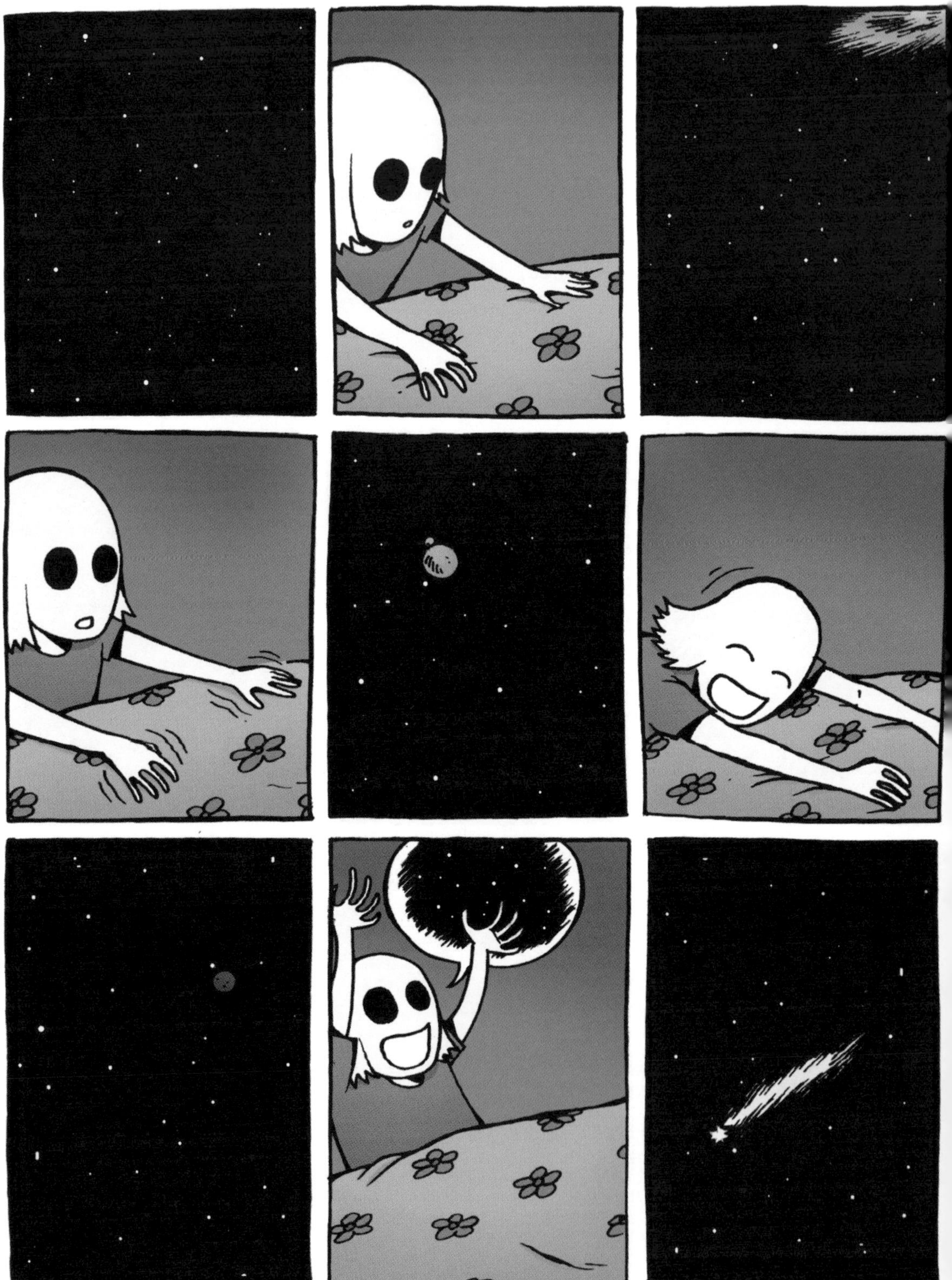

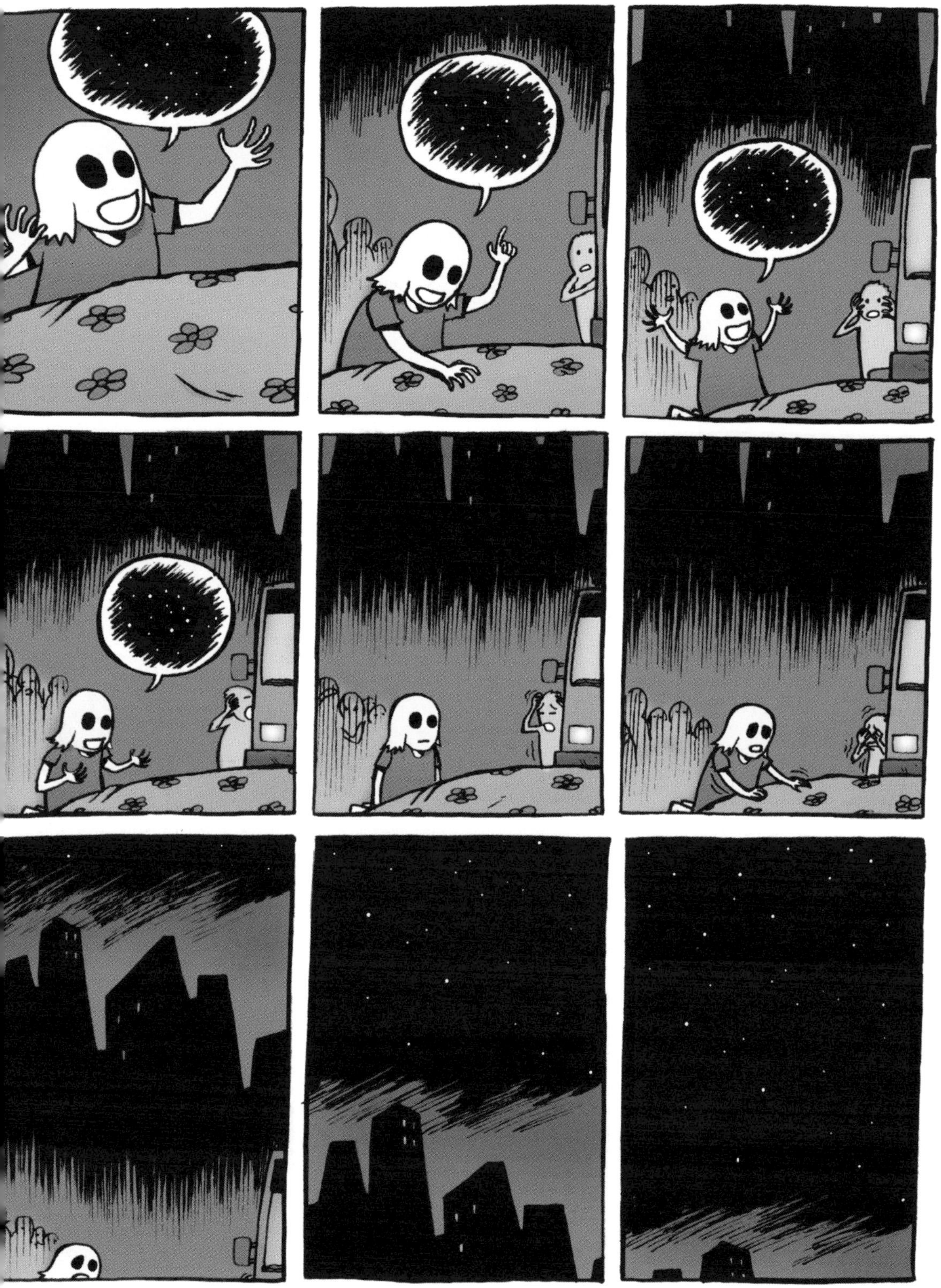

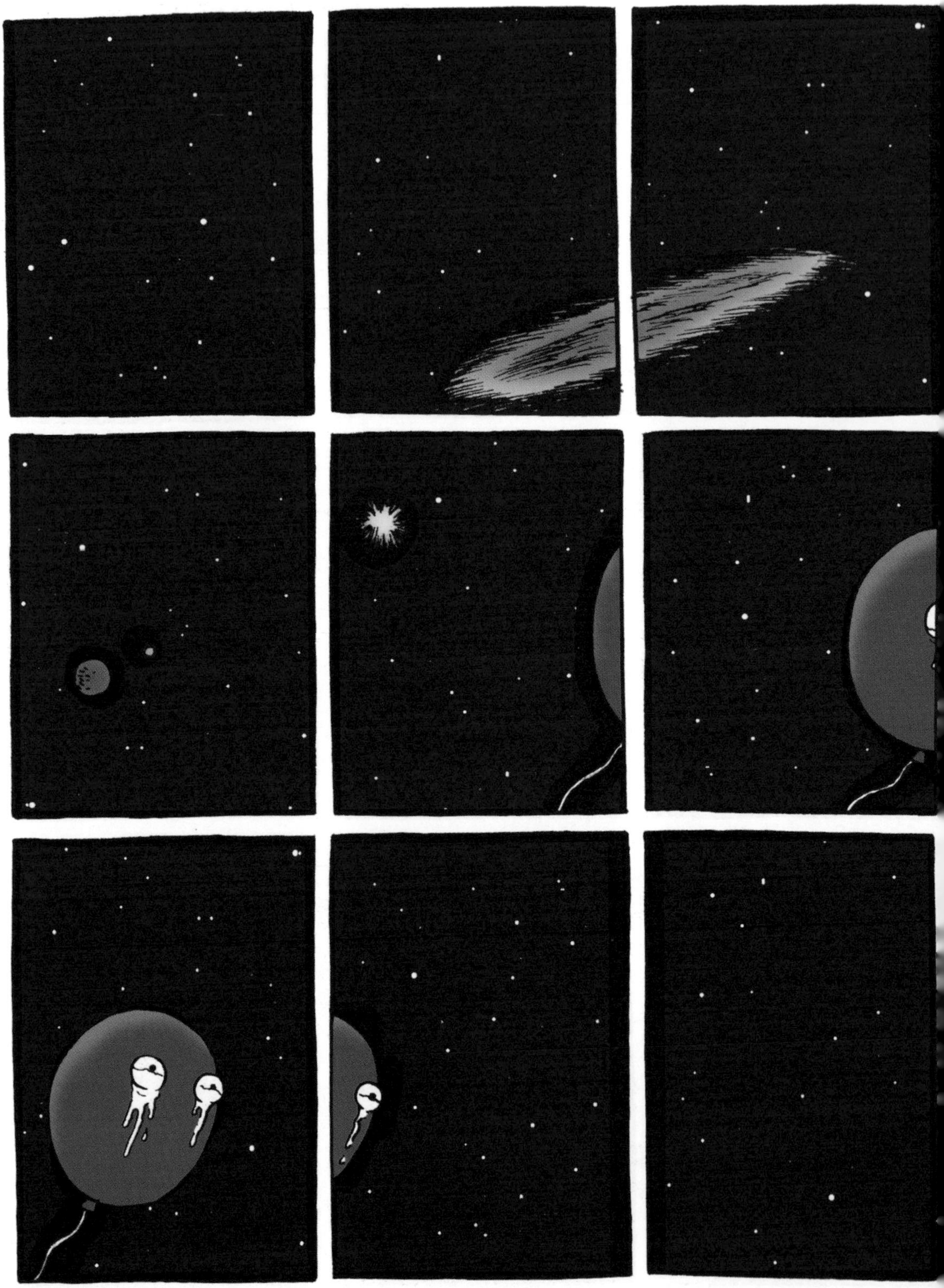

9

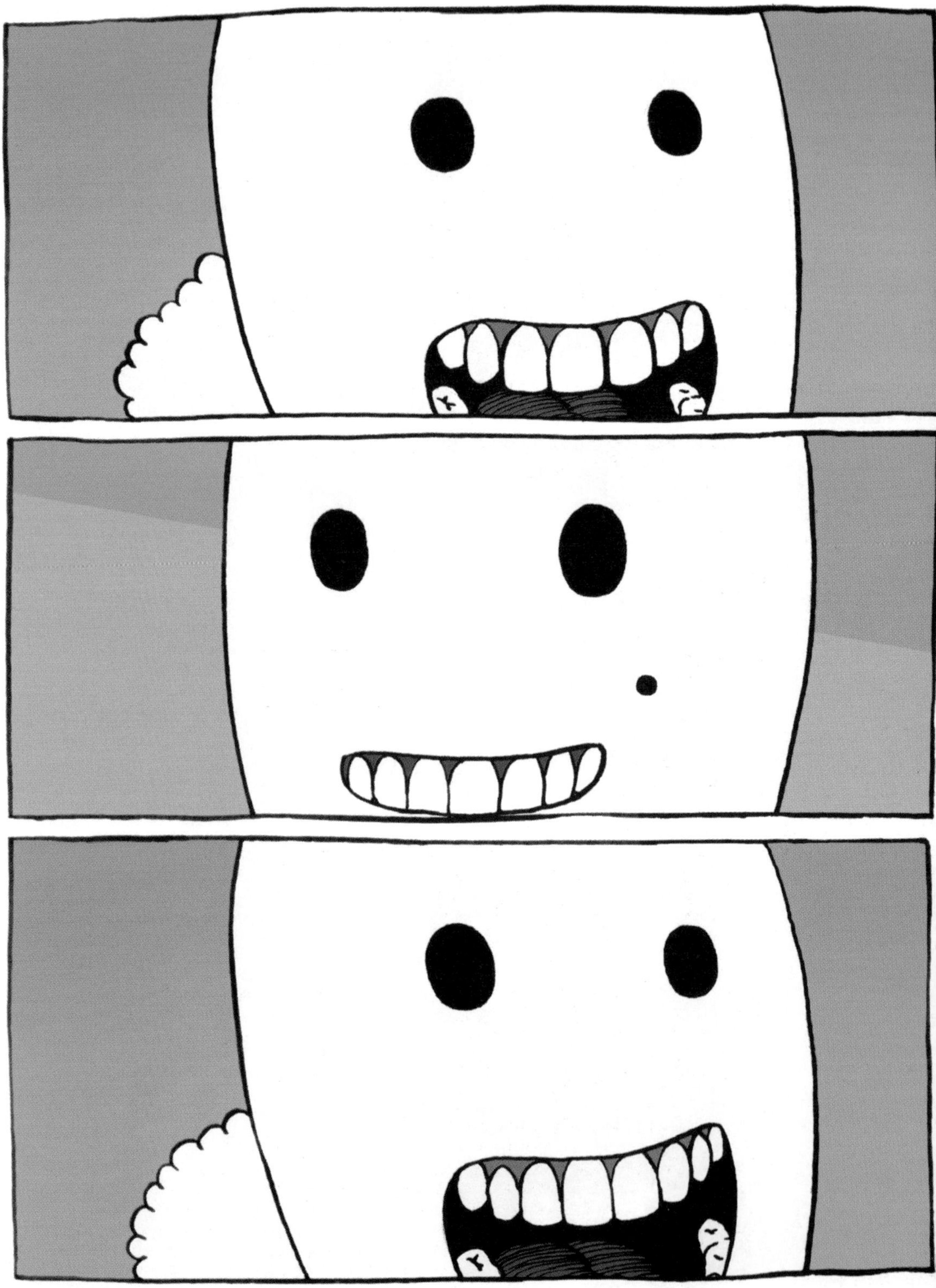

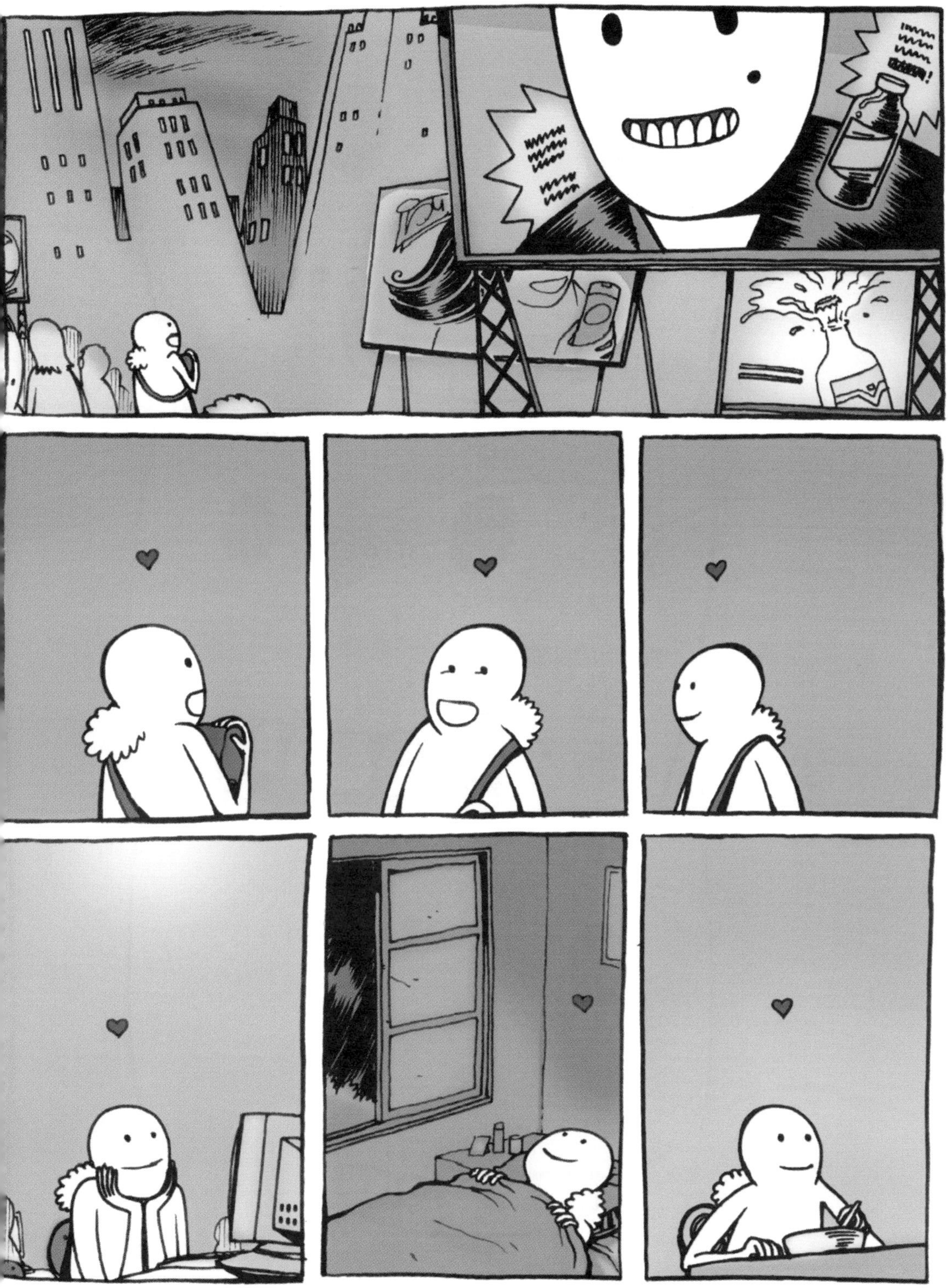

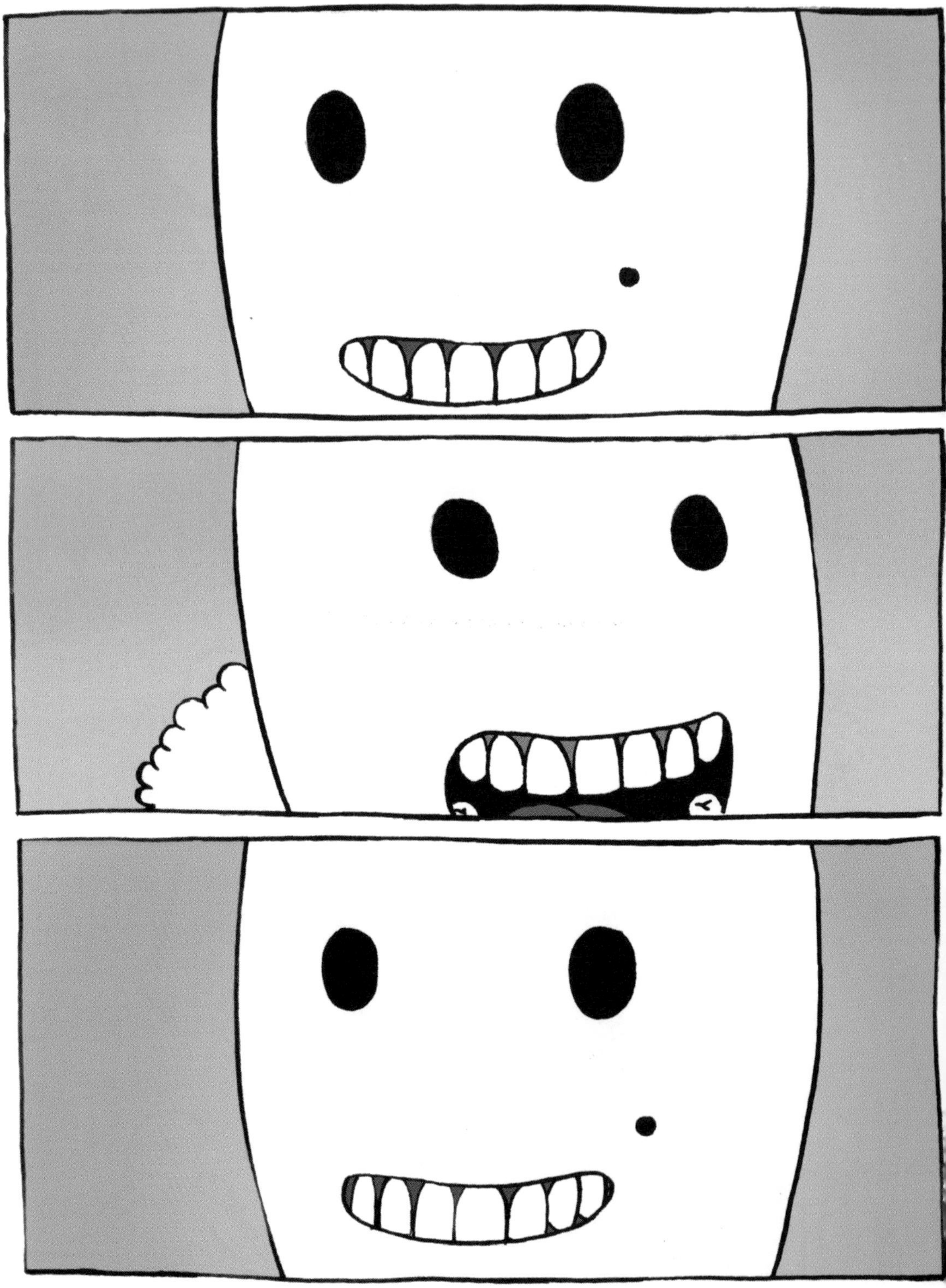

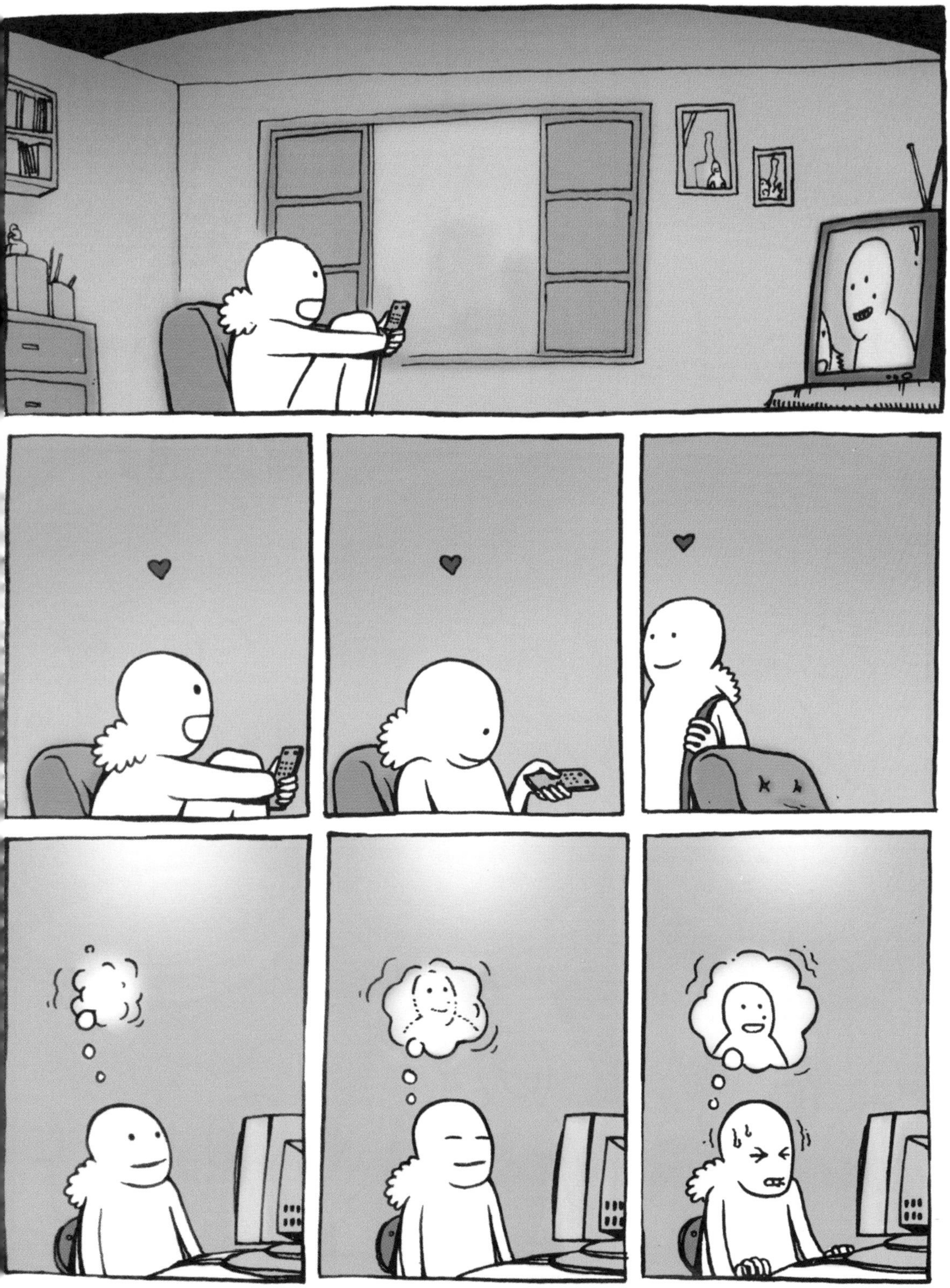

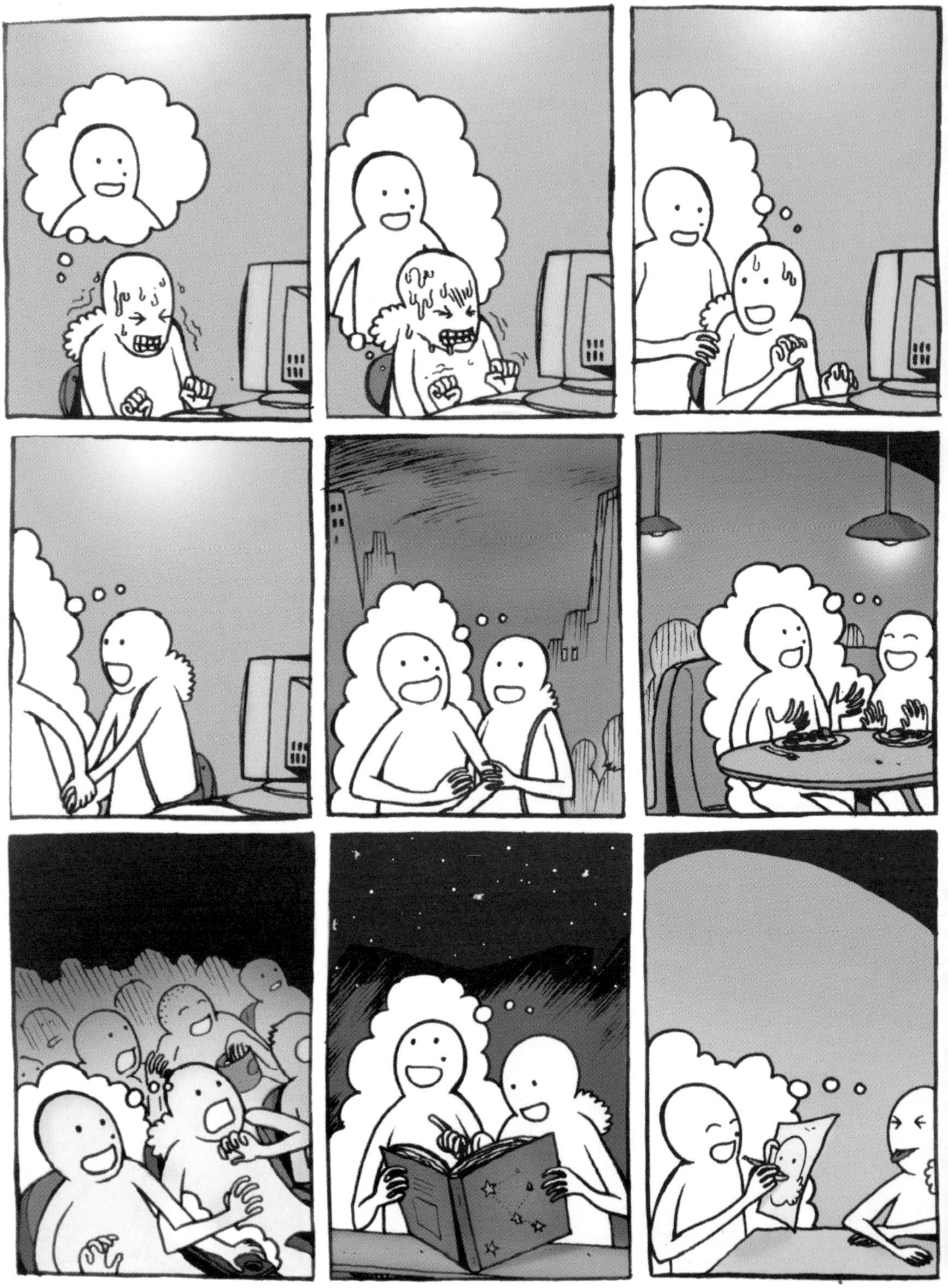

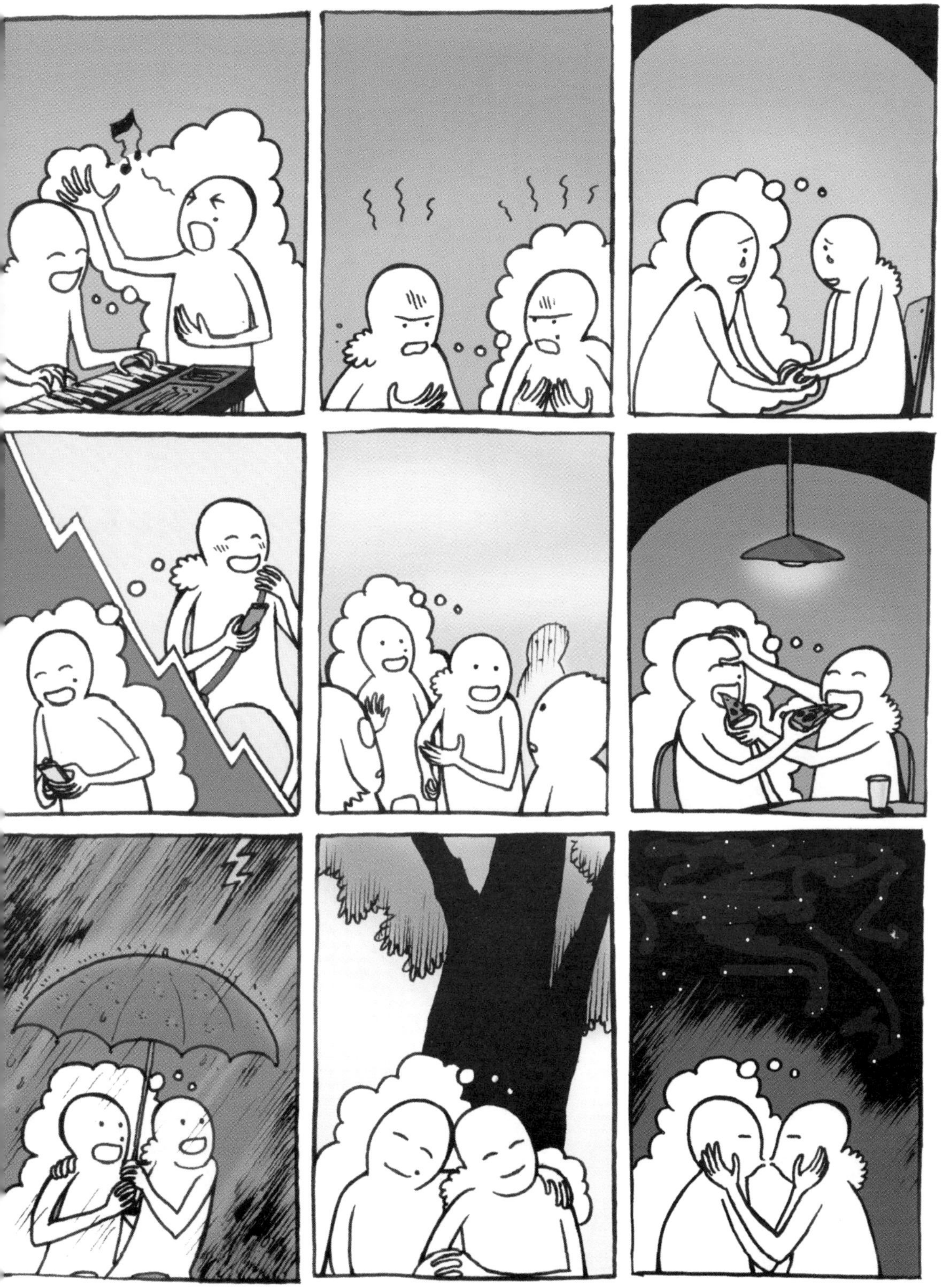

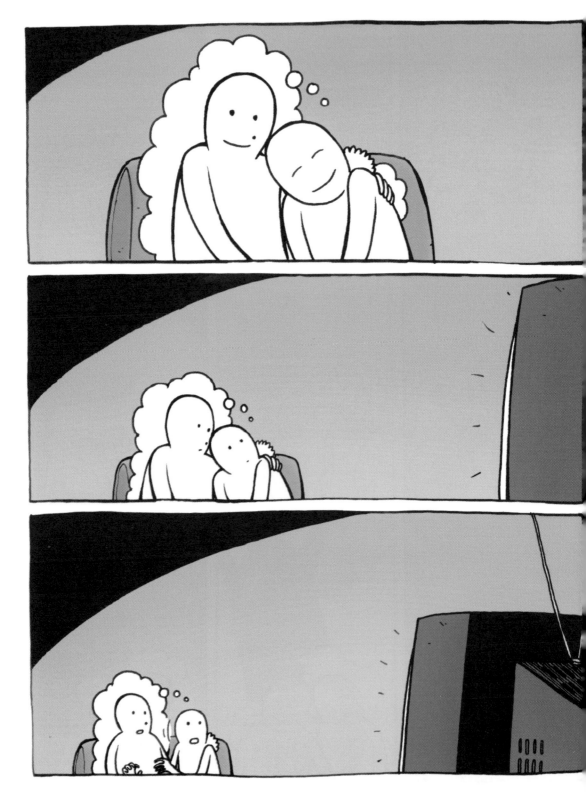

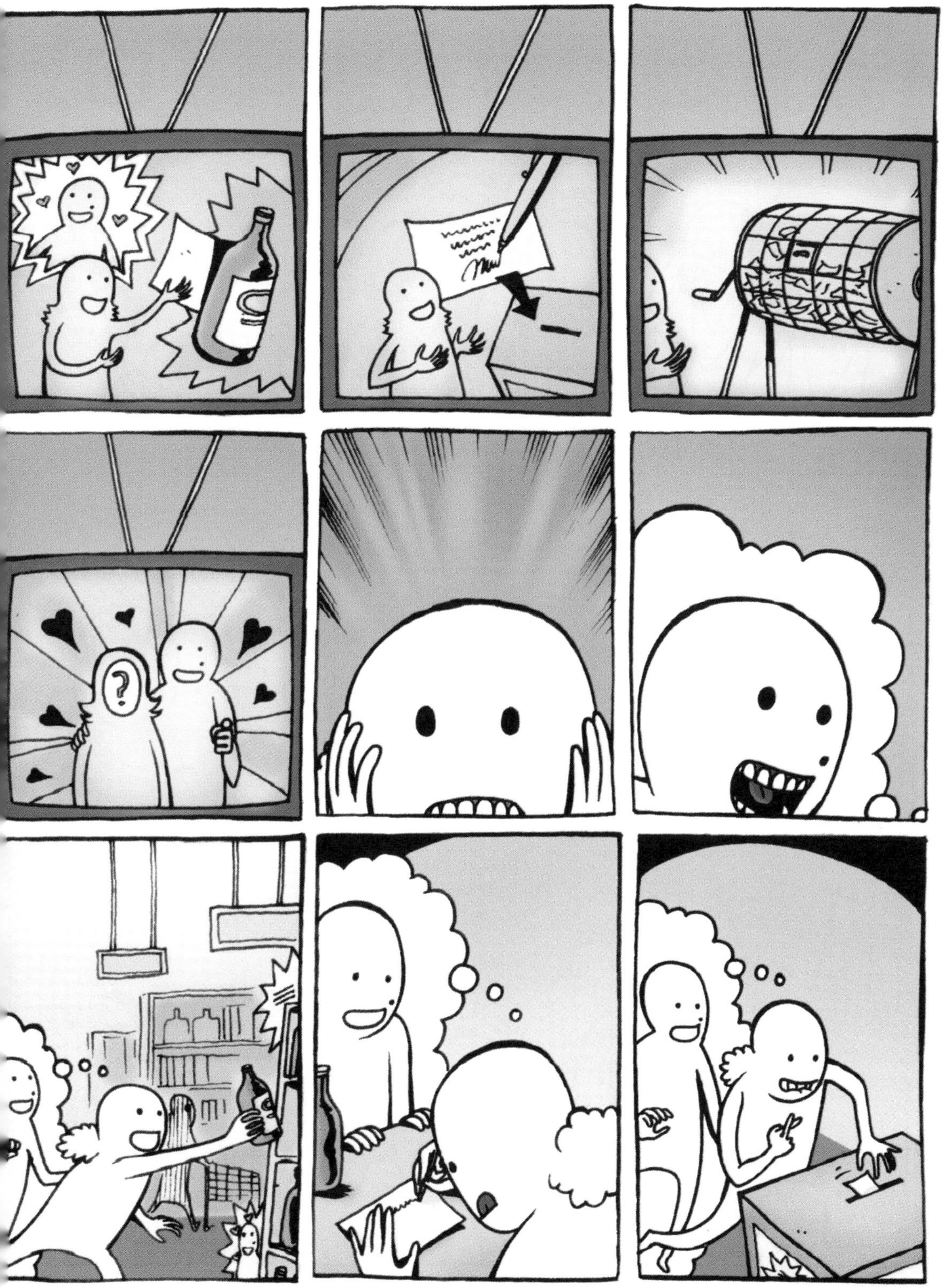

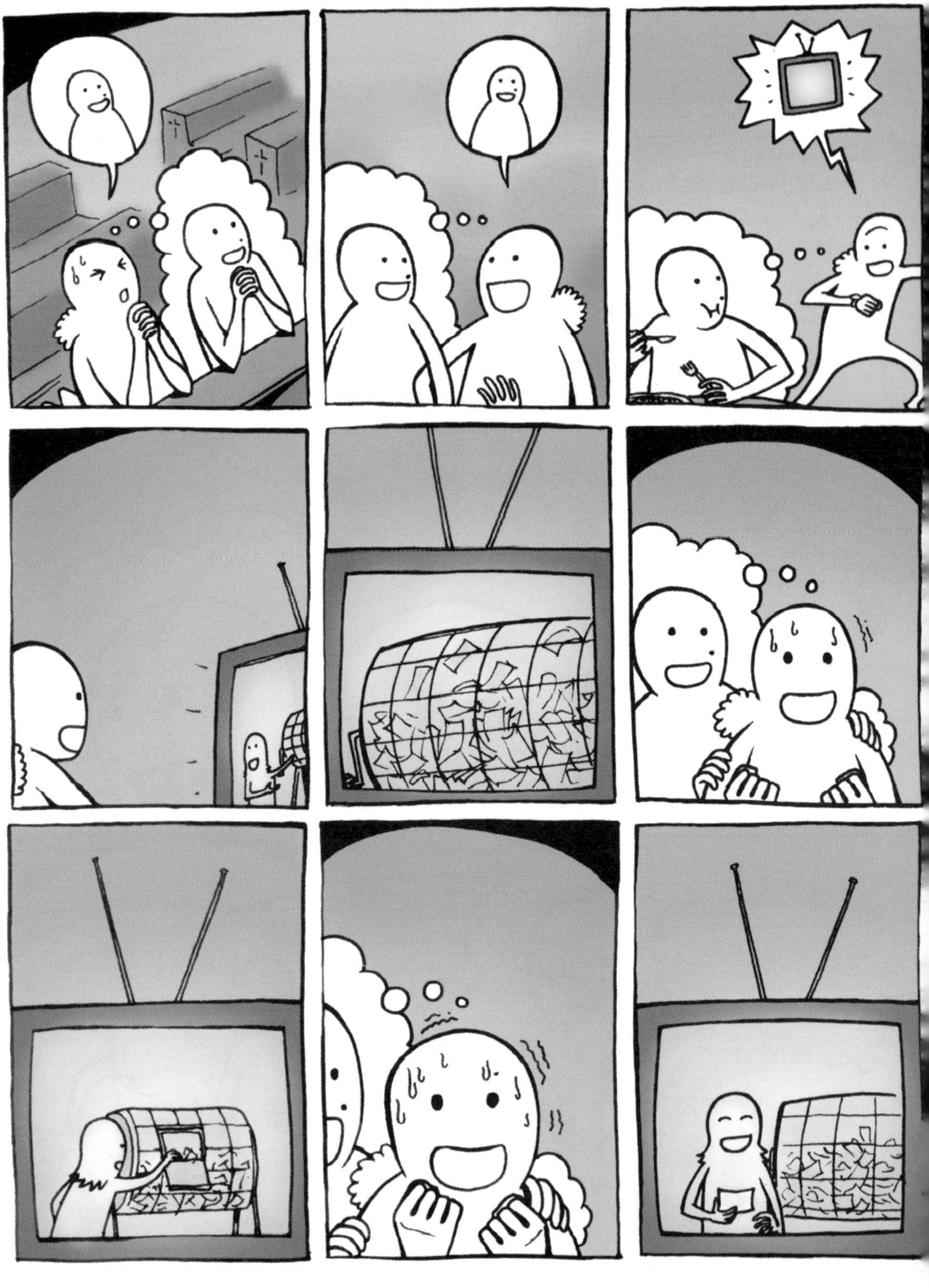

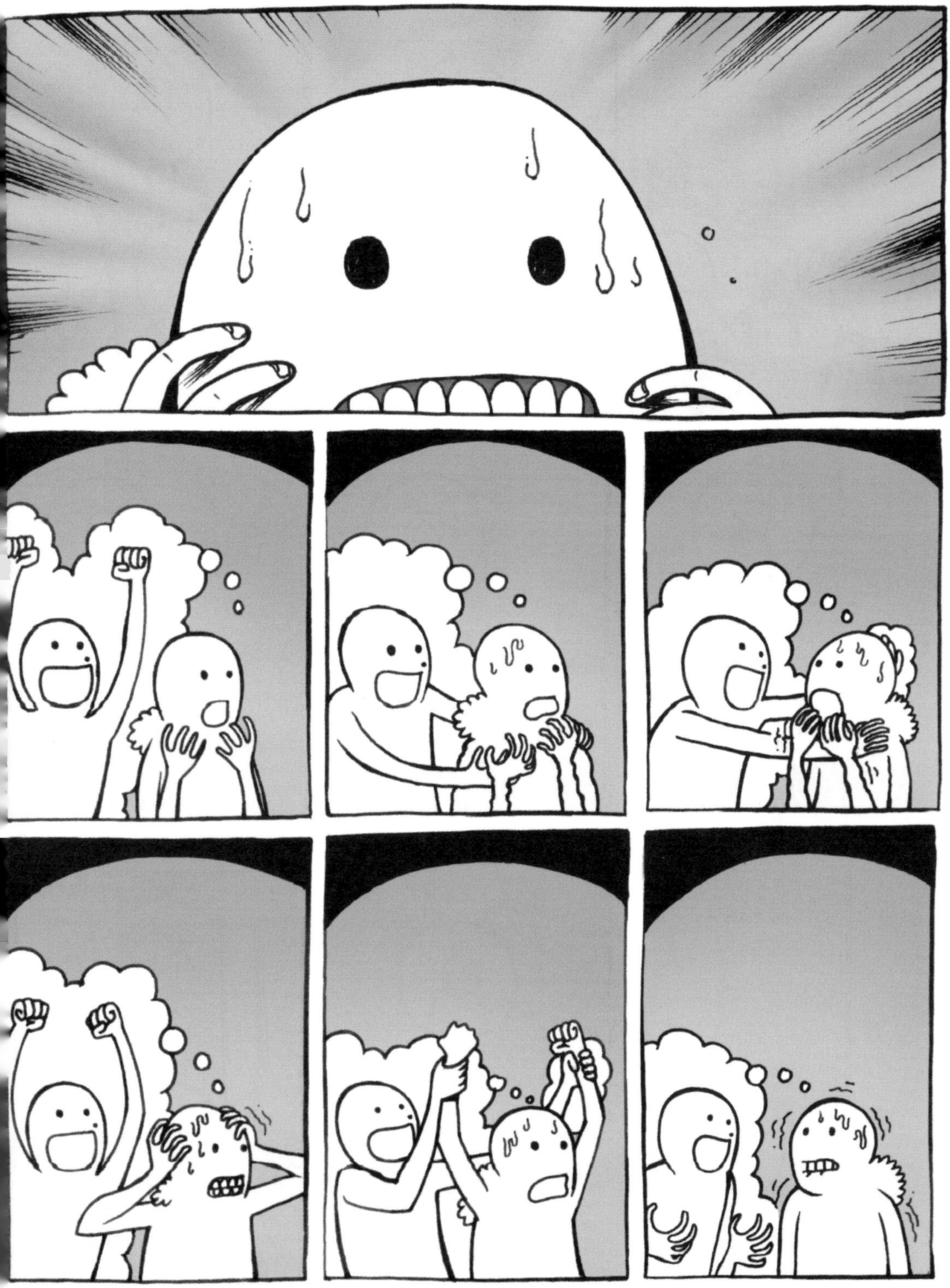

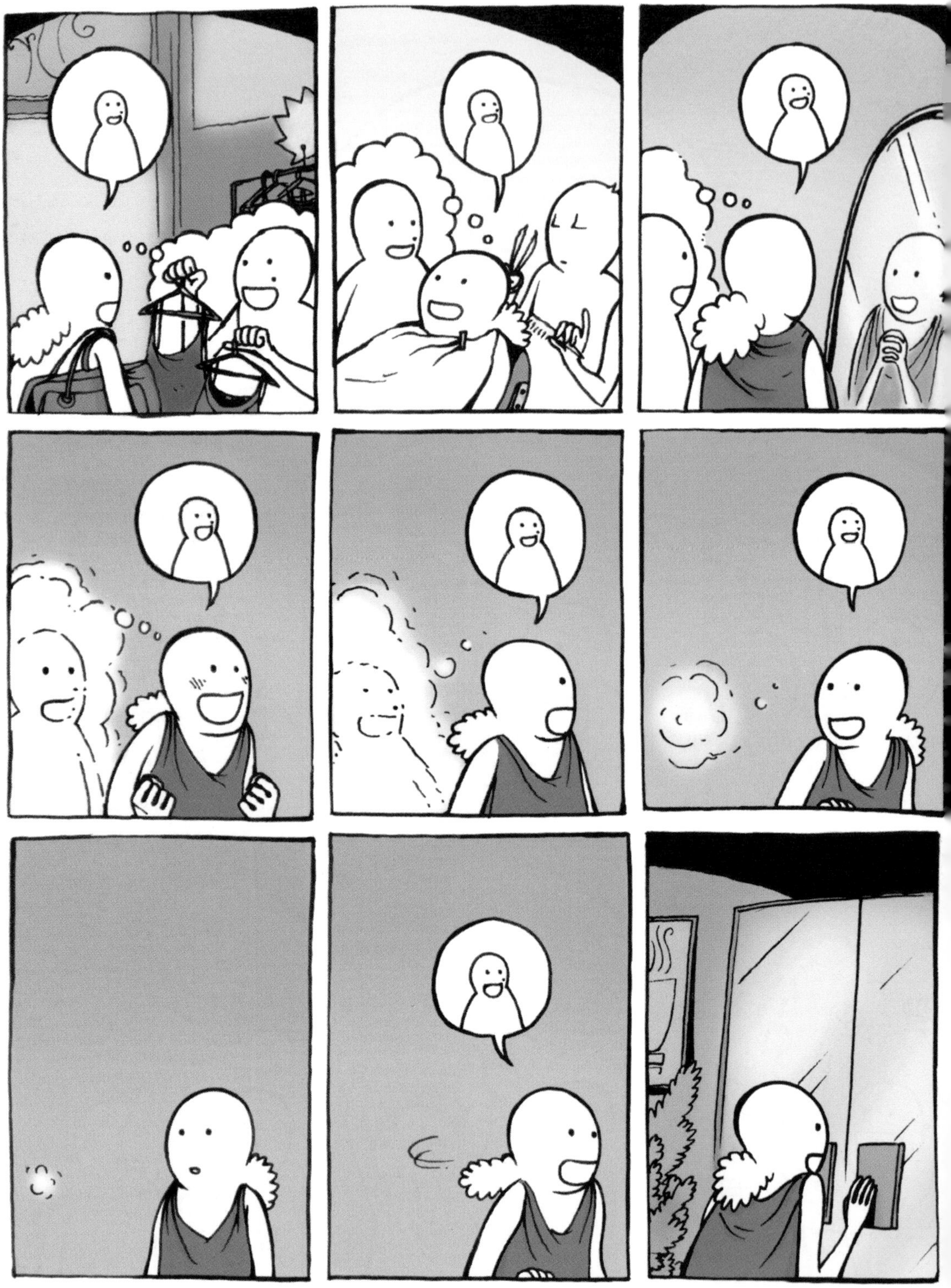

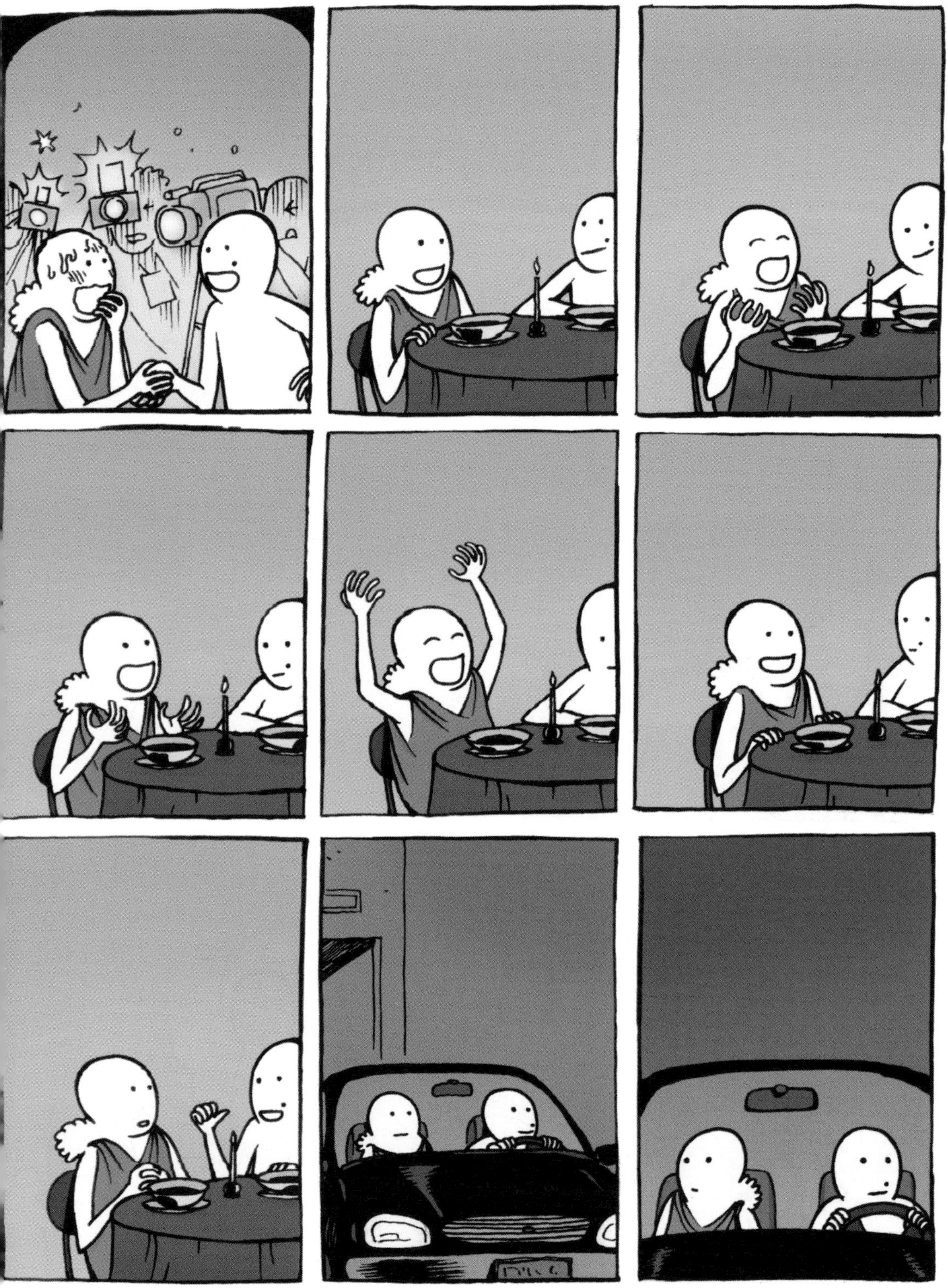

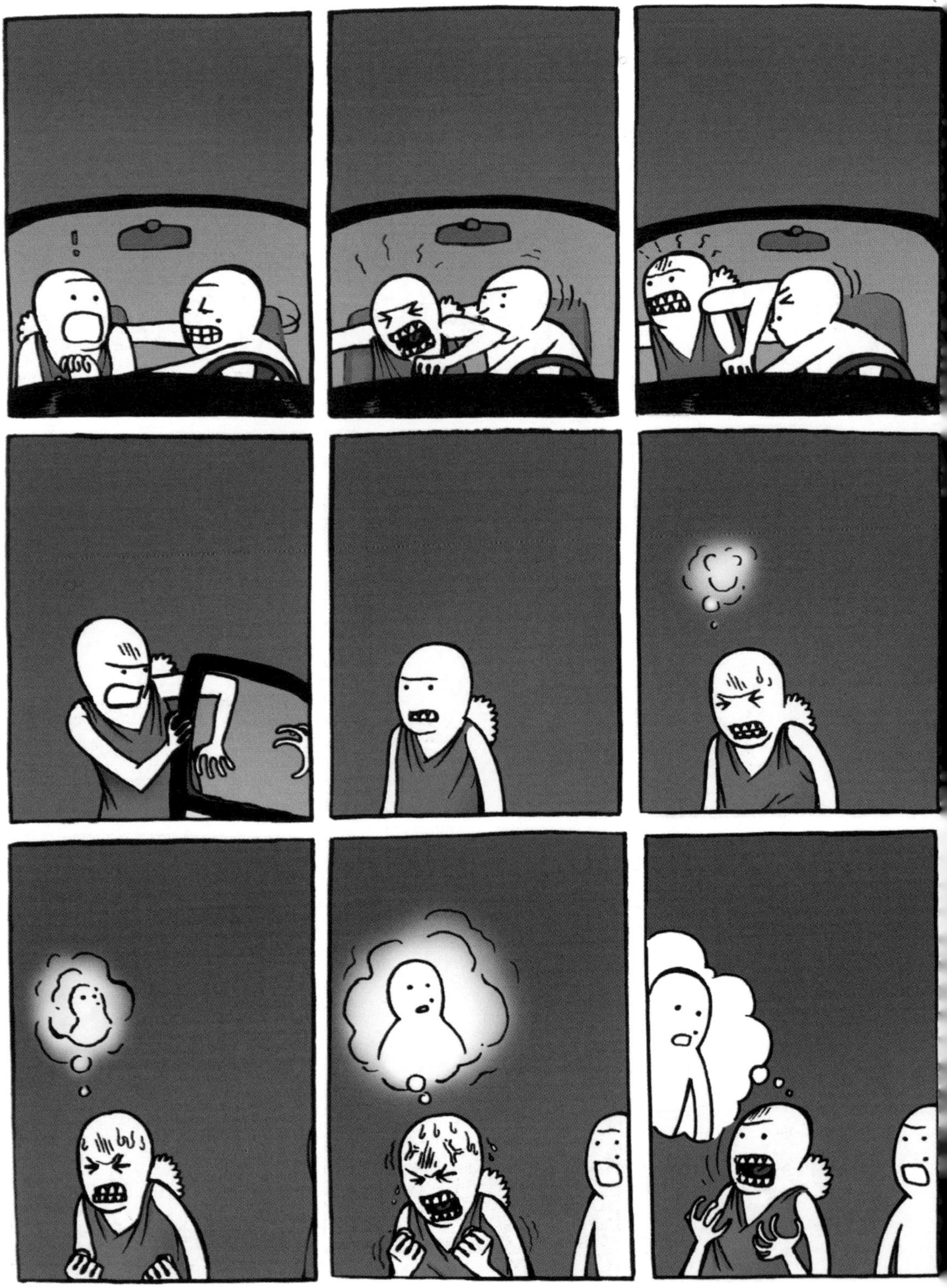

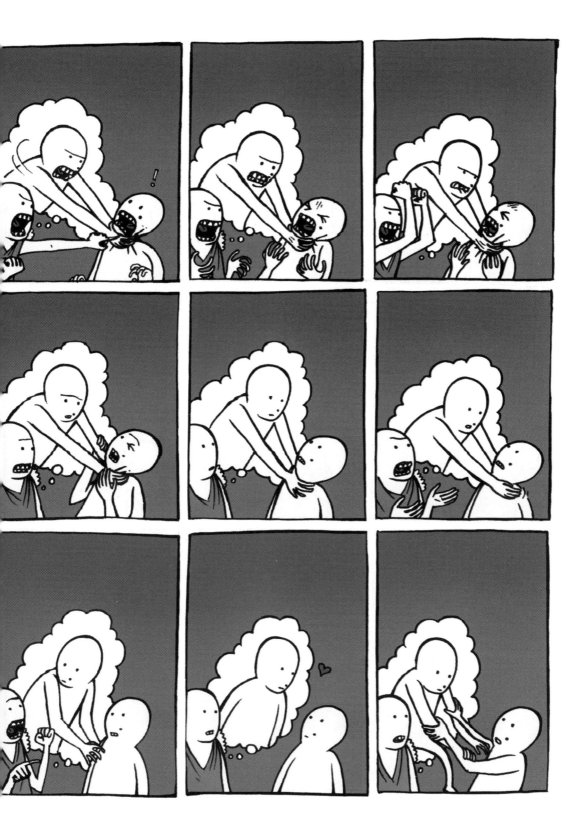

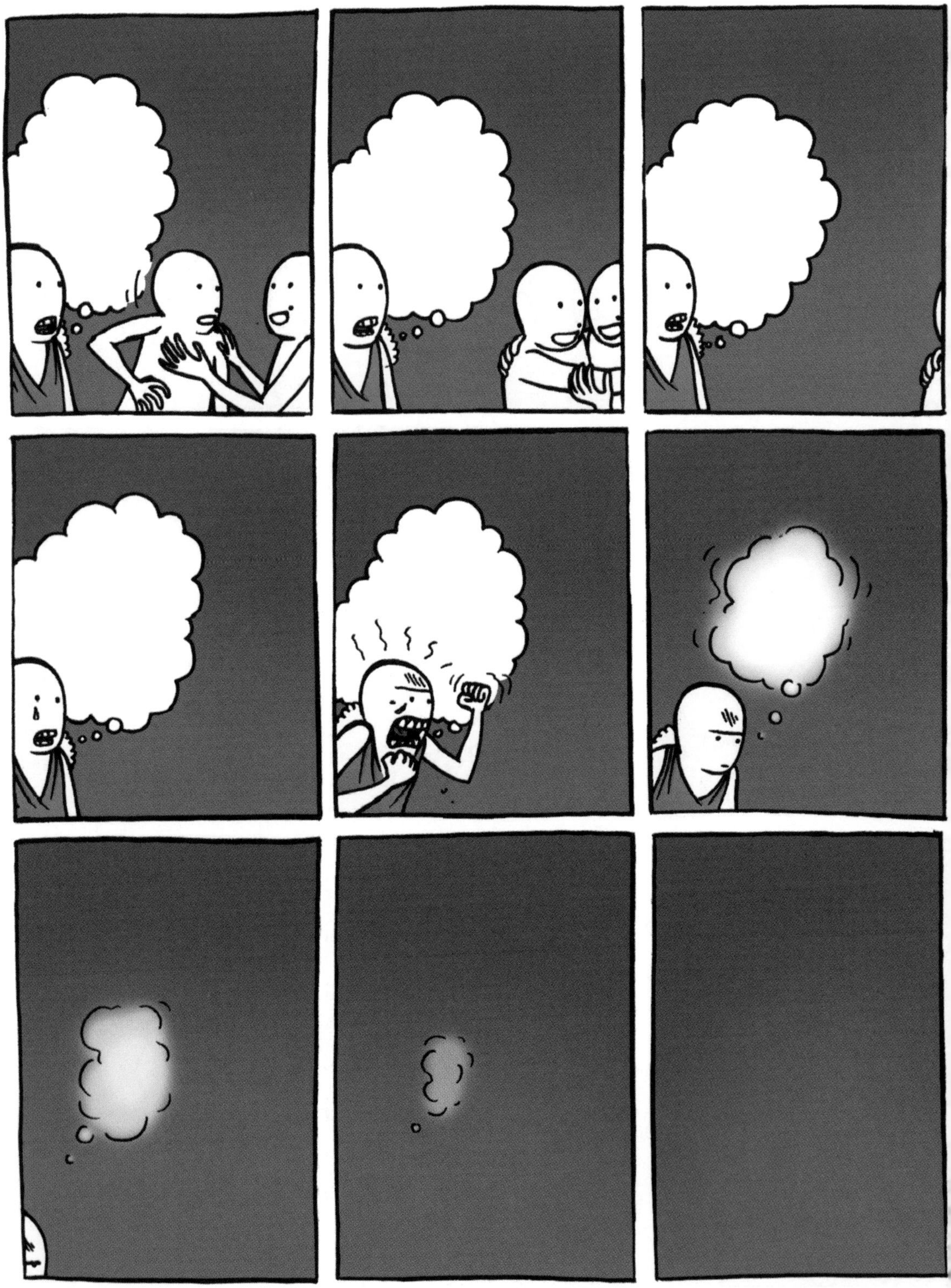

10

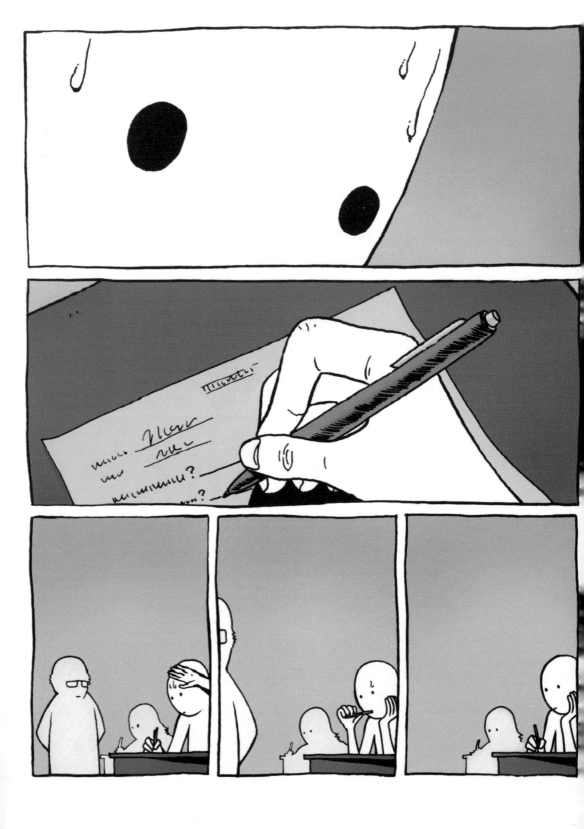

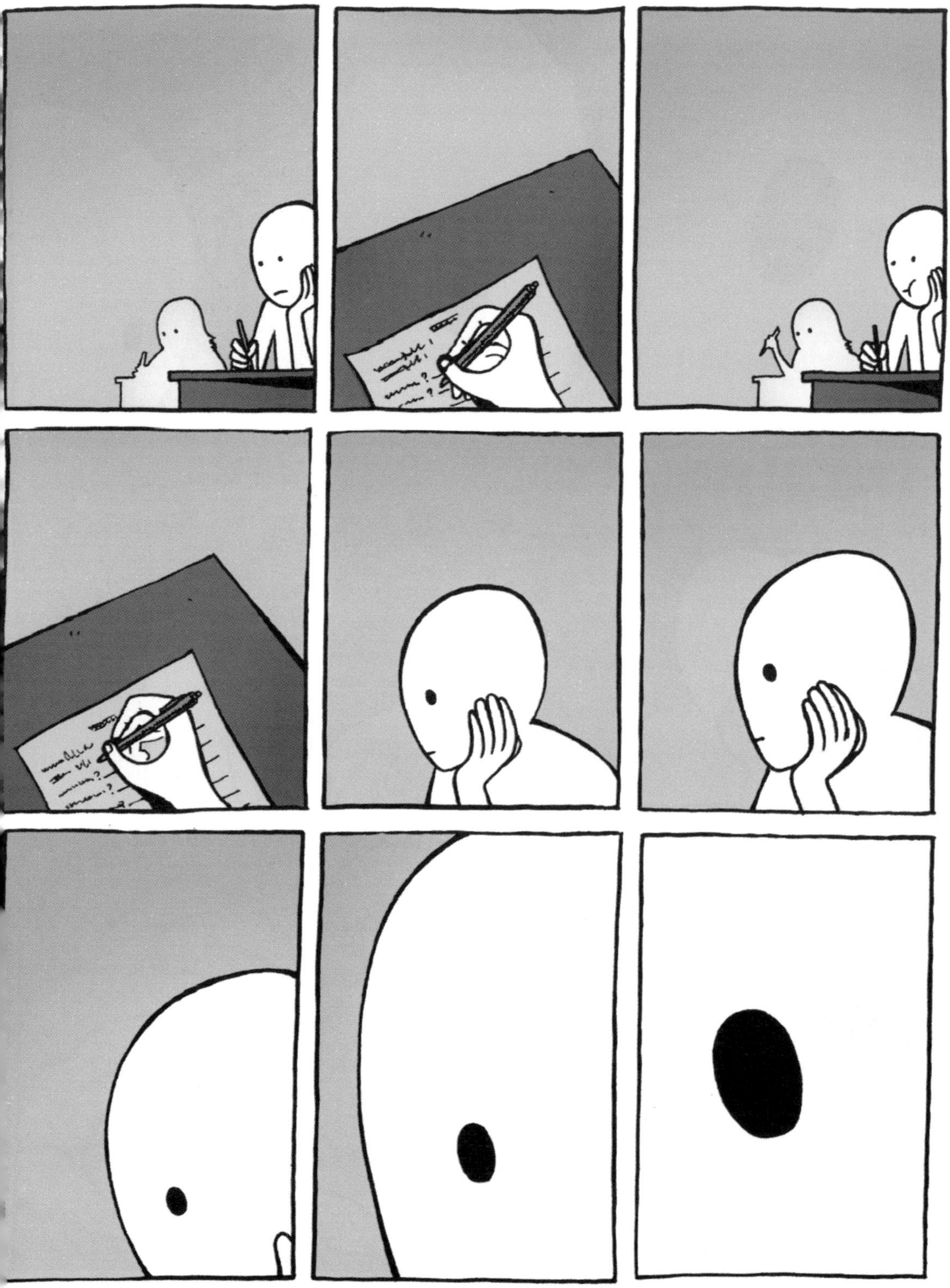

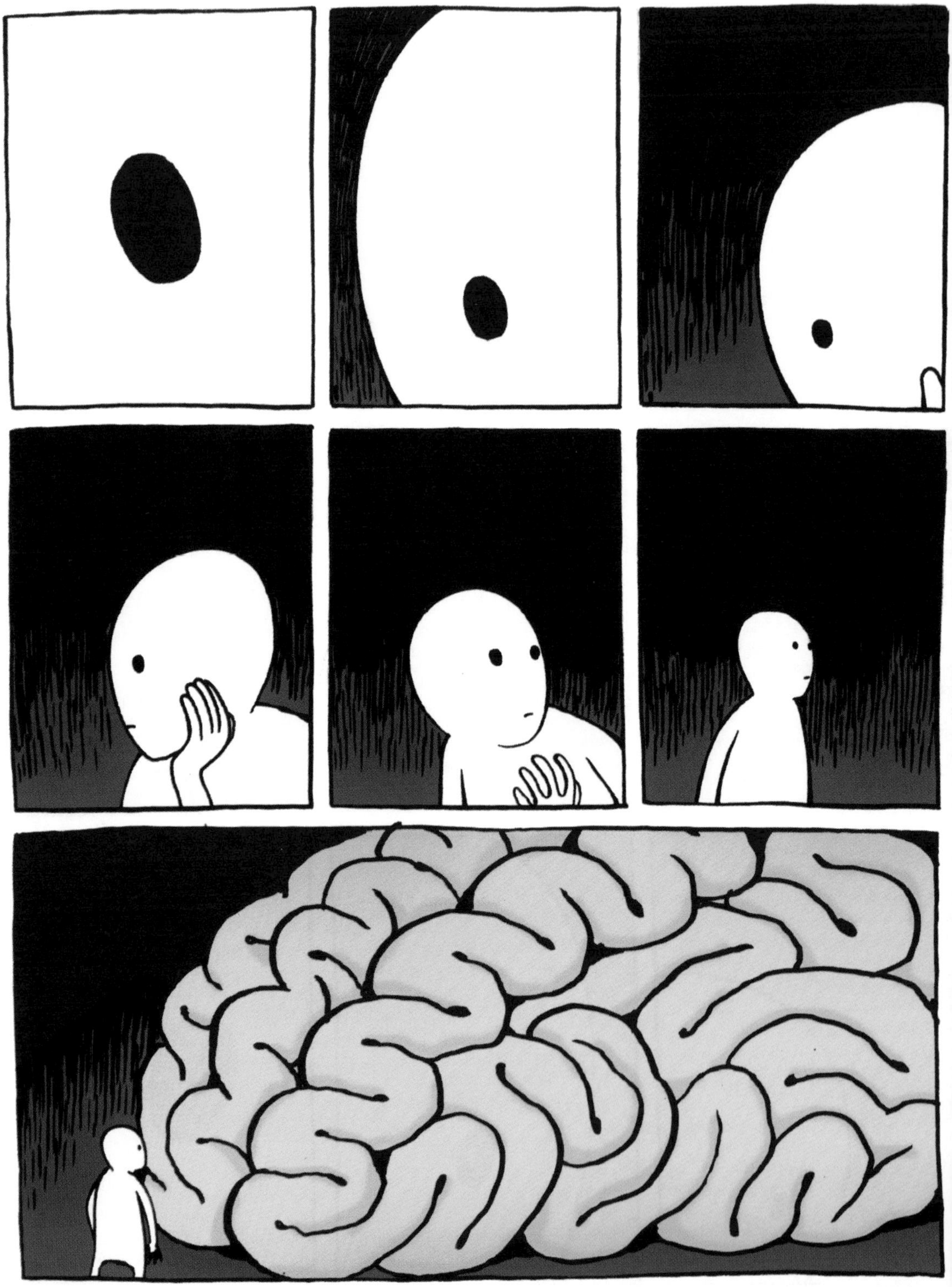

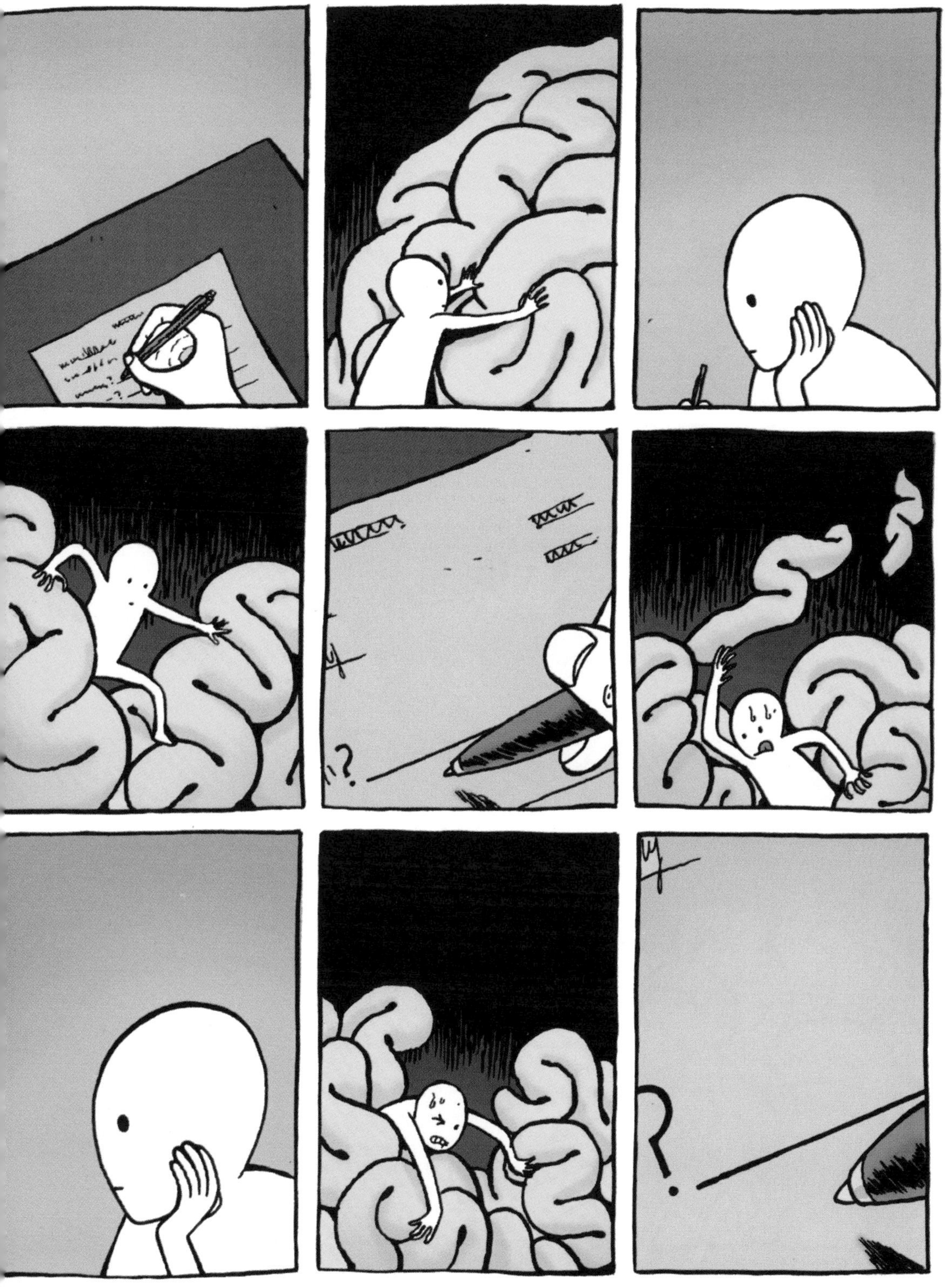
?
?

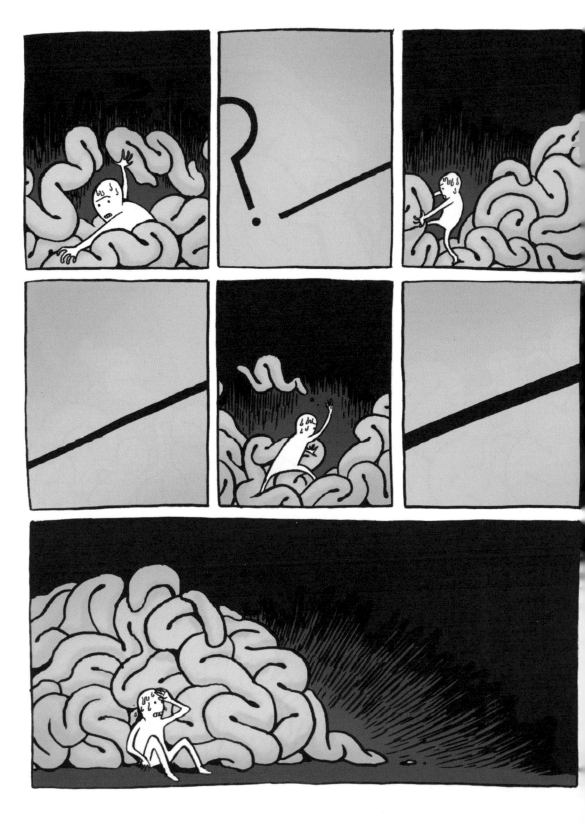

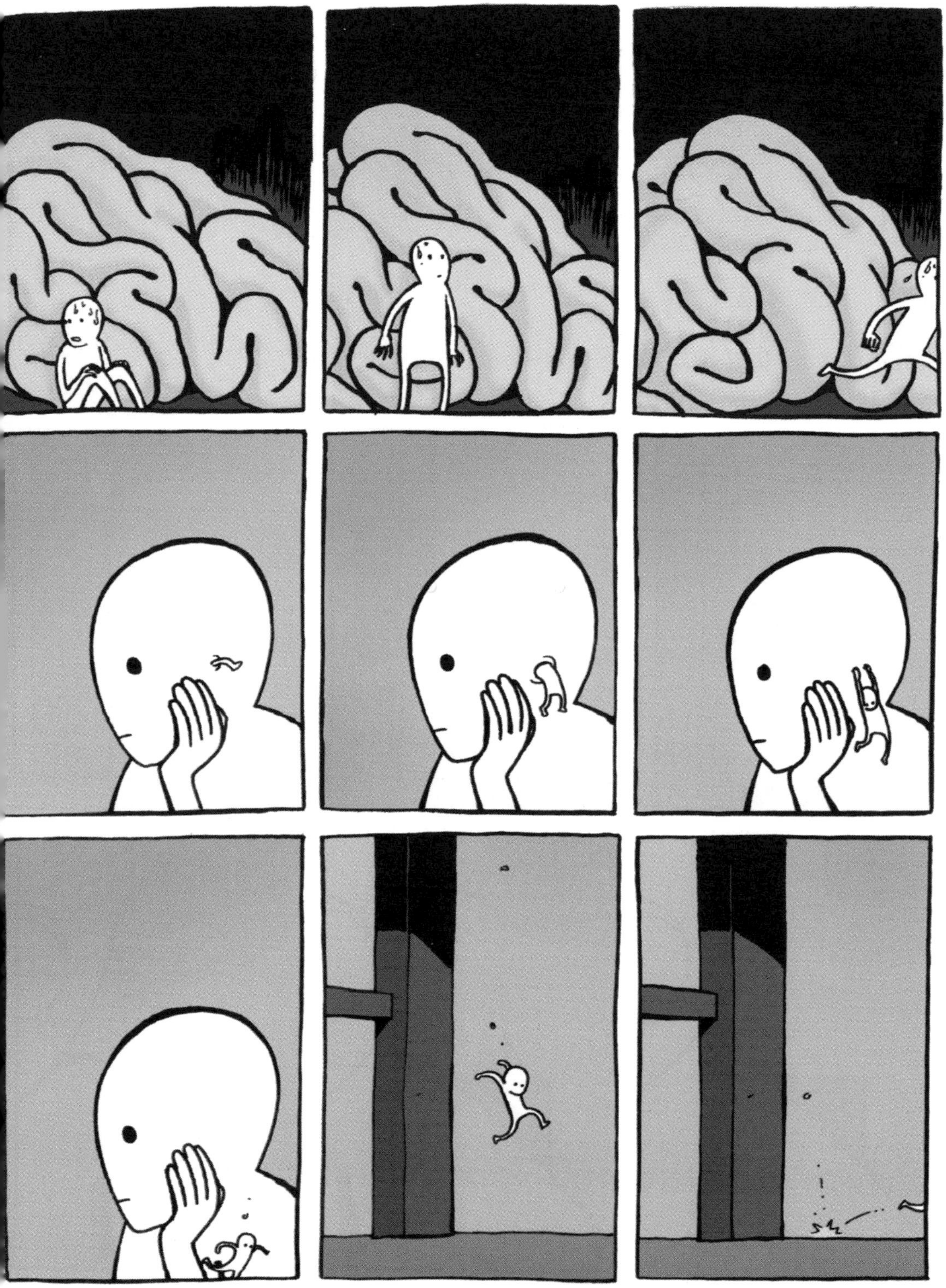

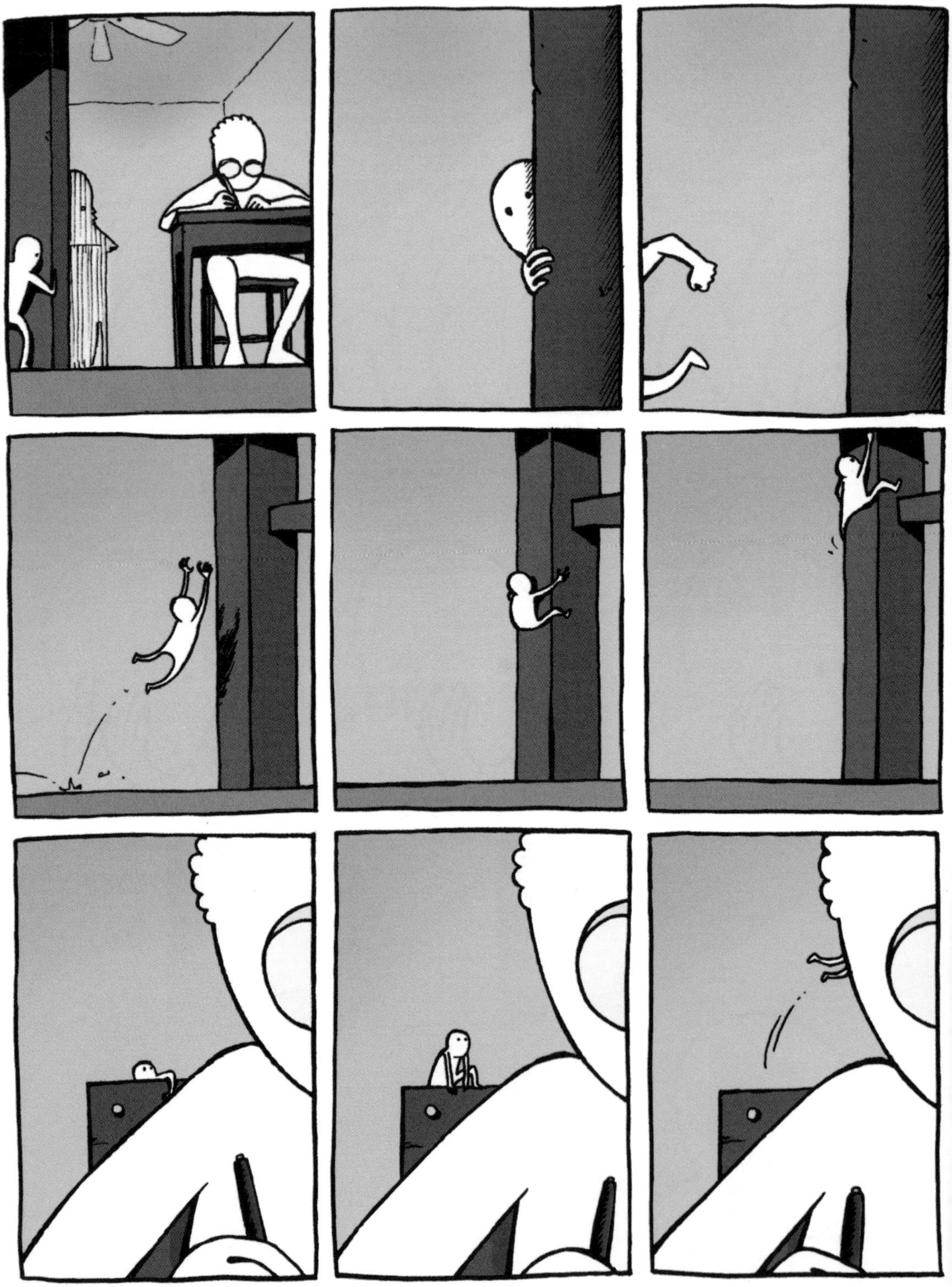

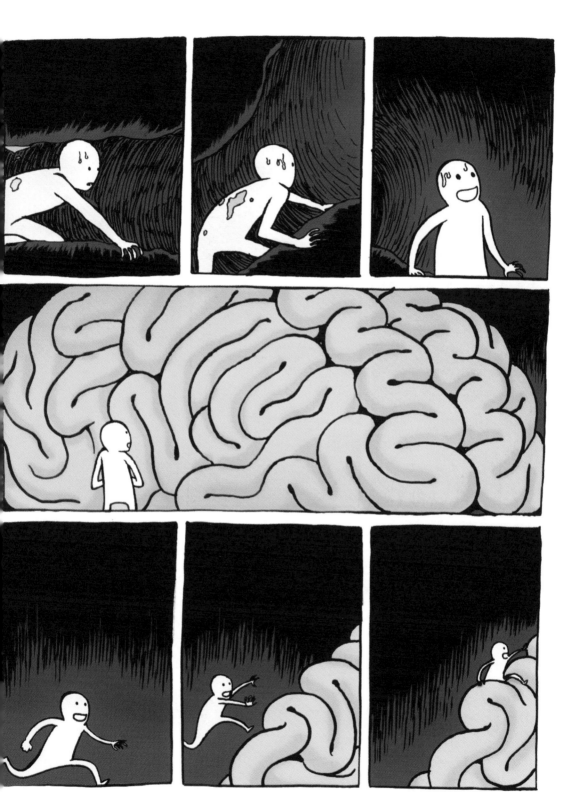

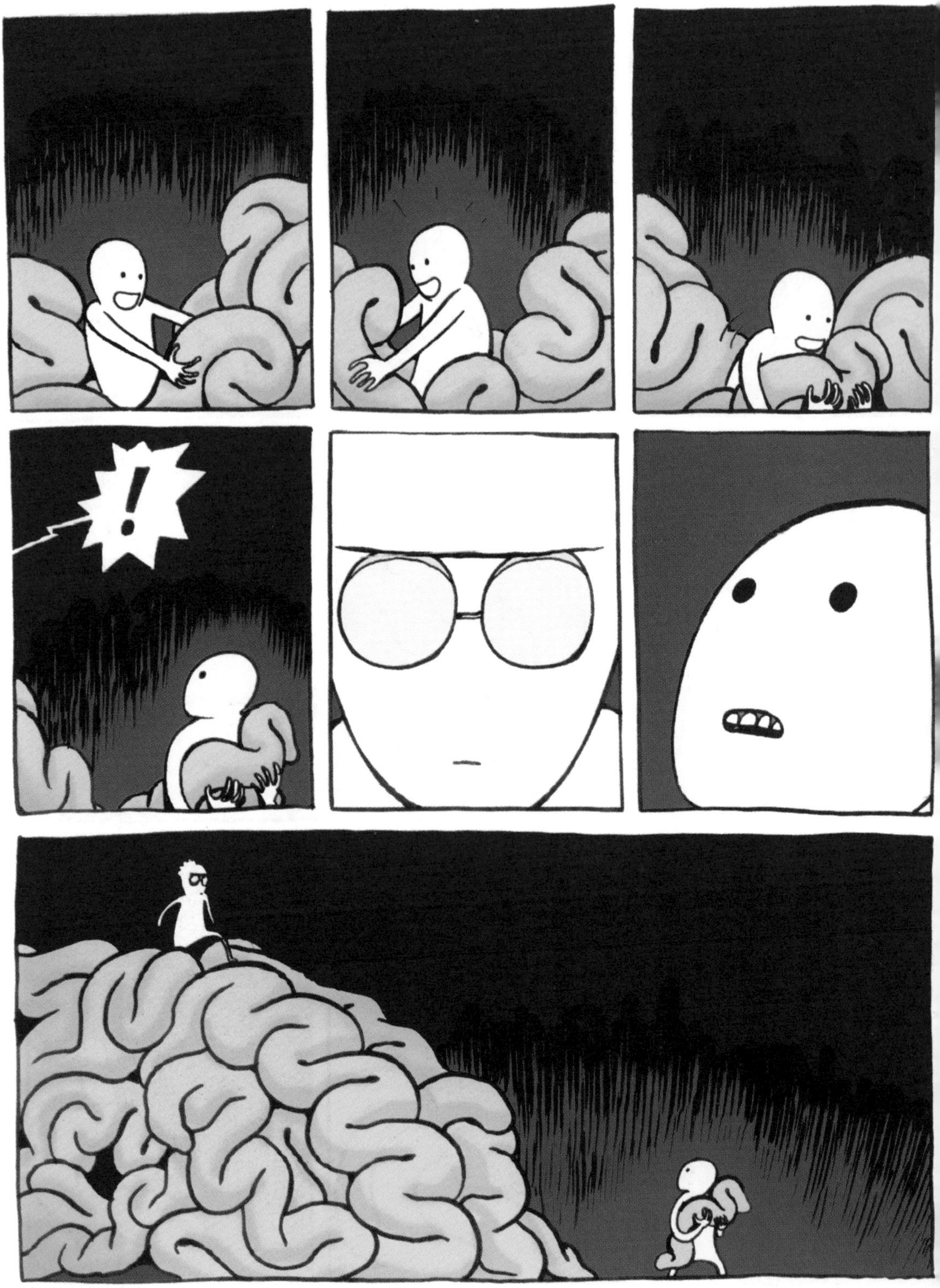
!

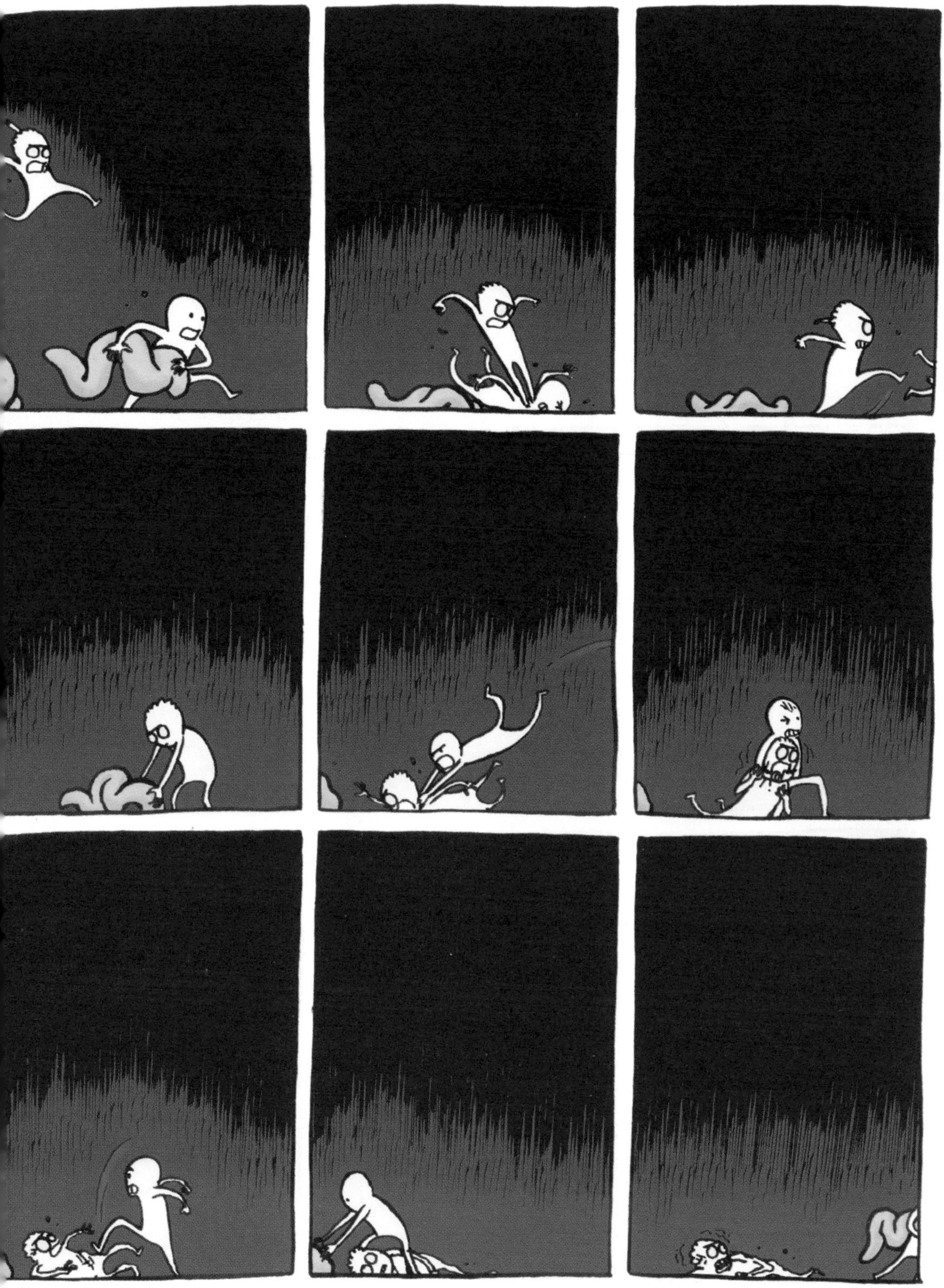

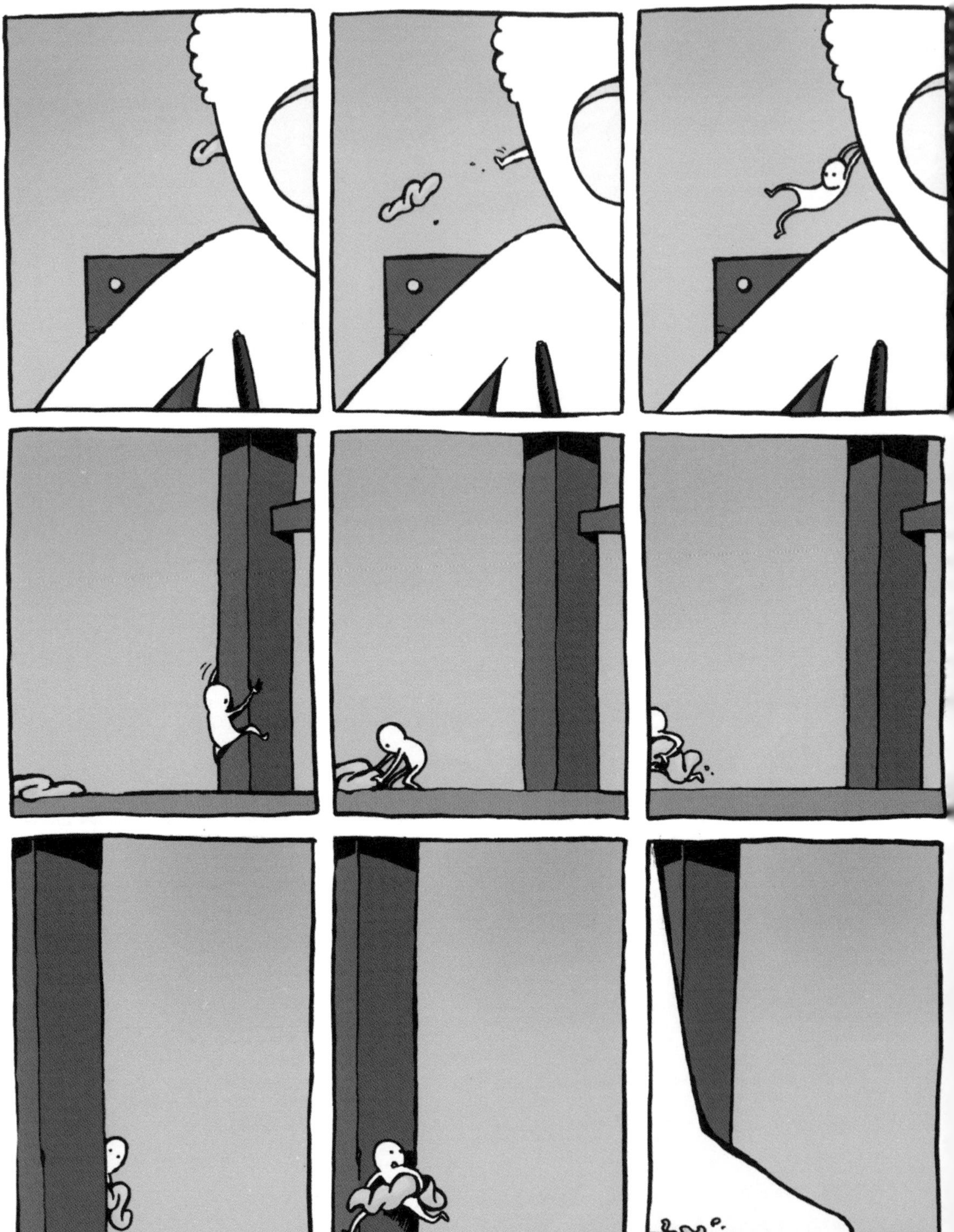

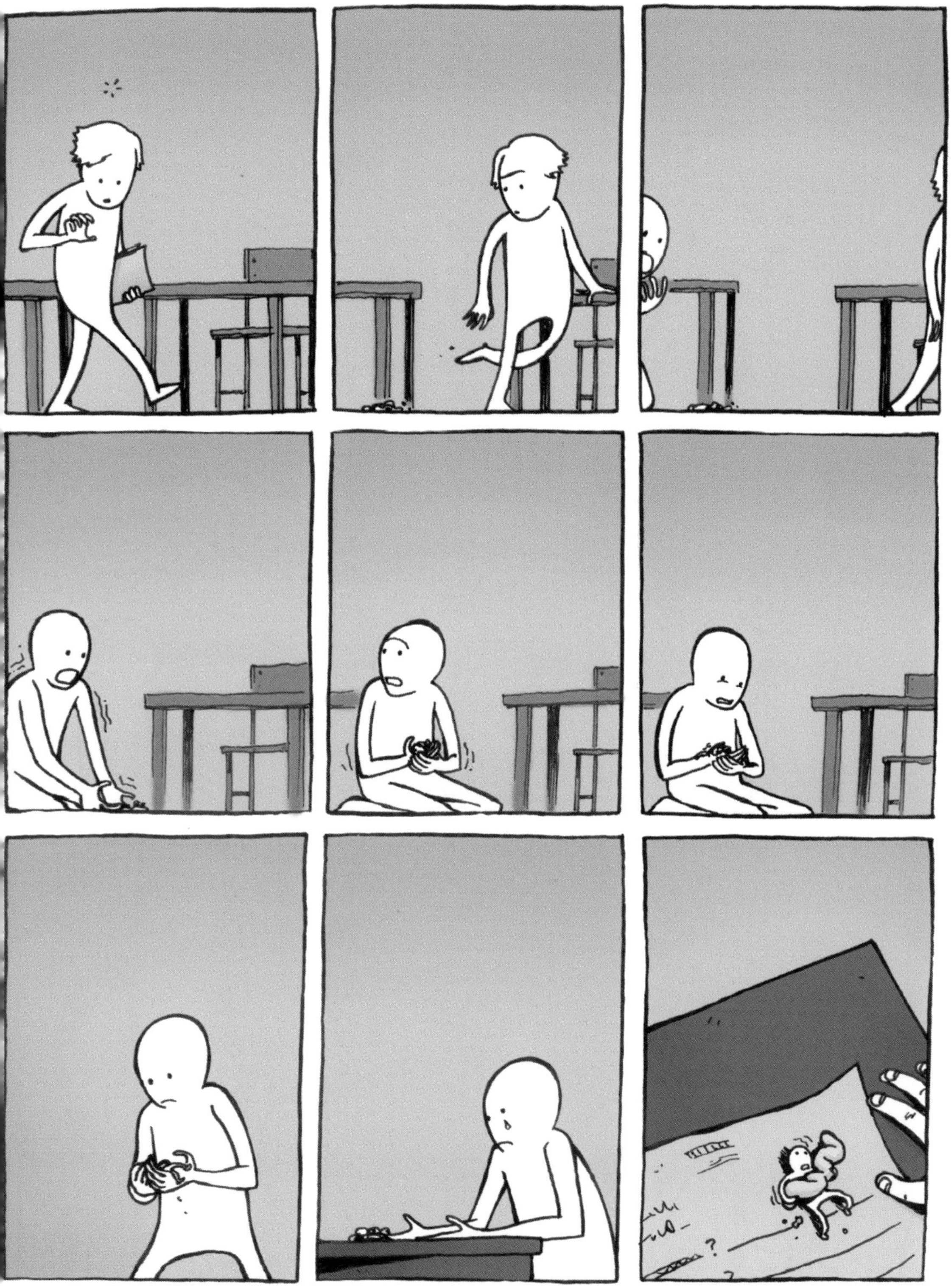

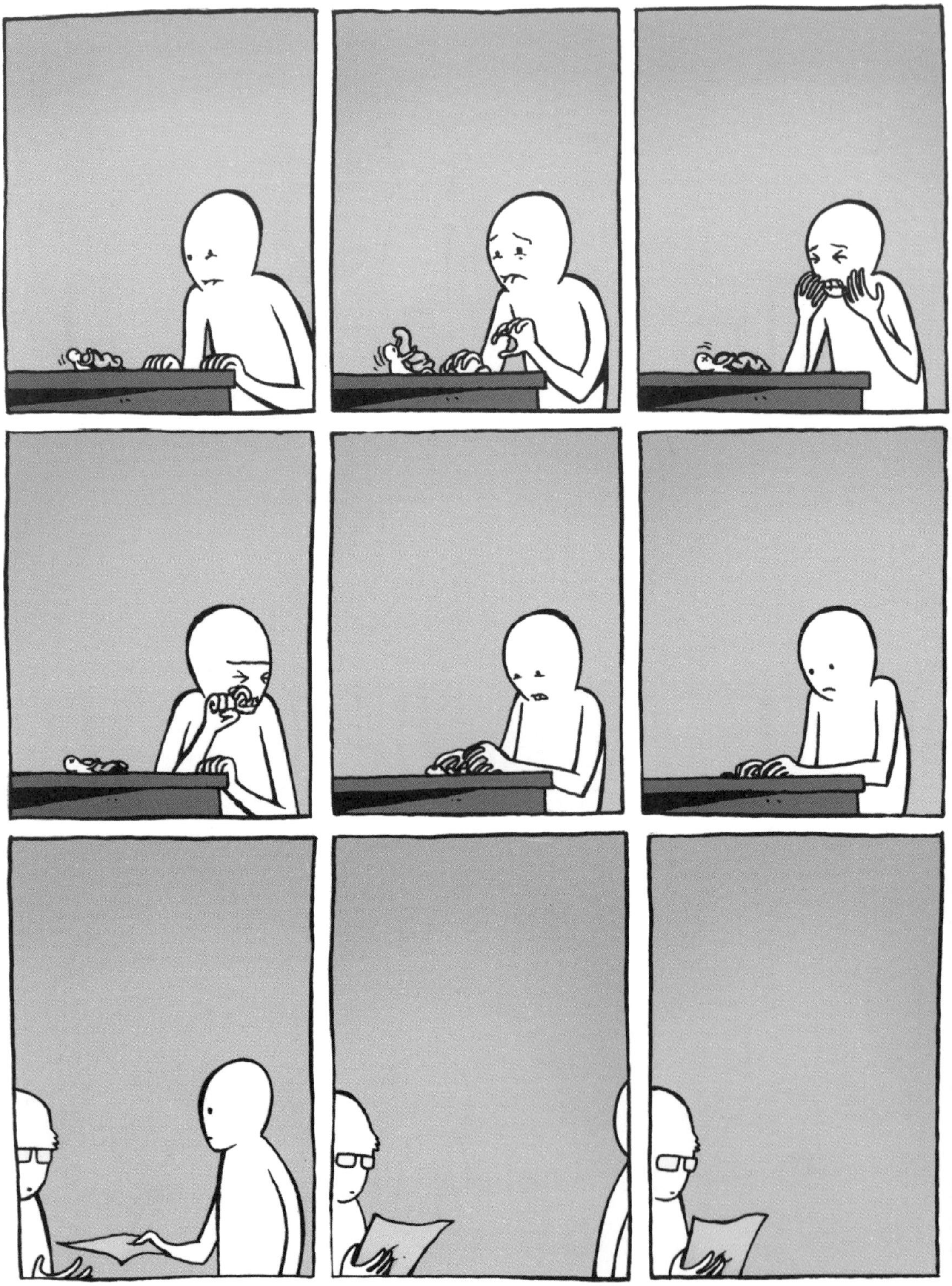

11

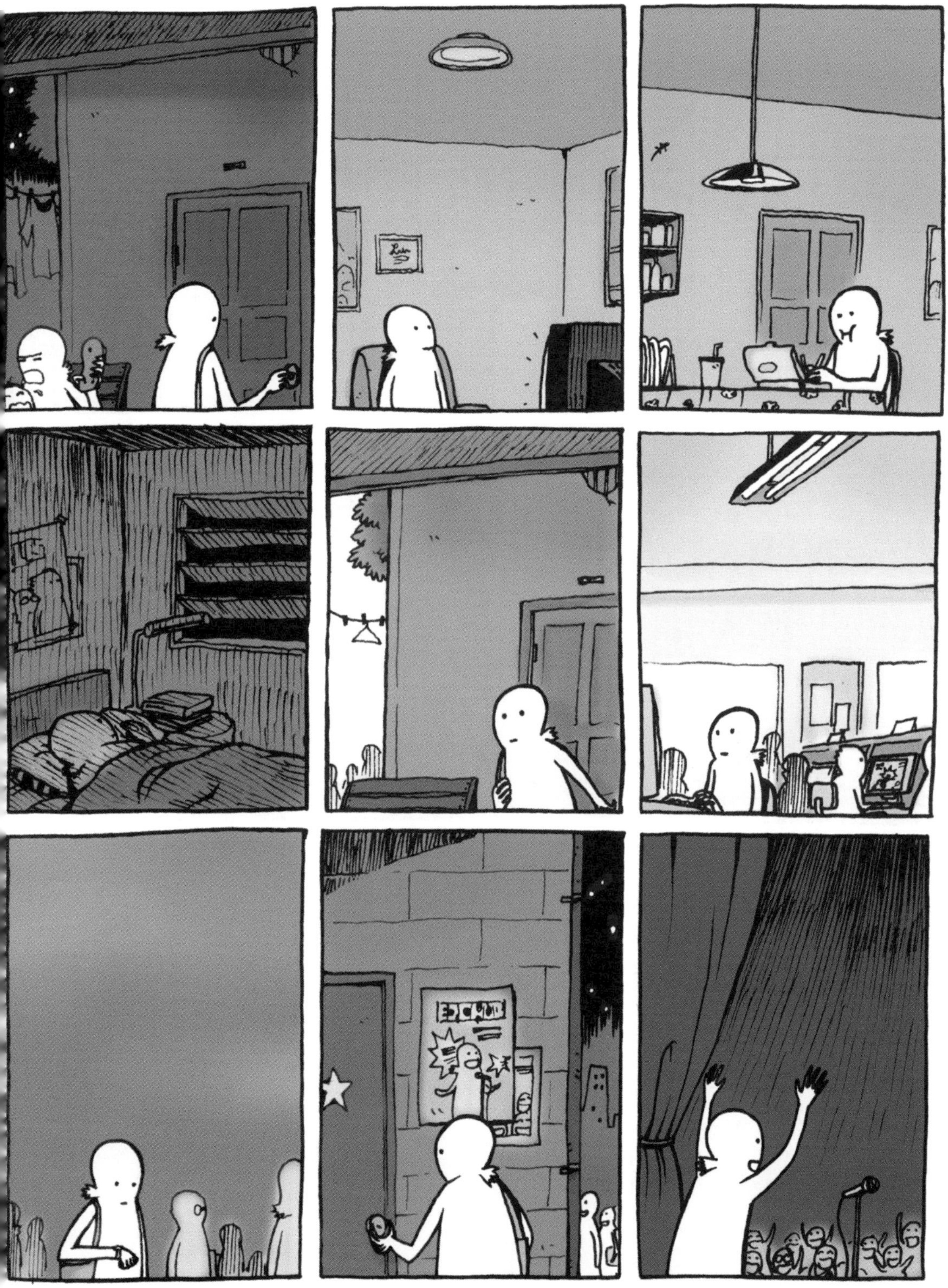

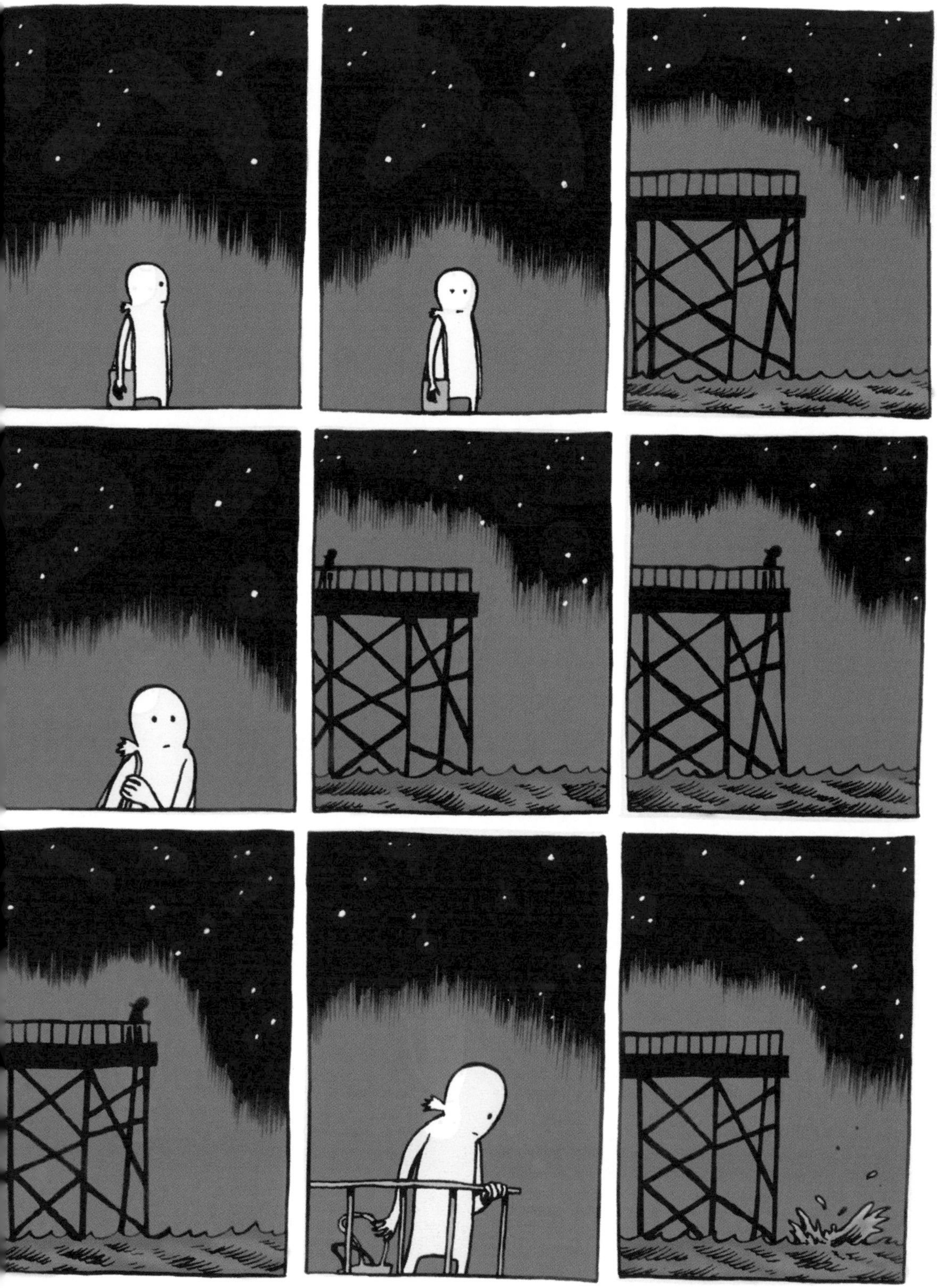

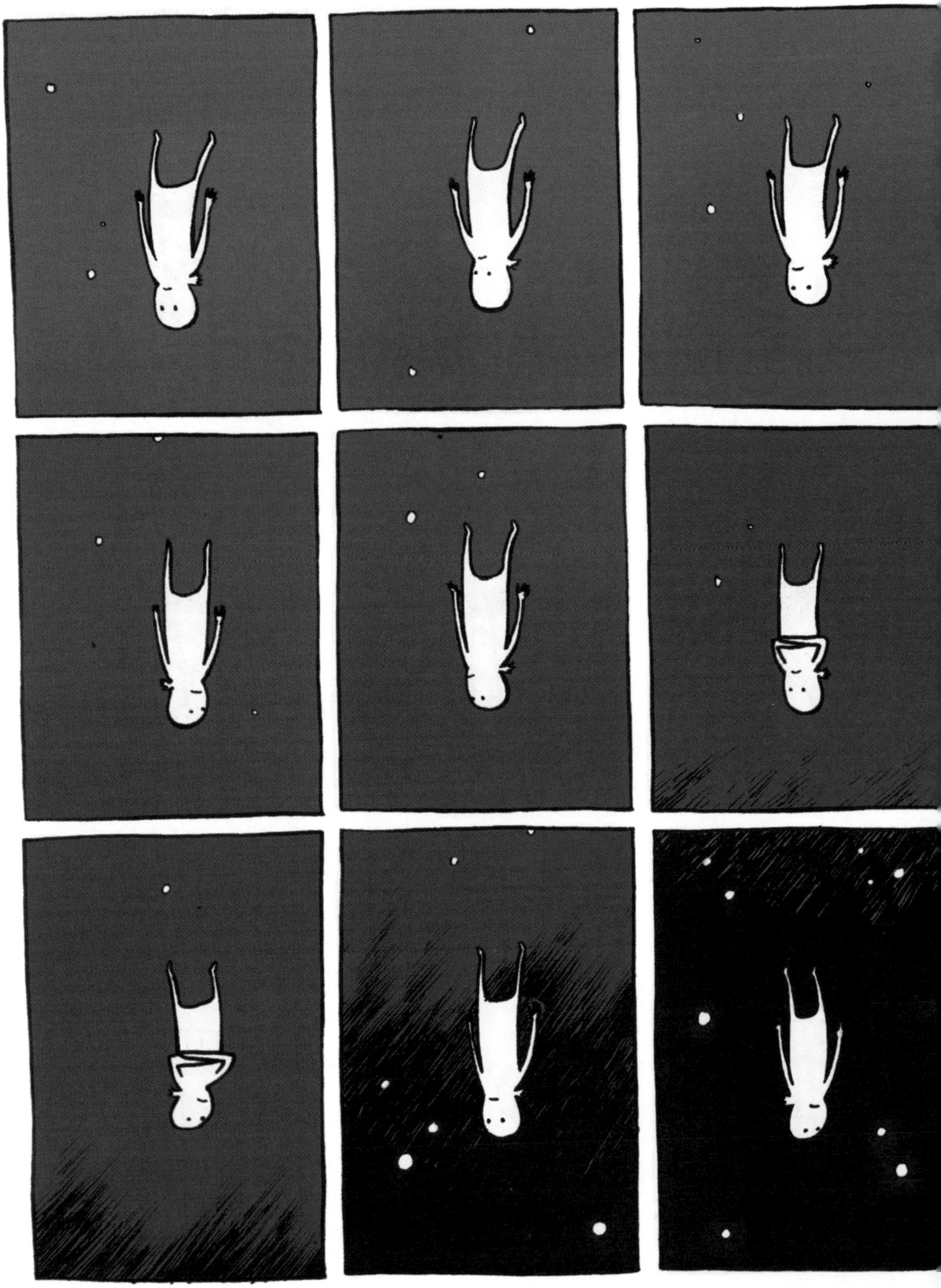

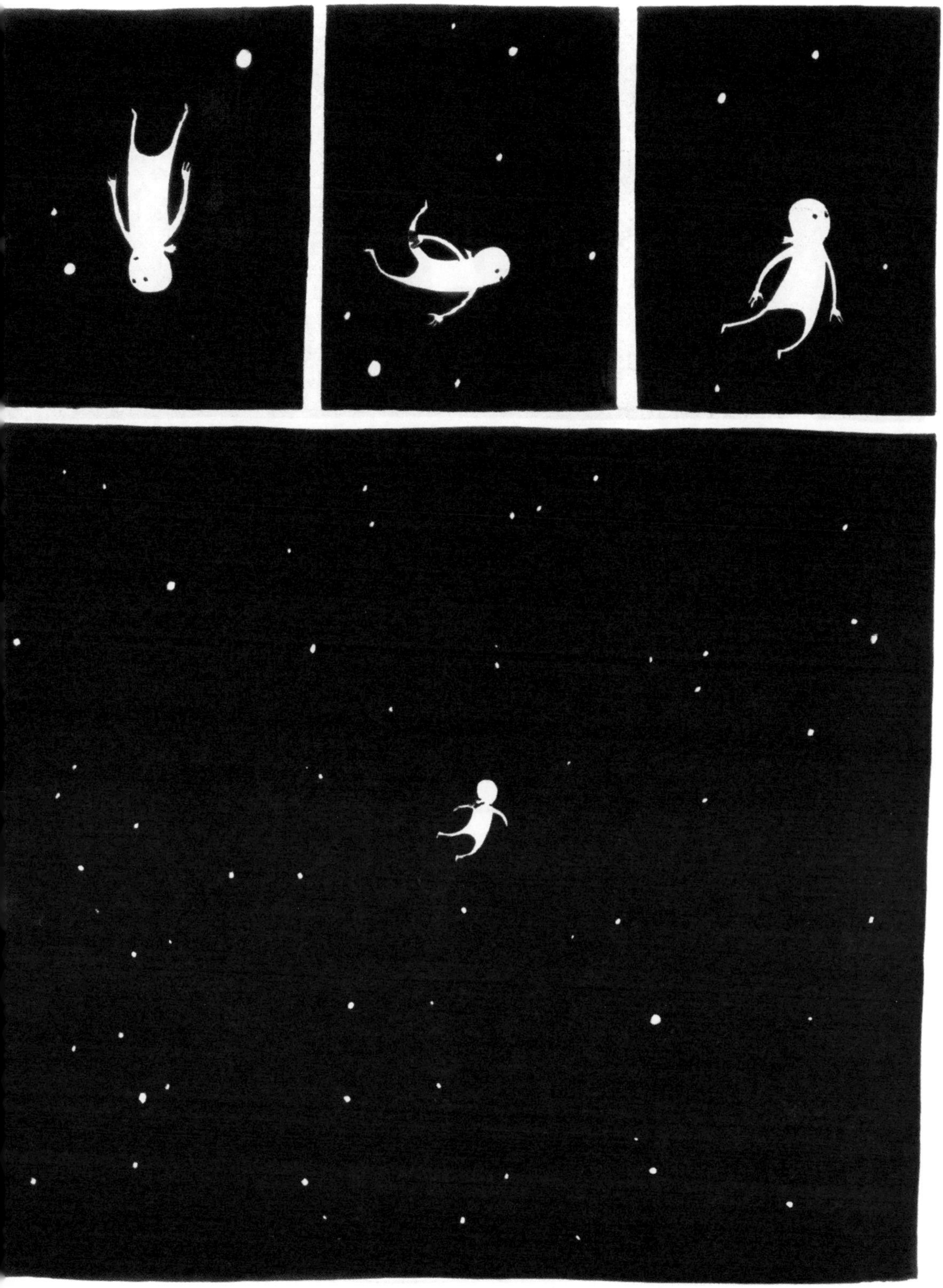

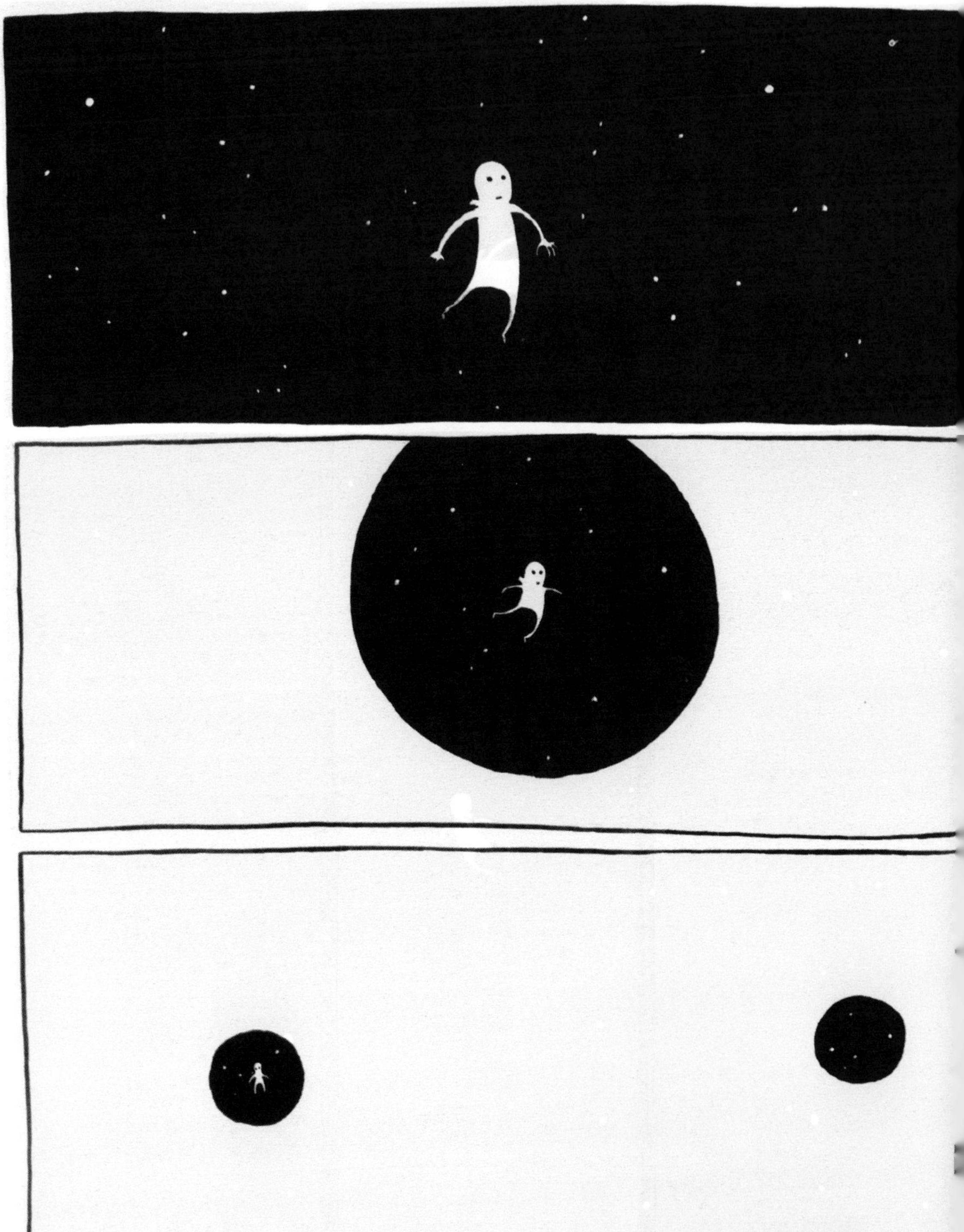

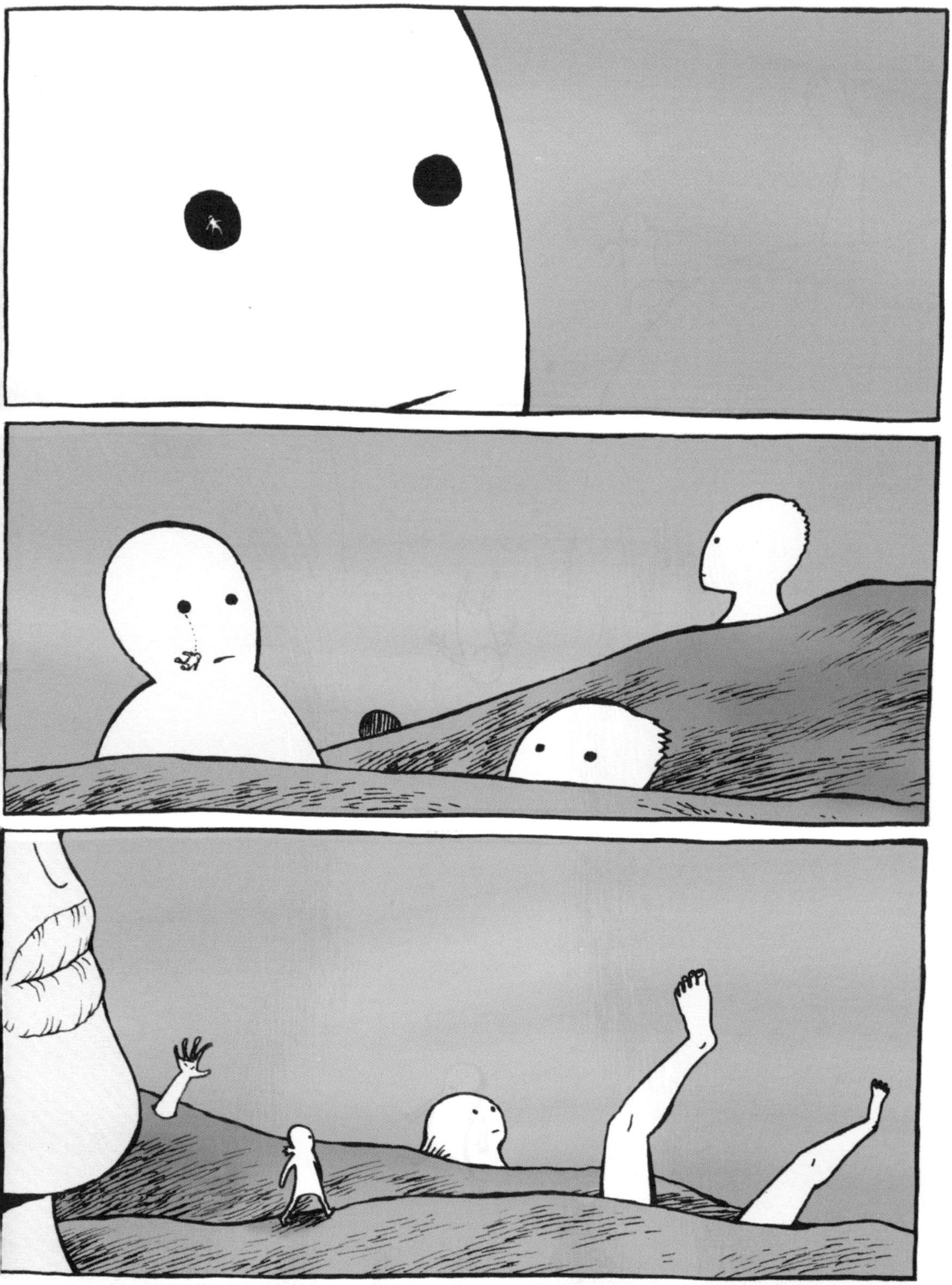

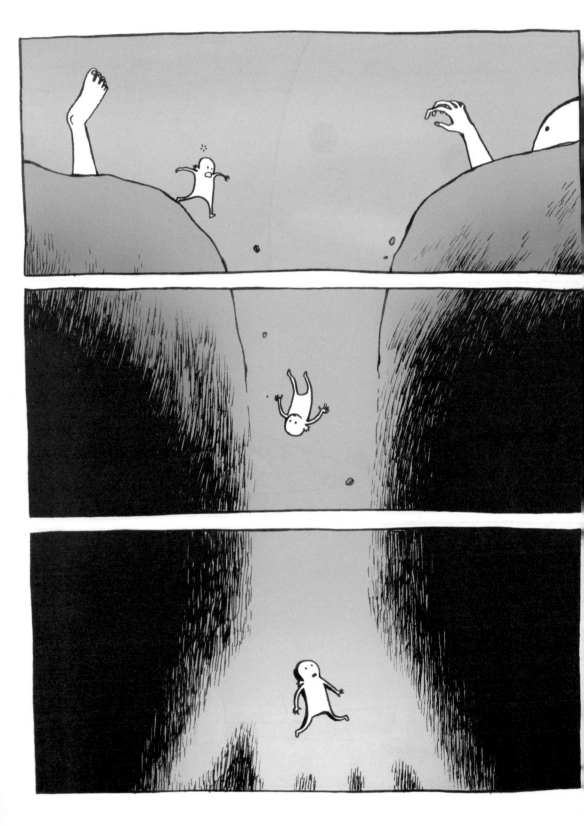

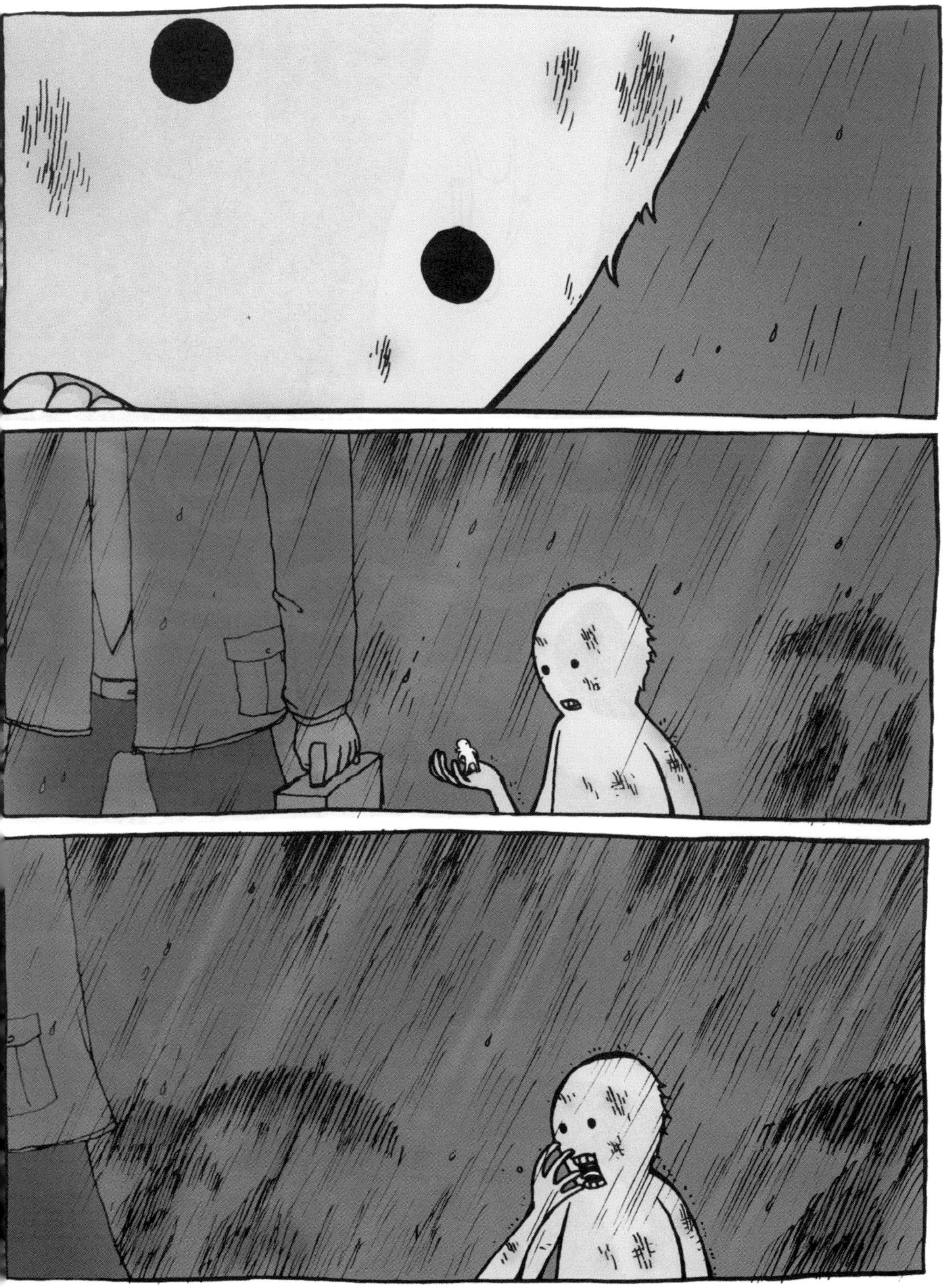

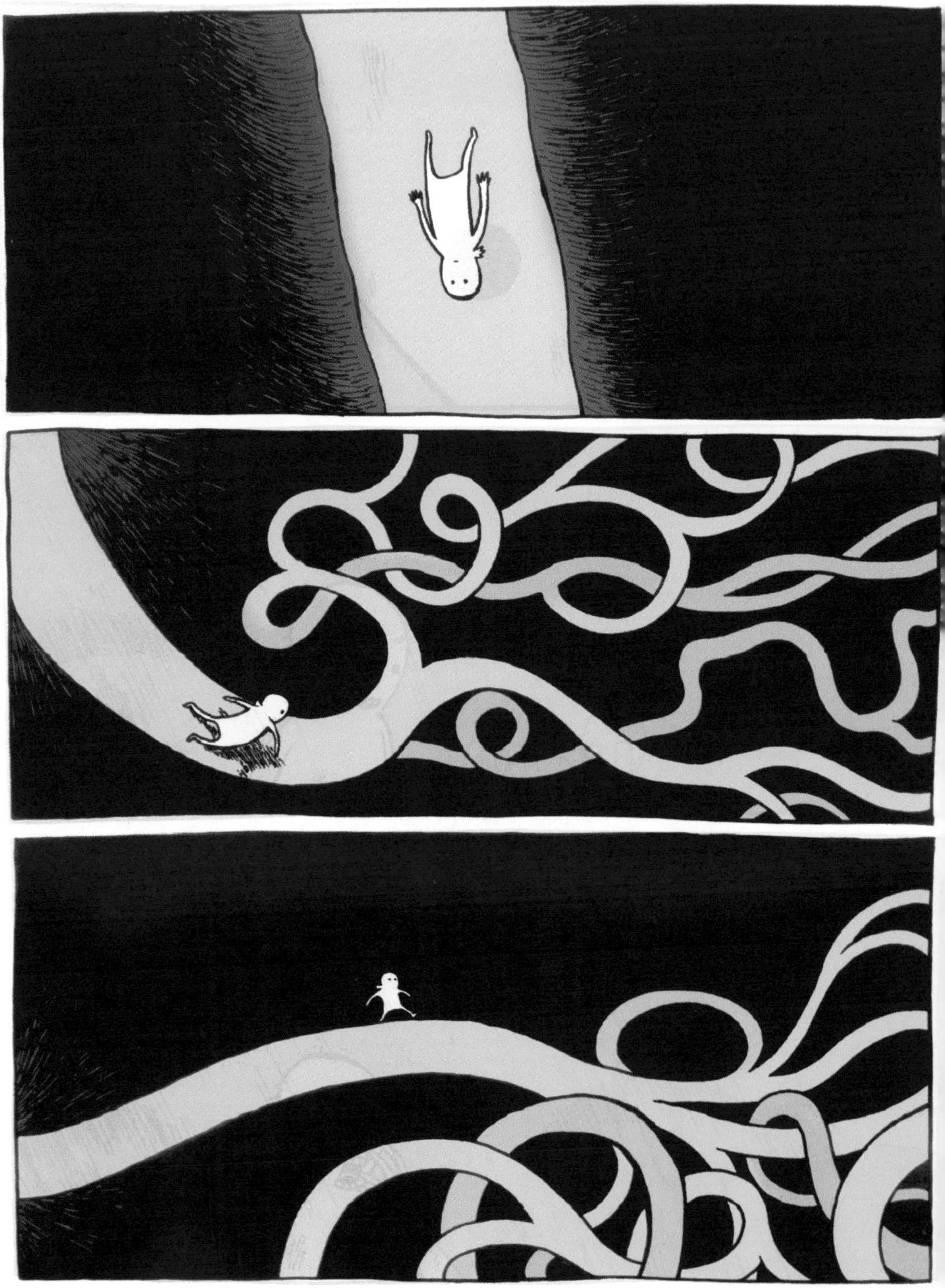

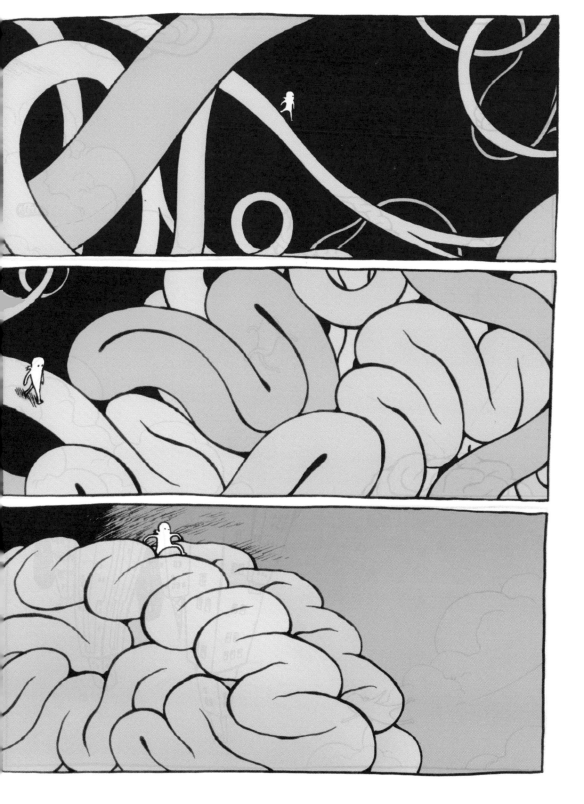

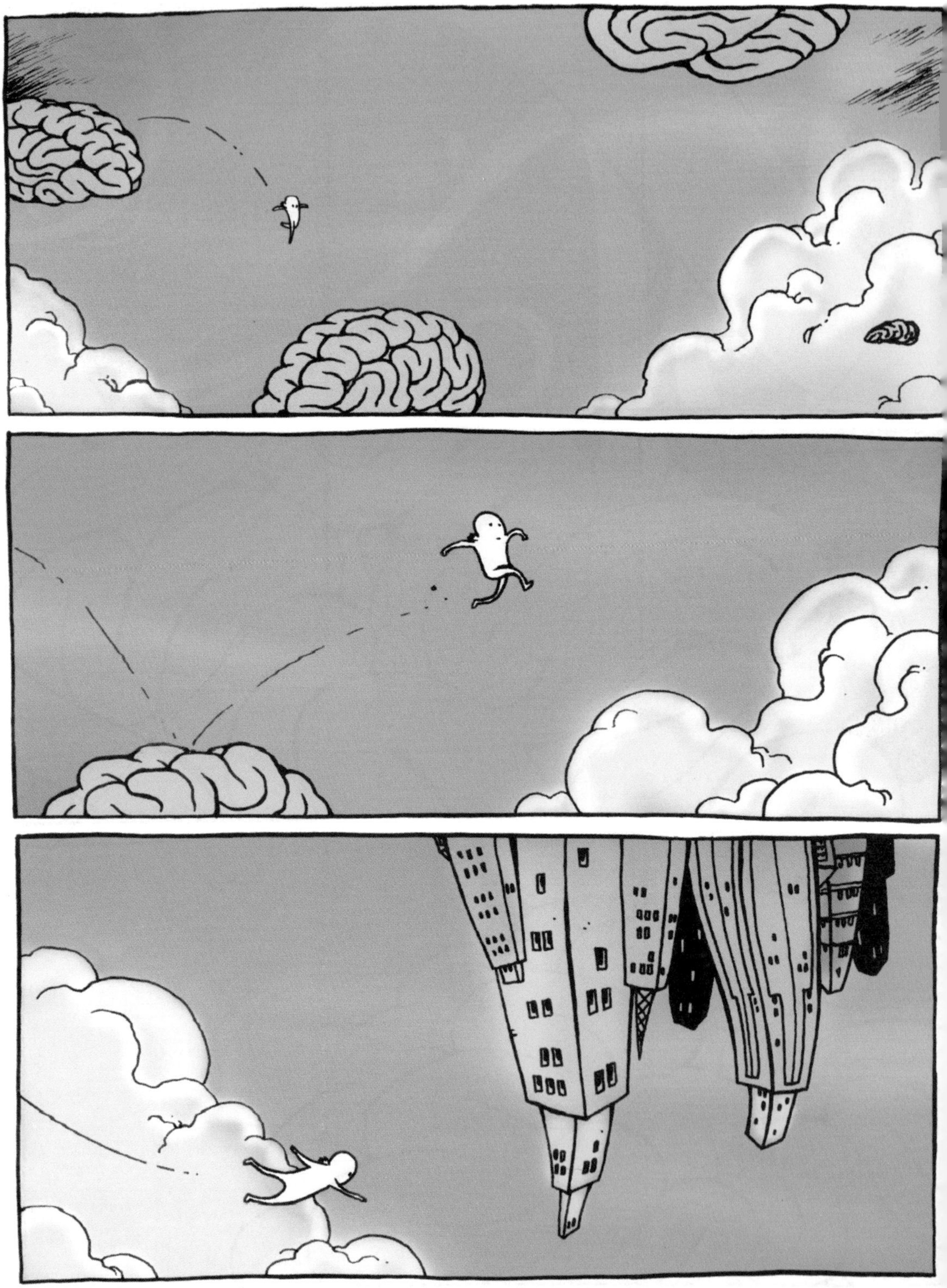

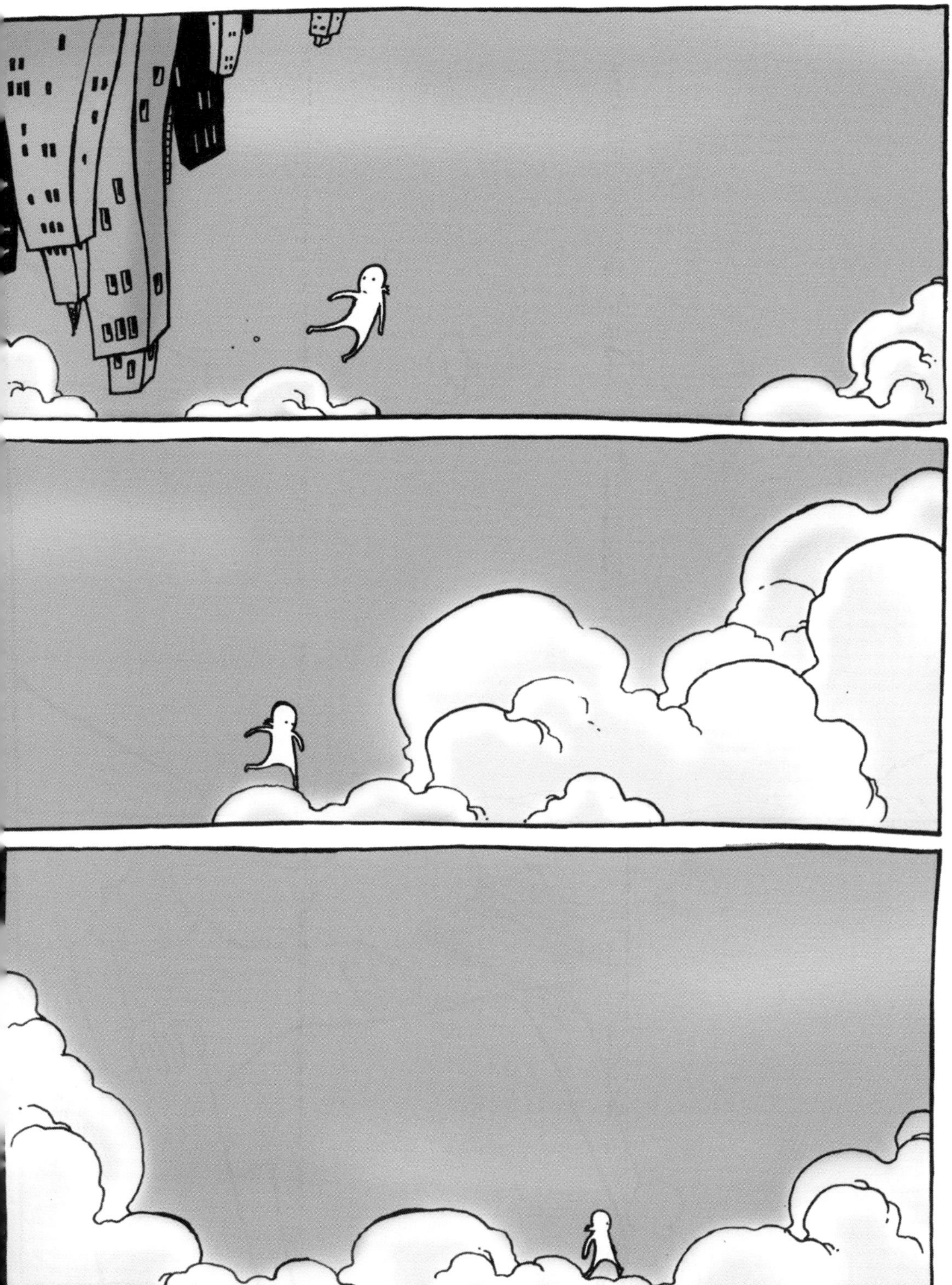

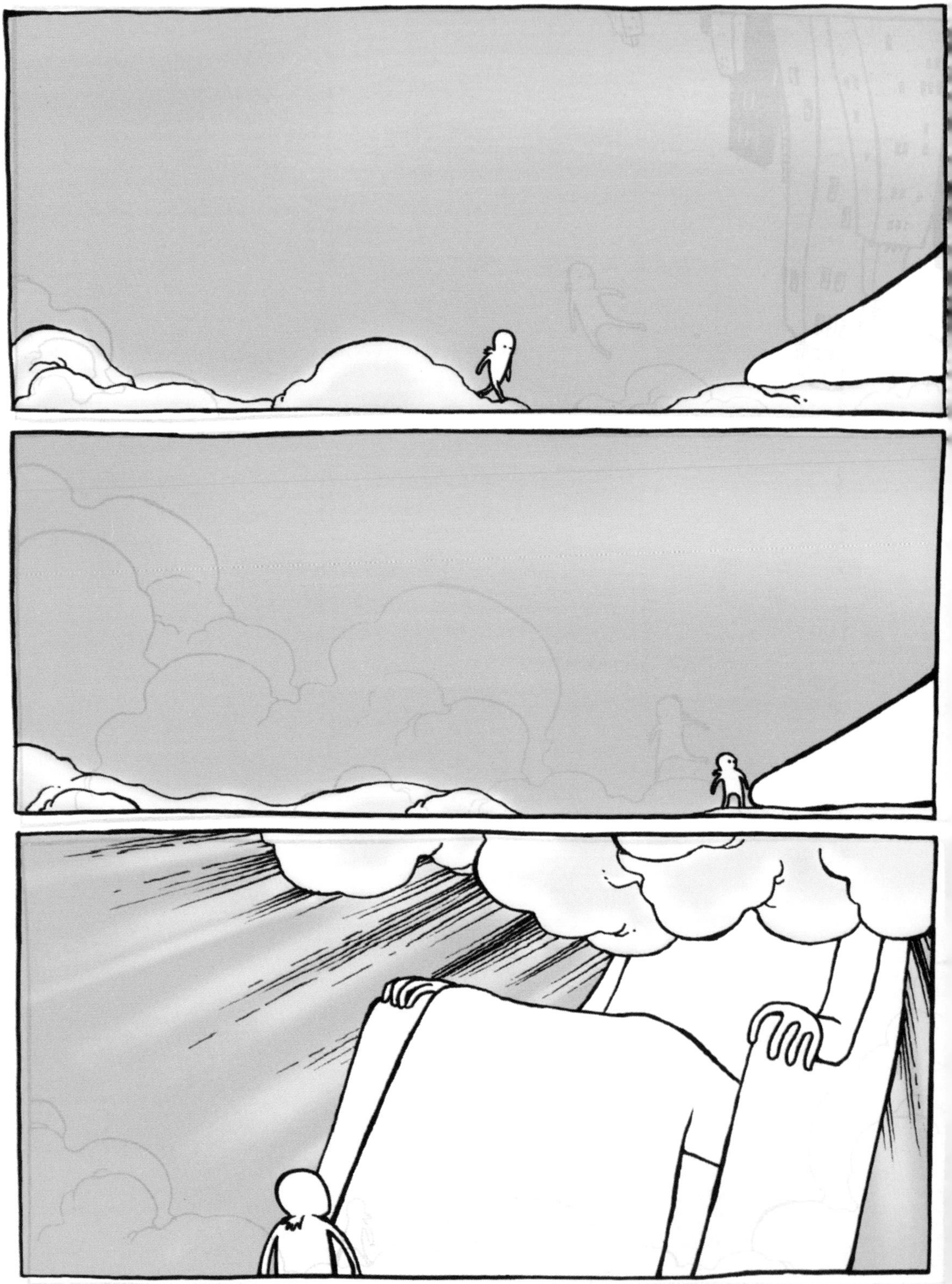

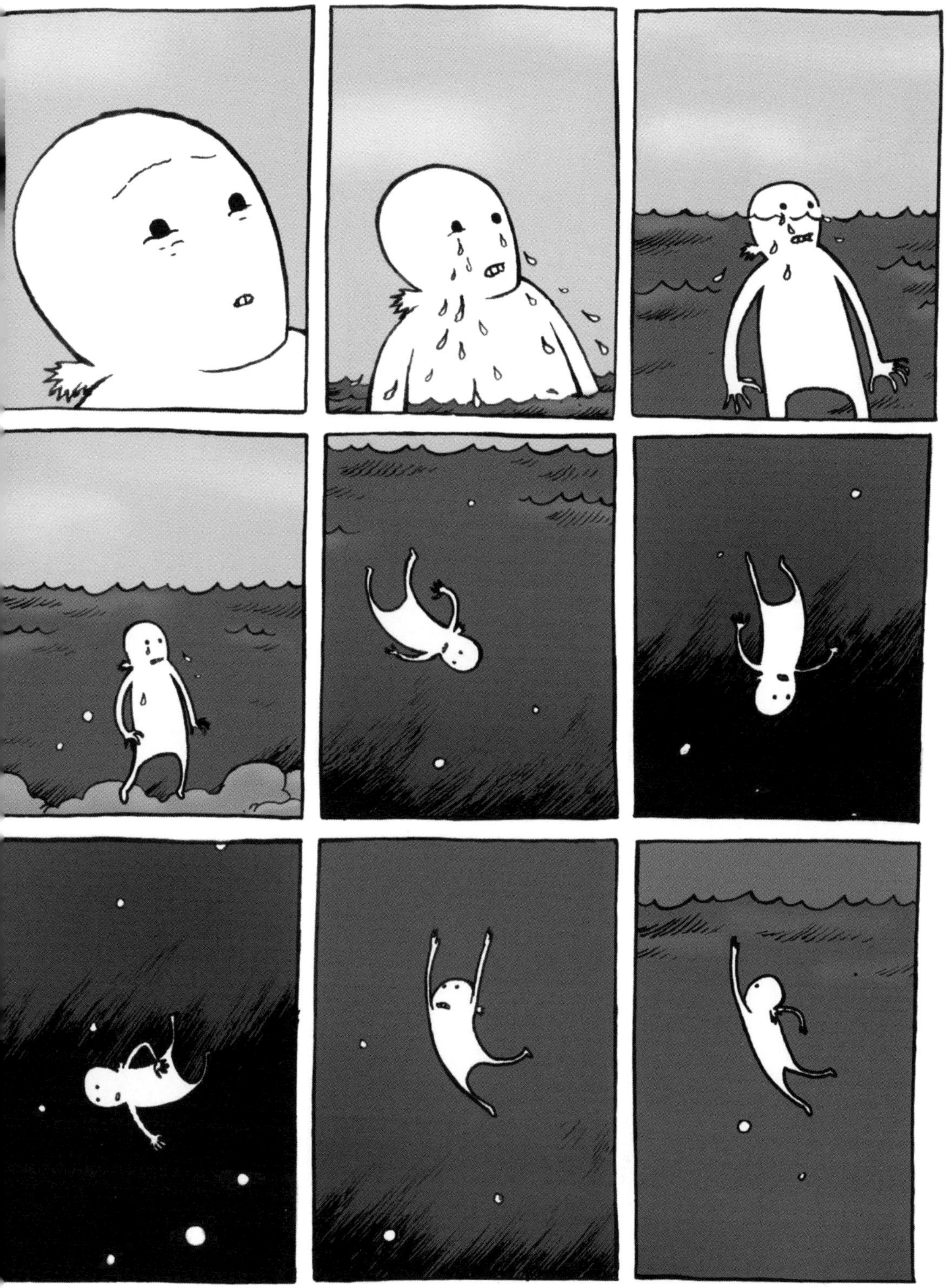

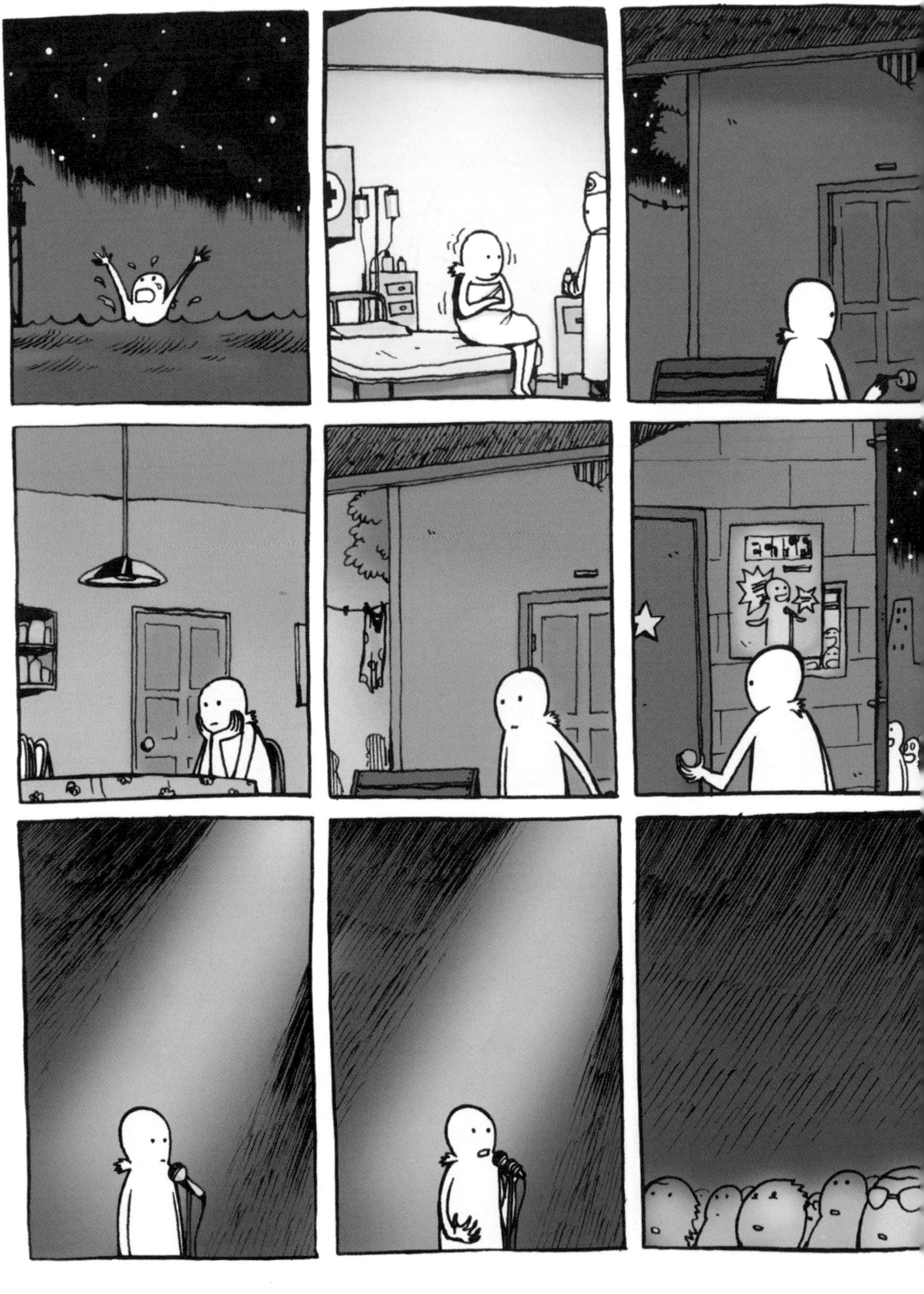

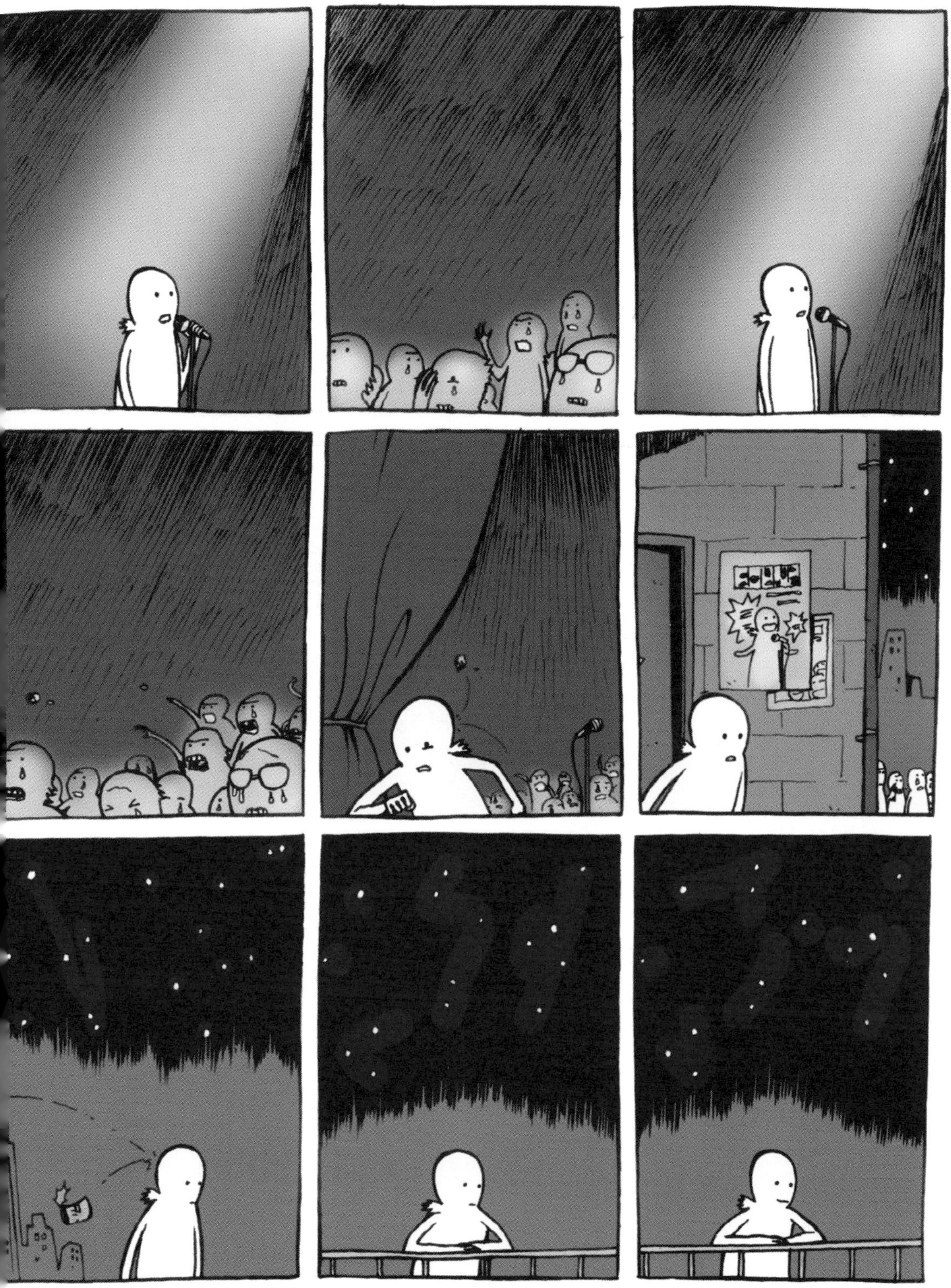

12

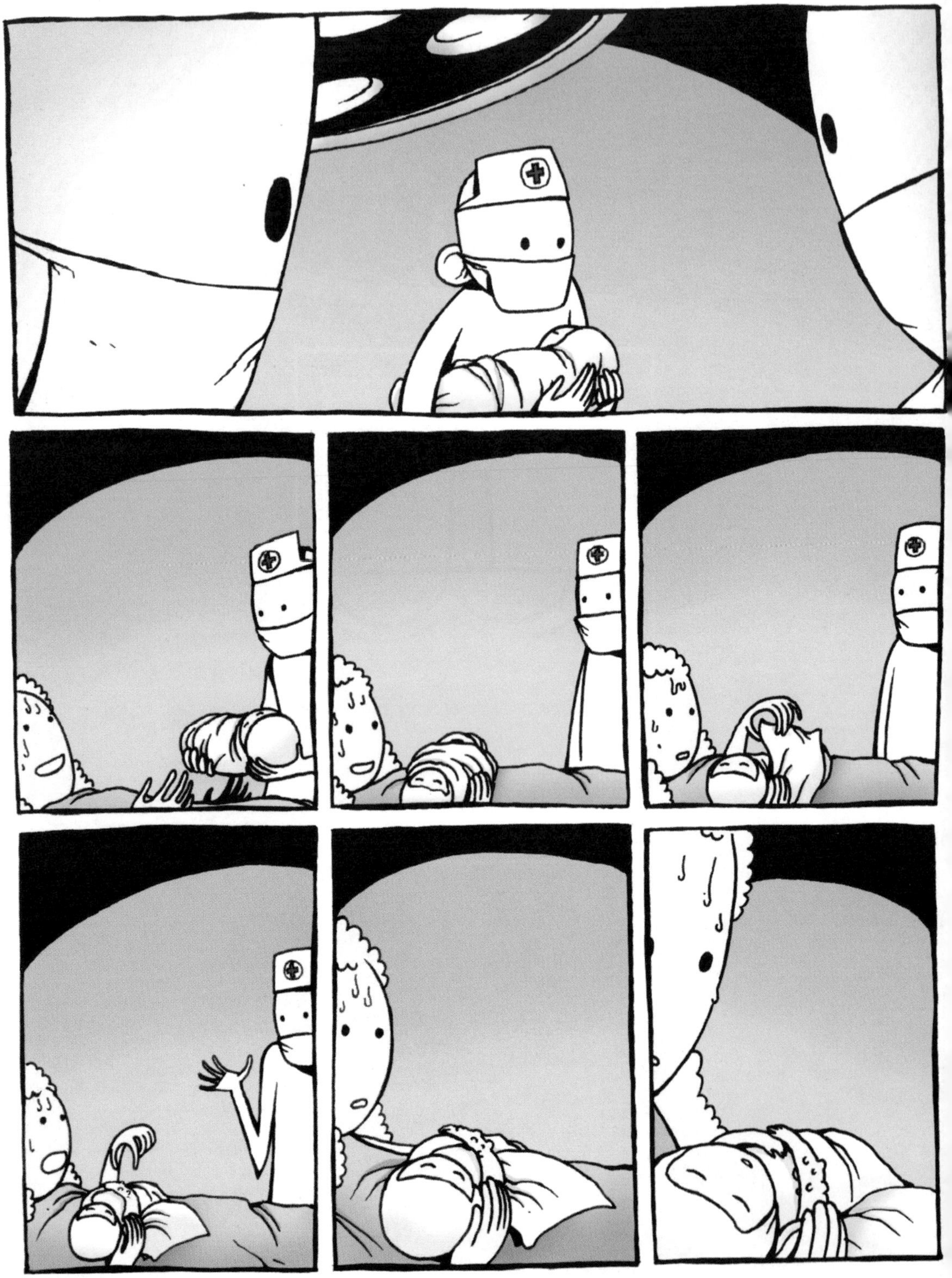

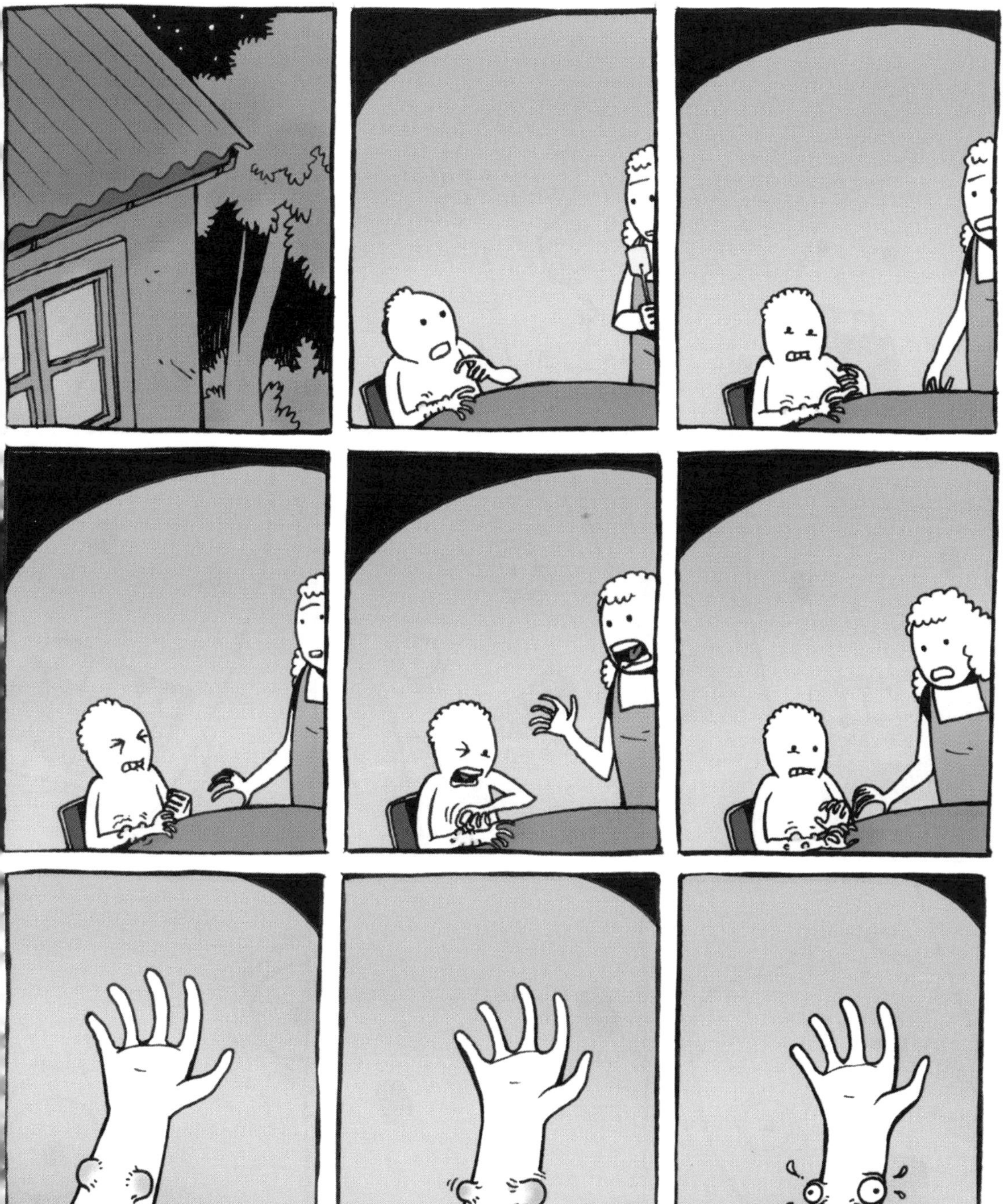

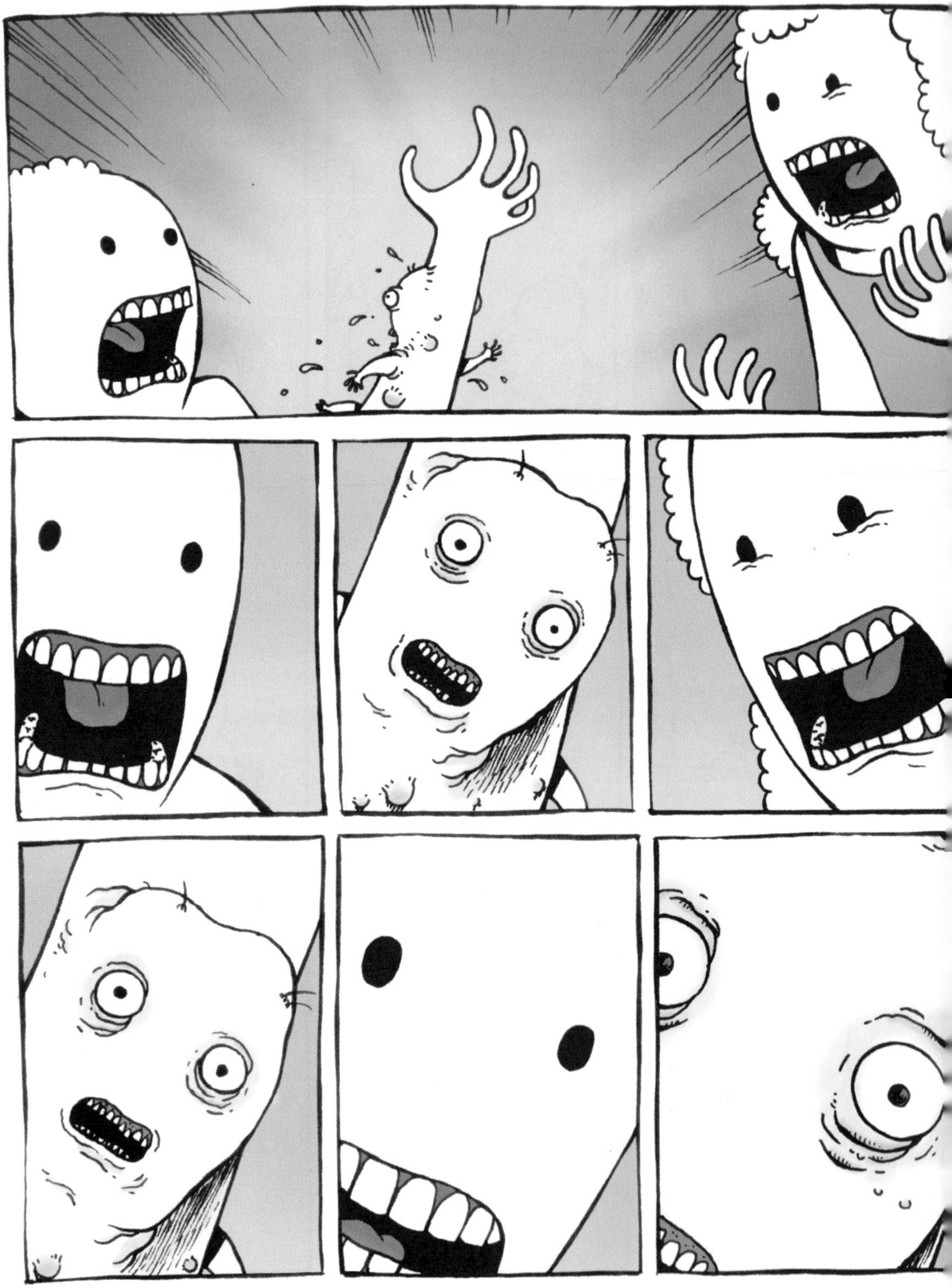

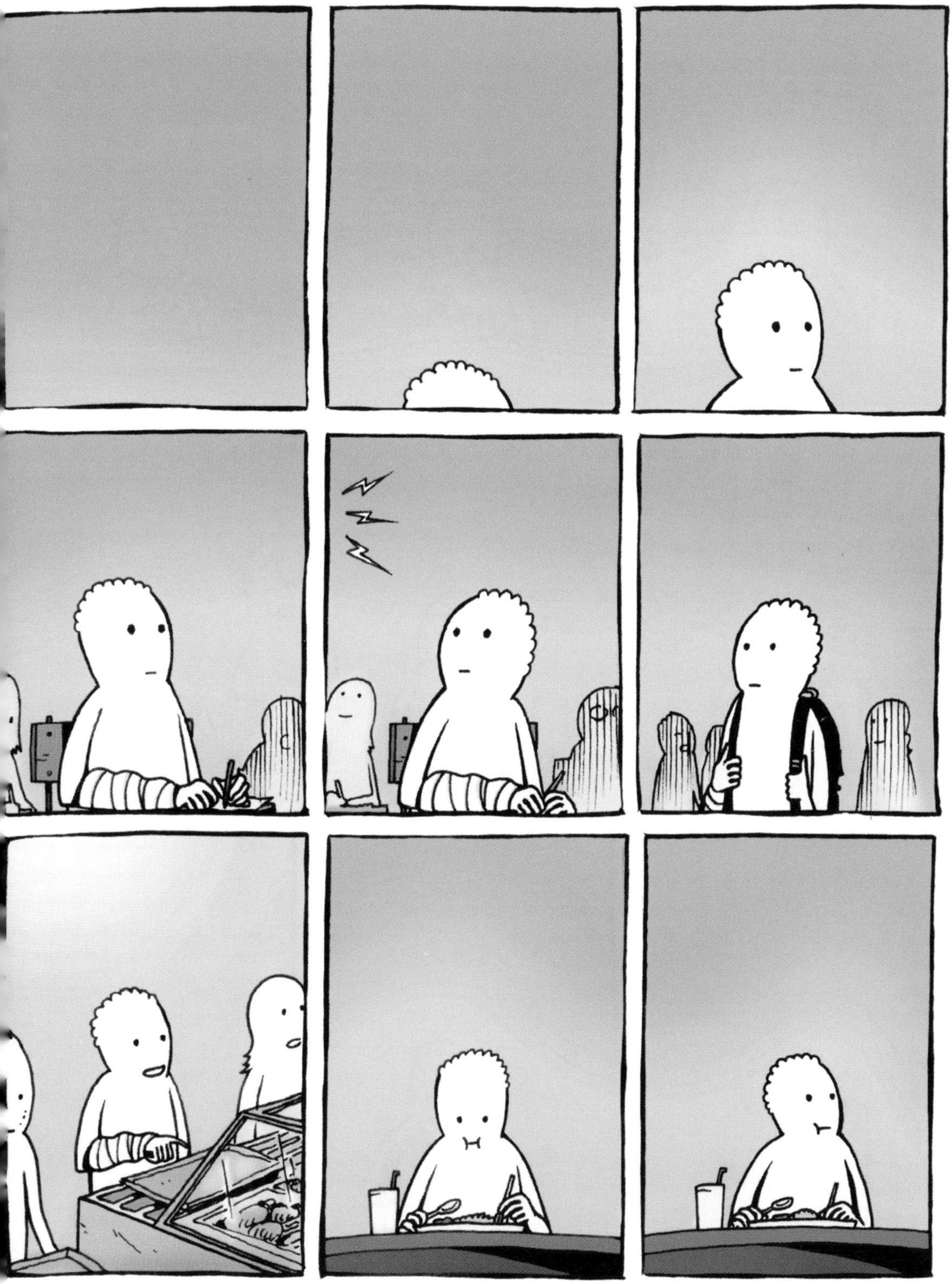

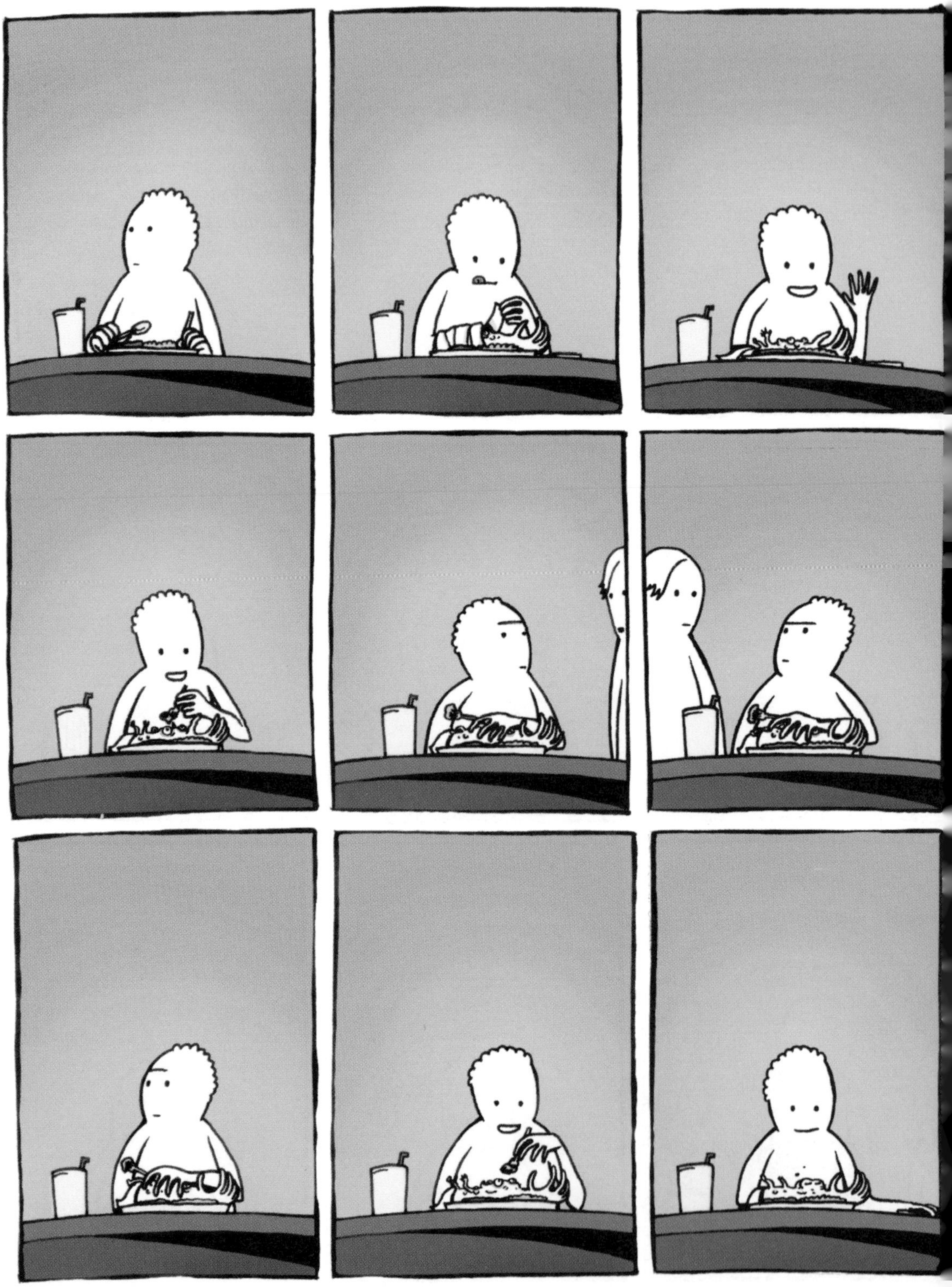

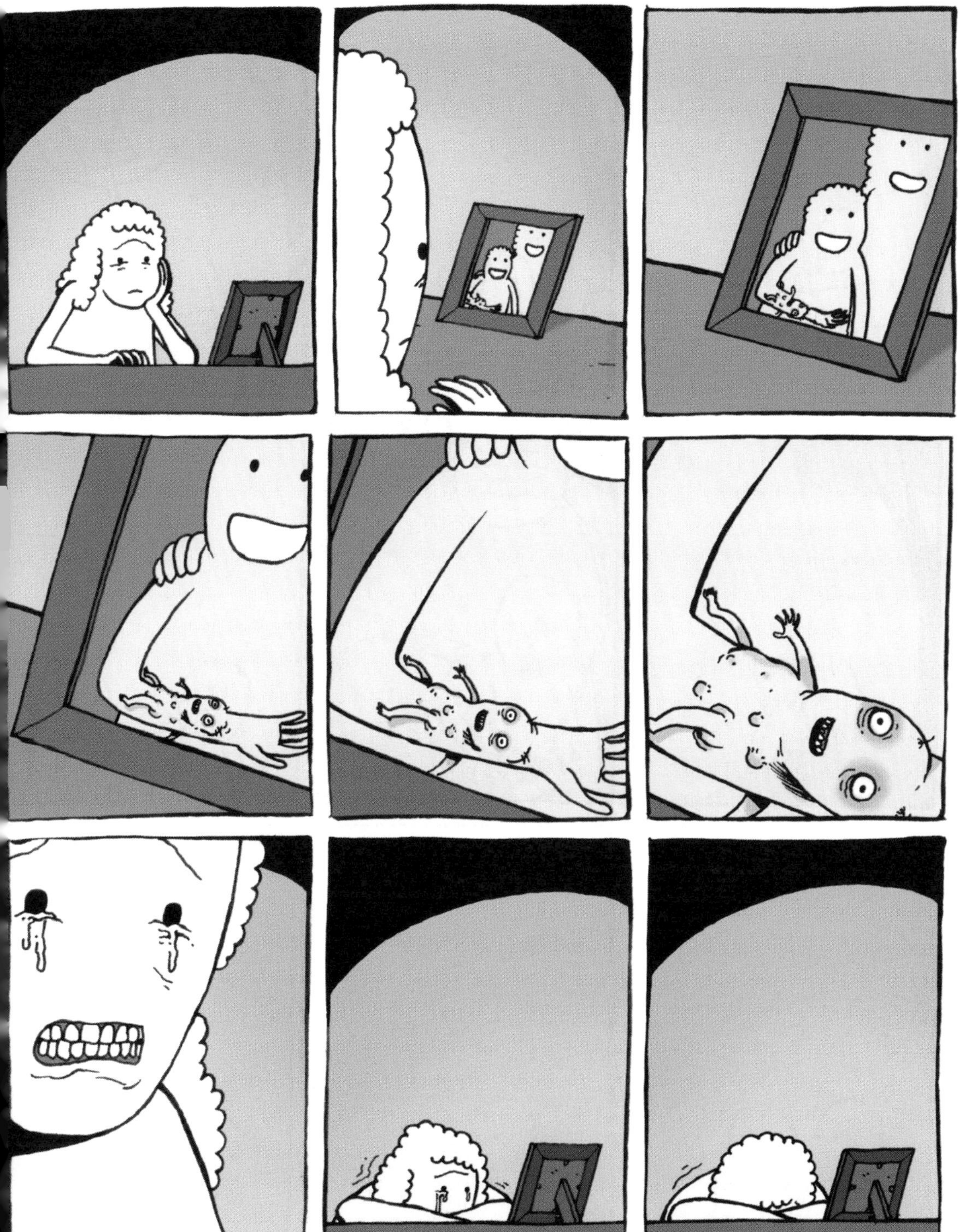

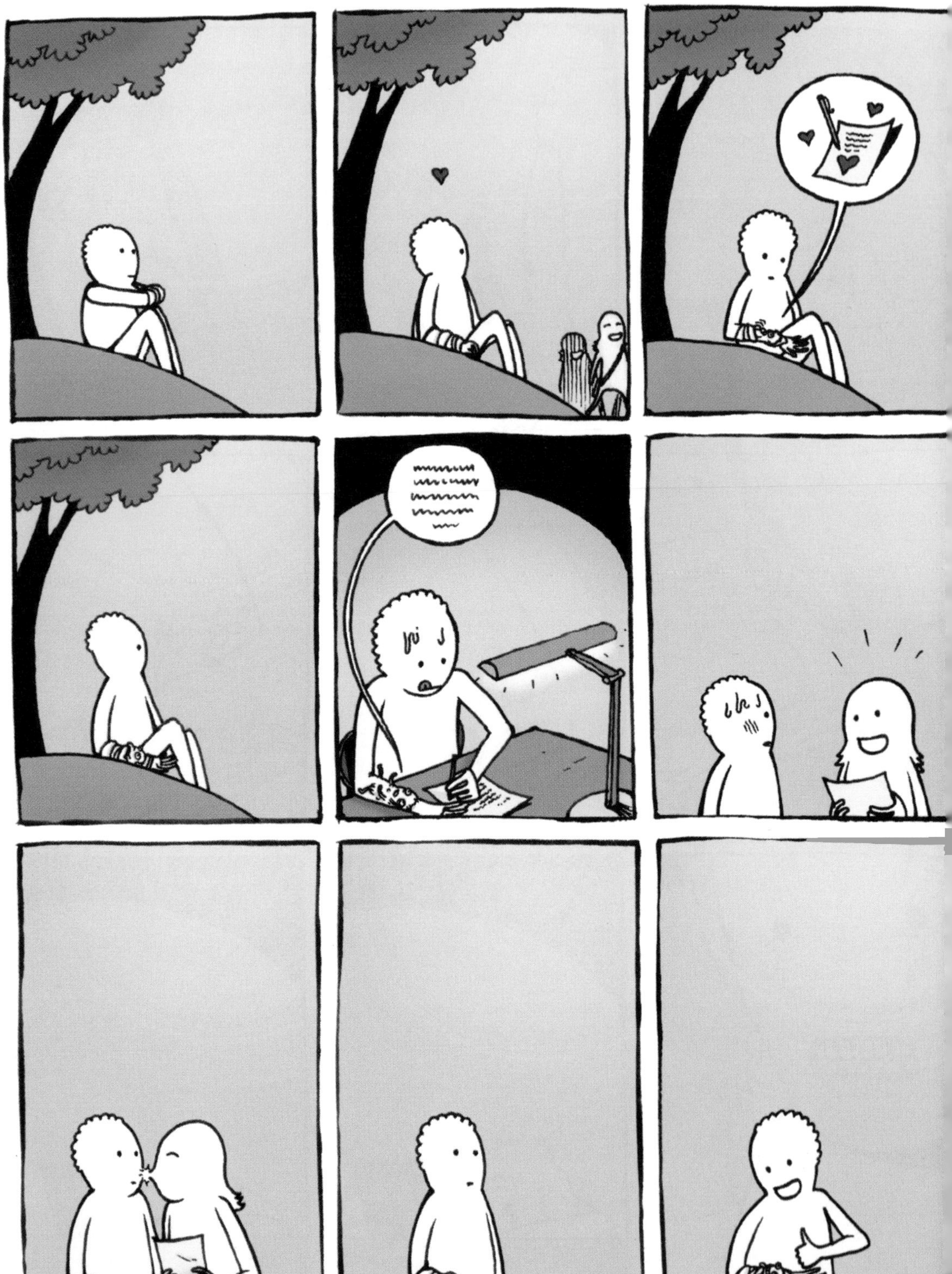

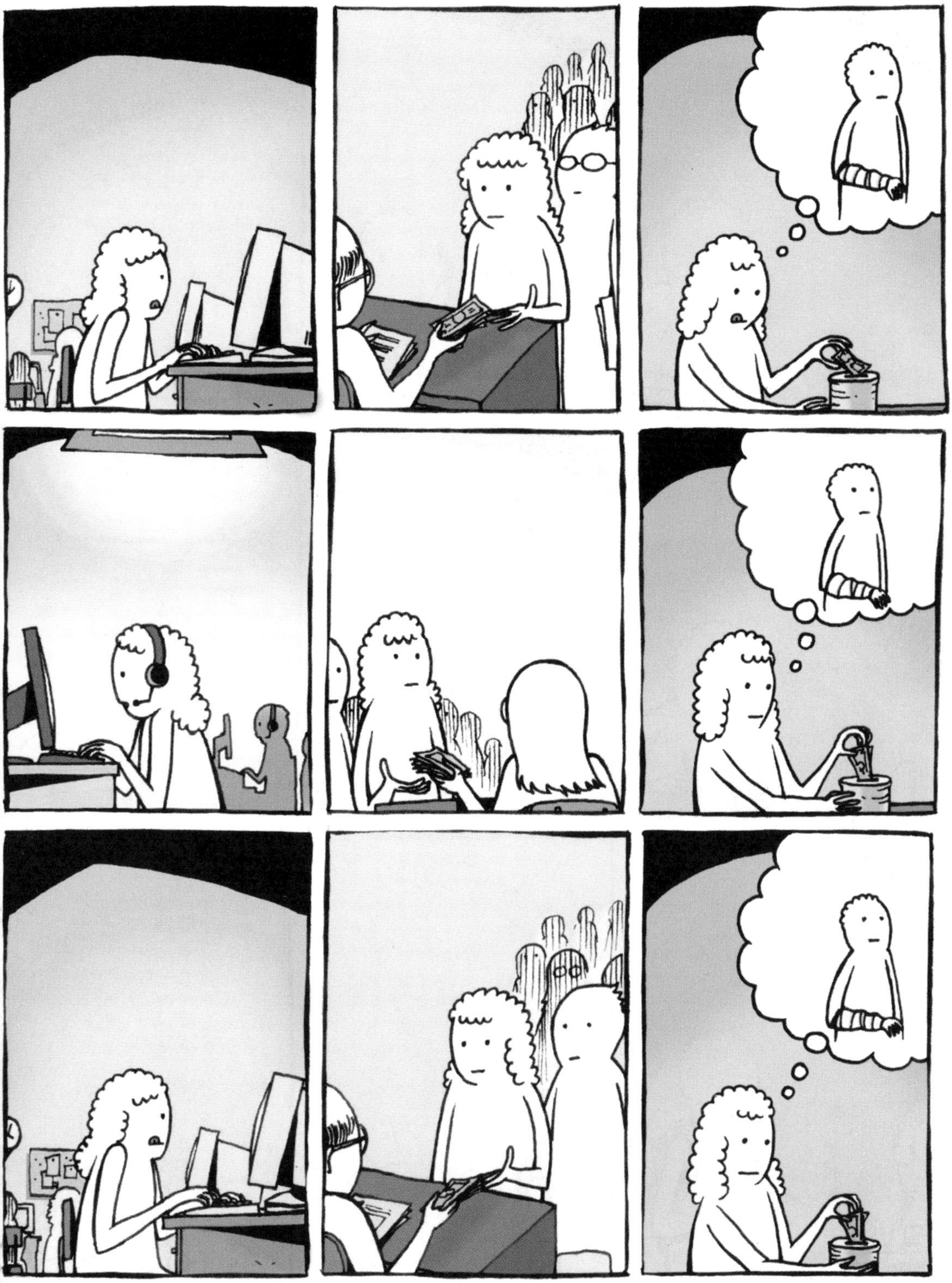

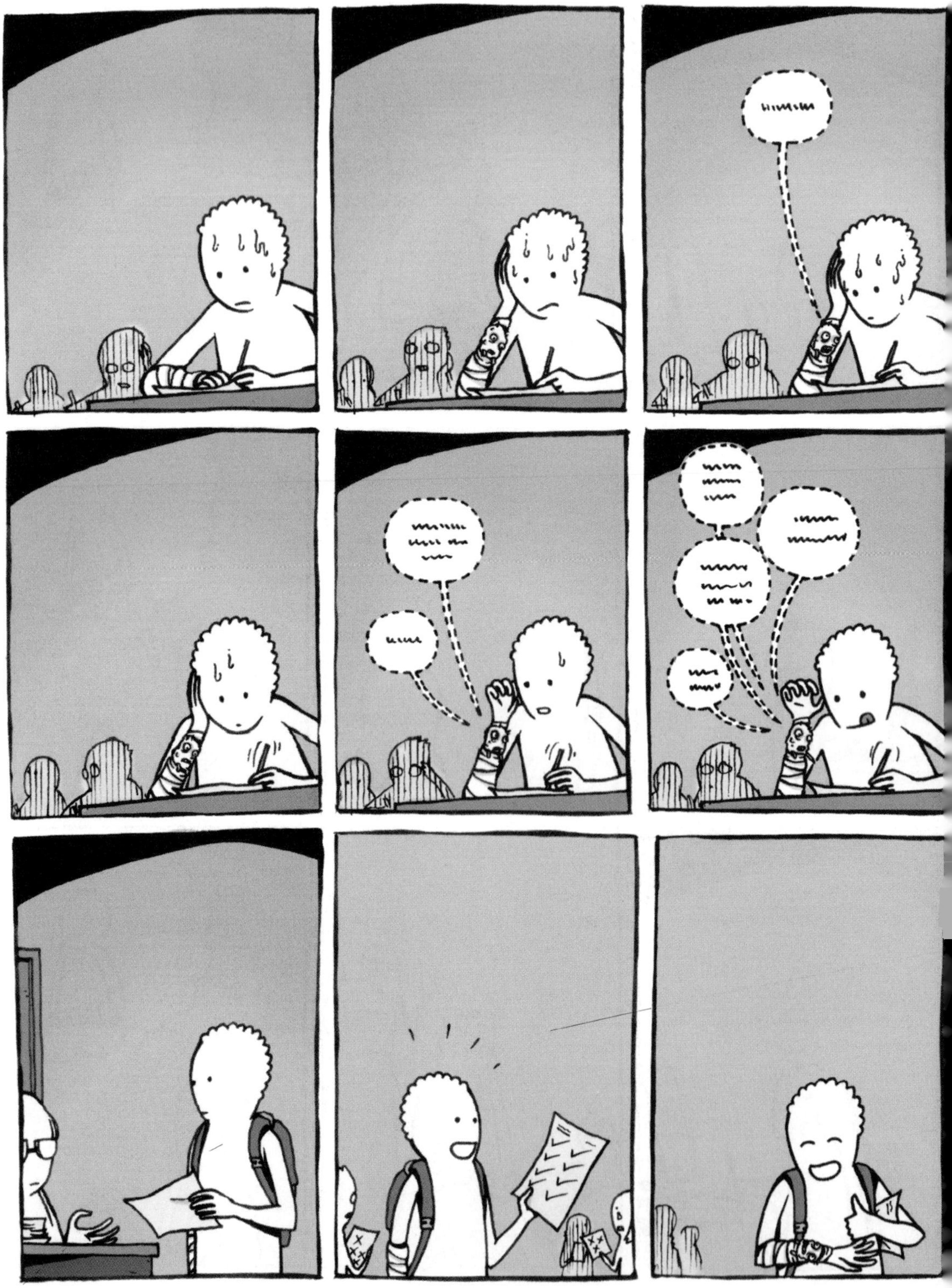

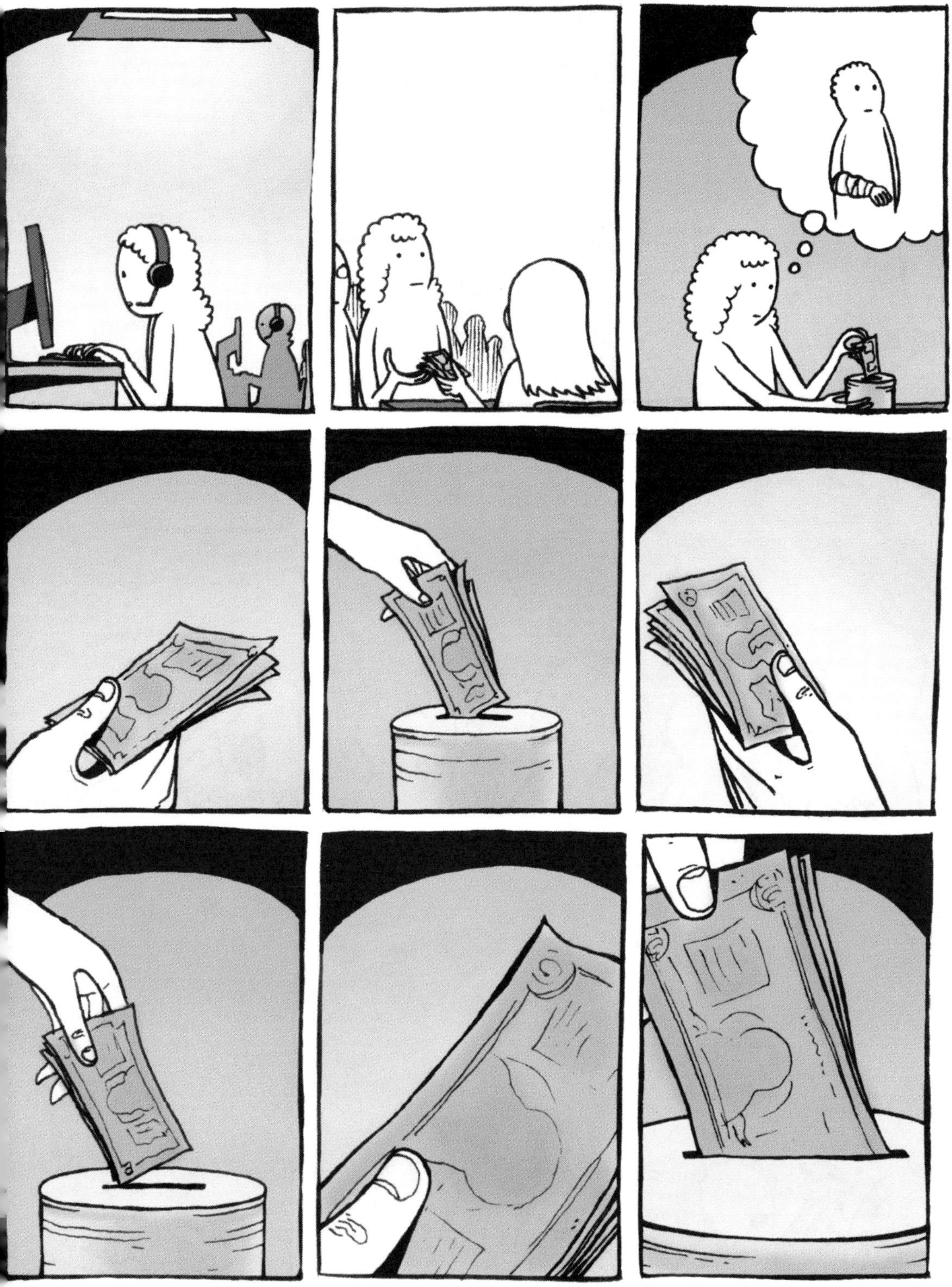

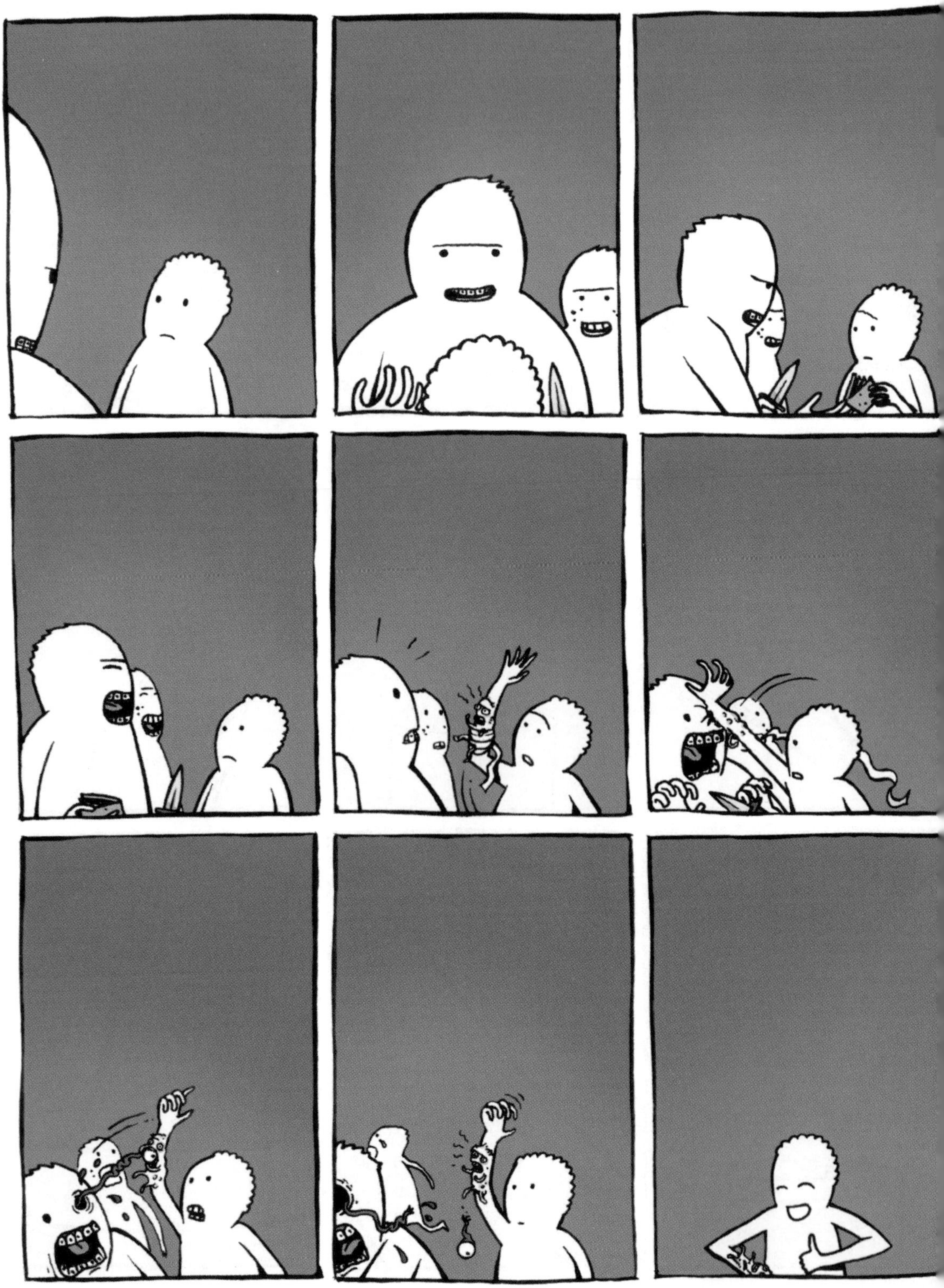

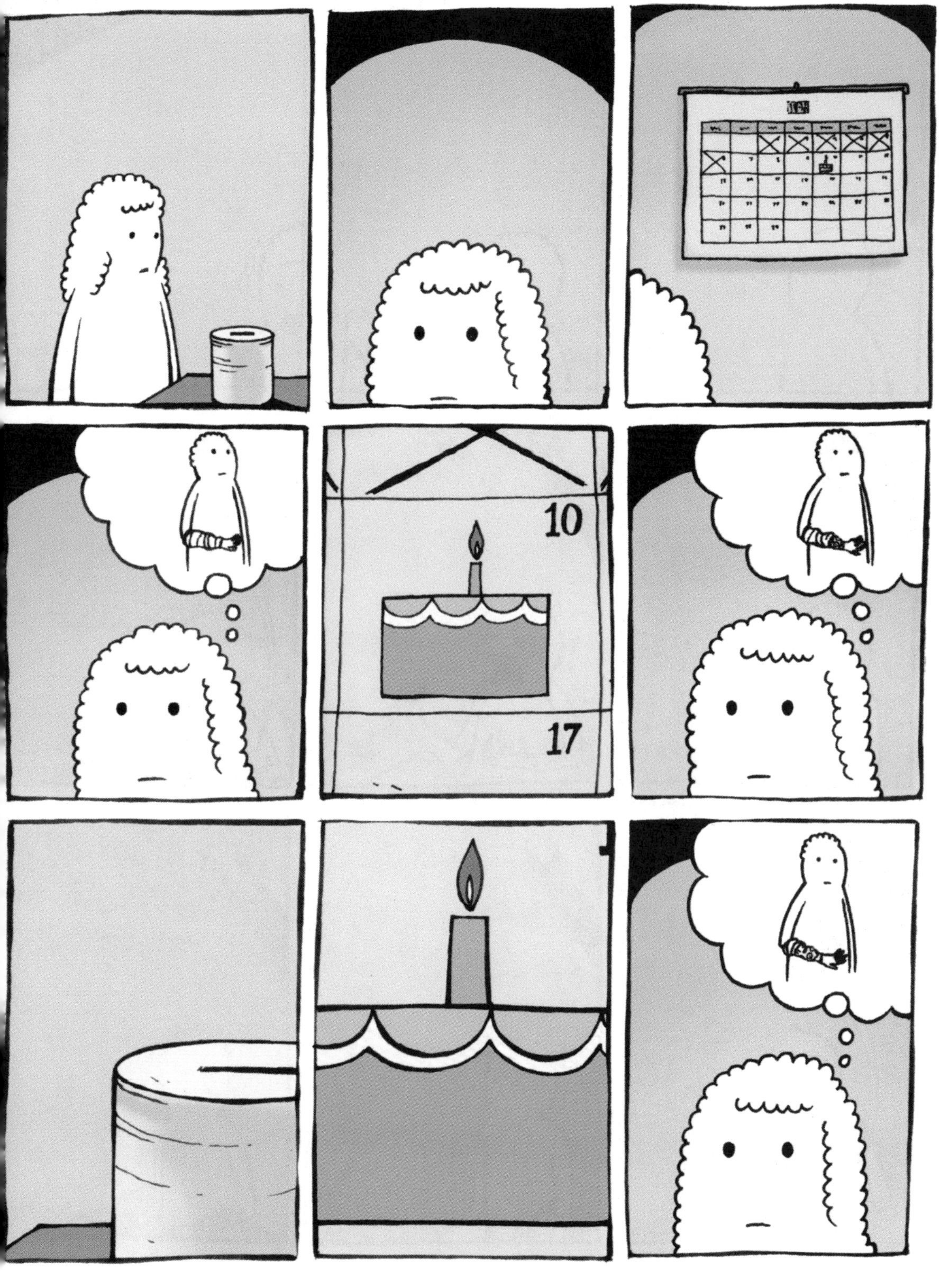
10
17

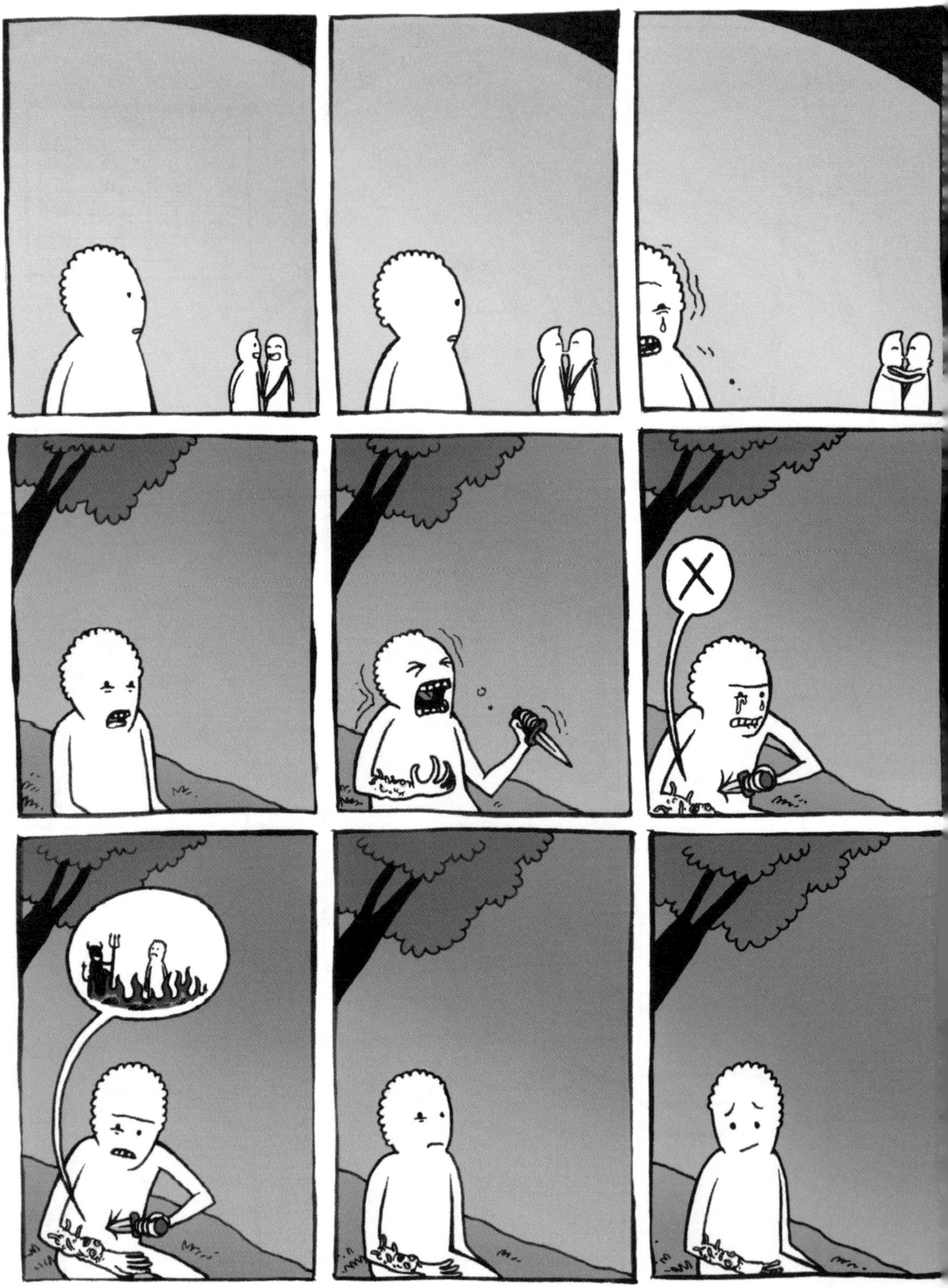

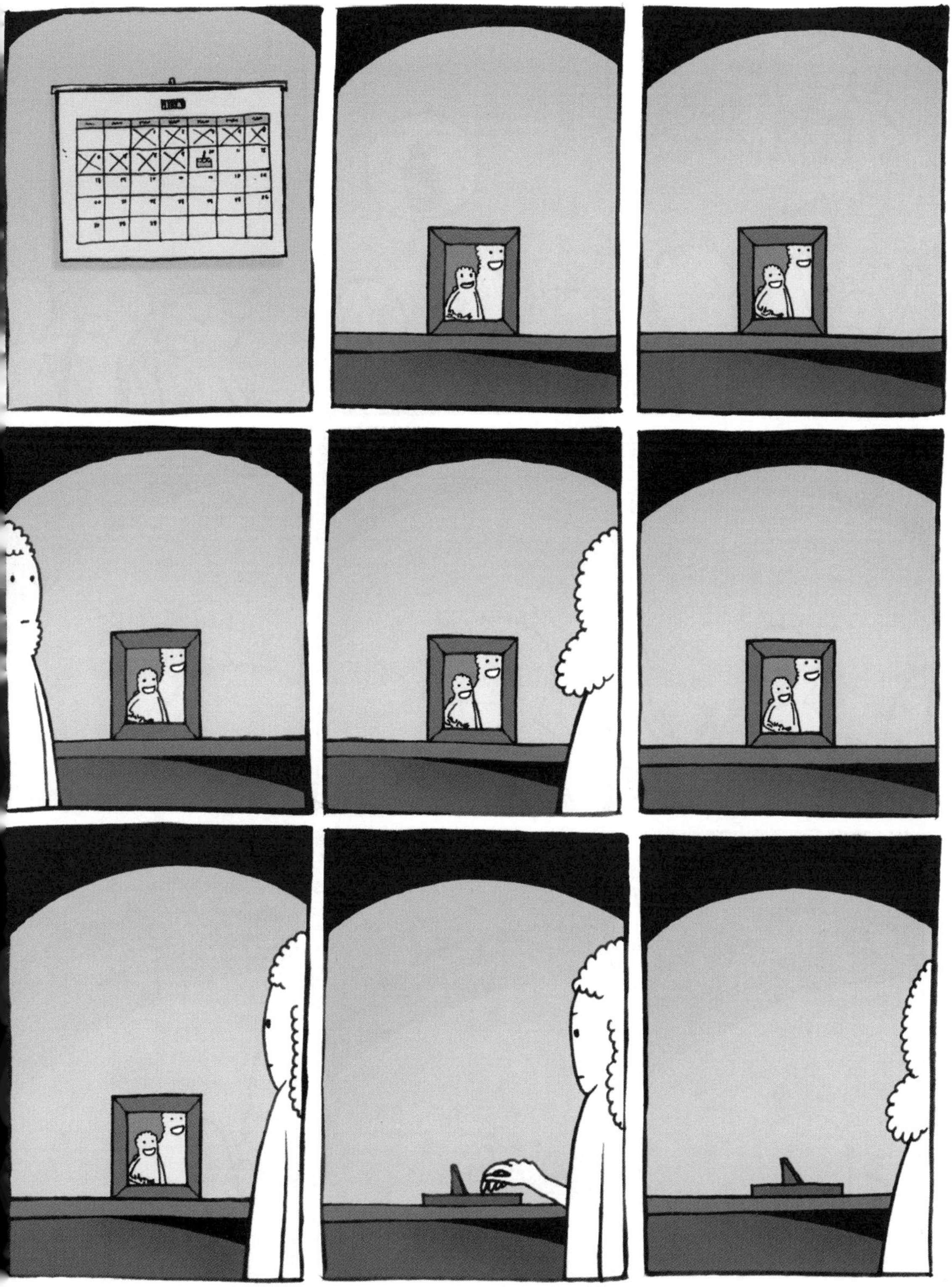

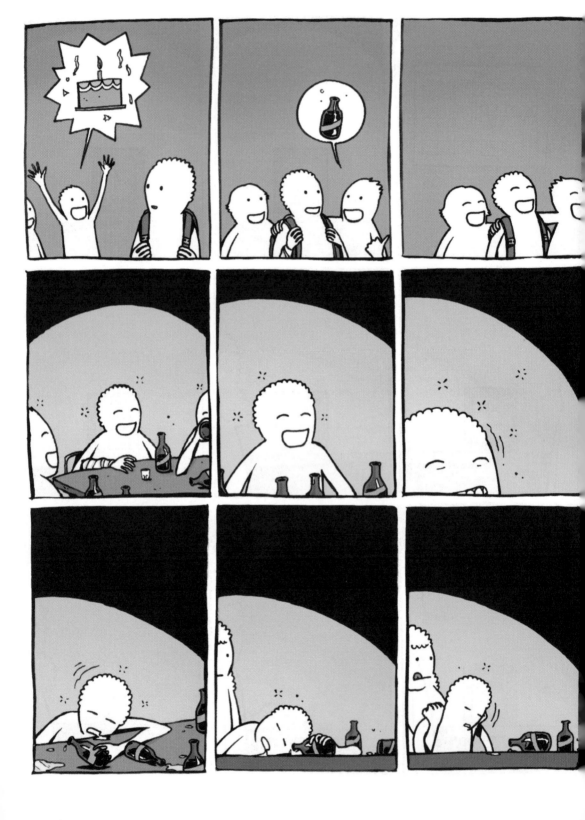

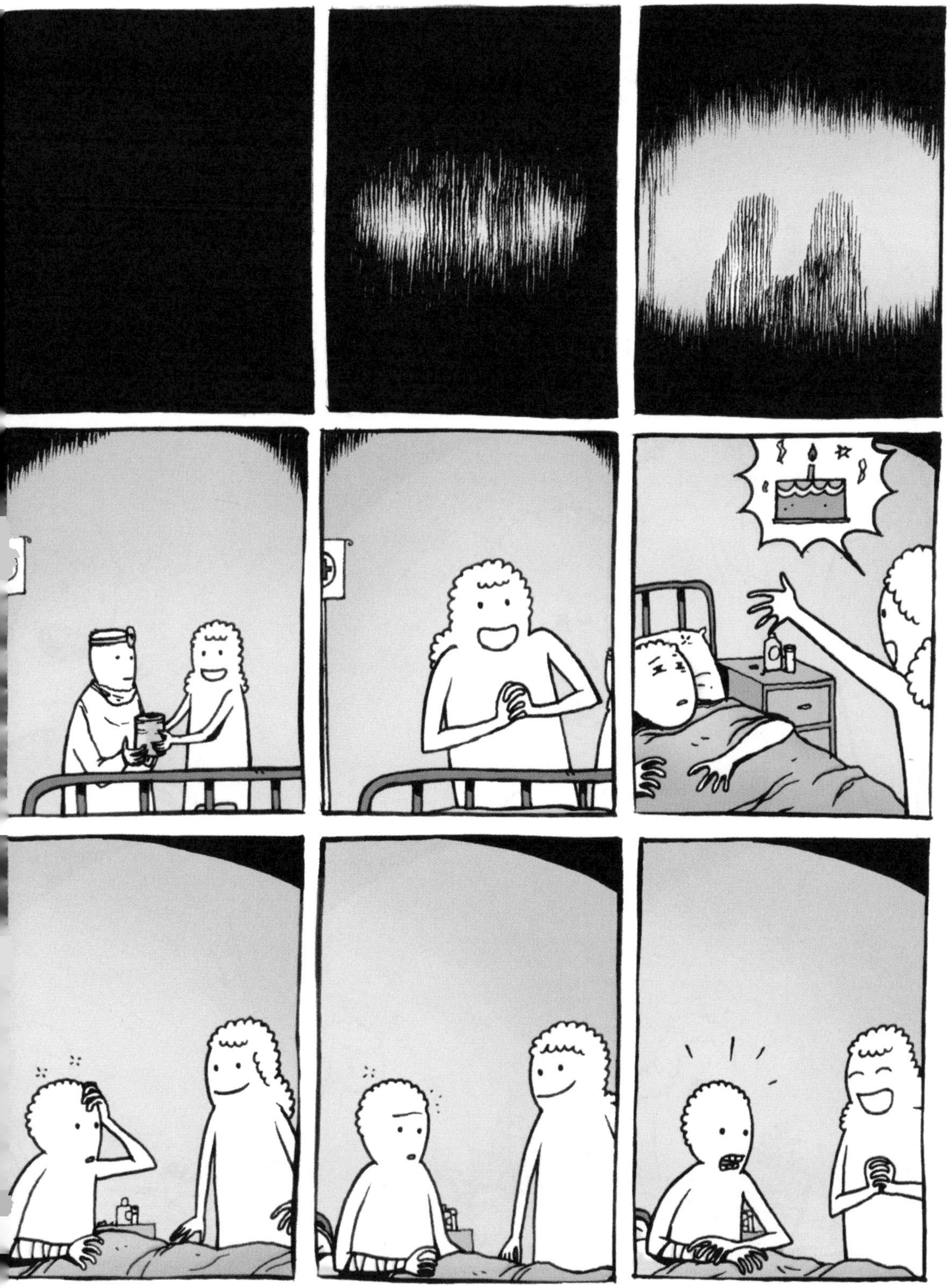

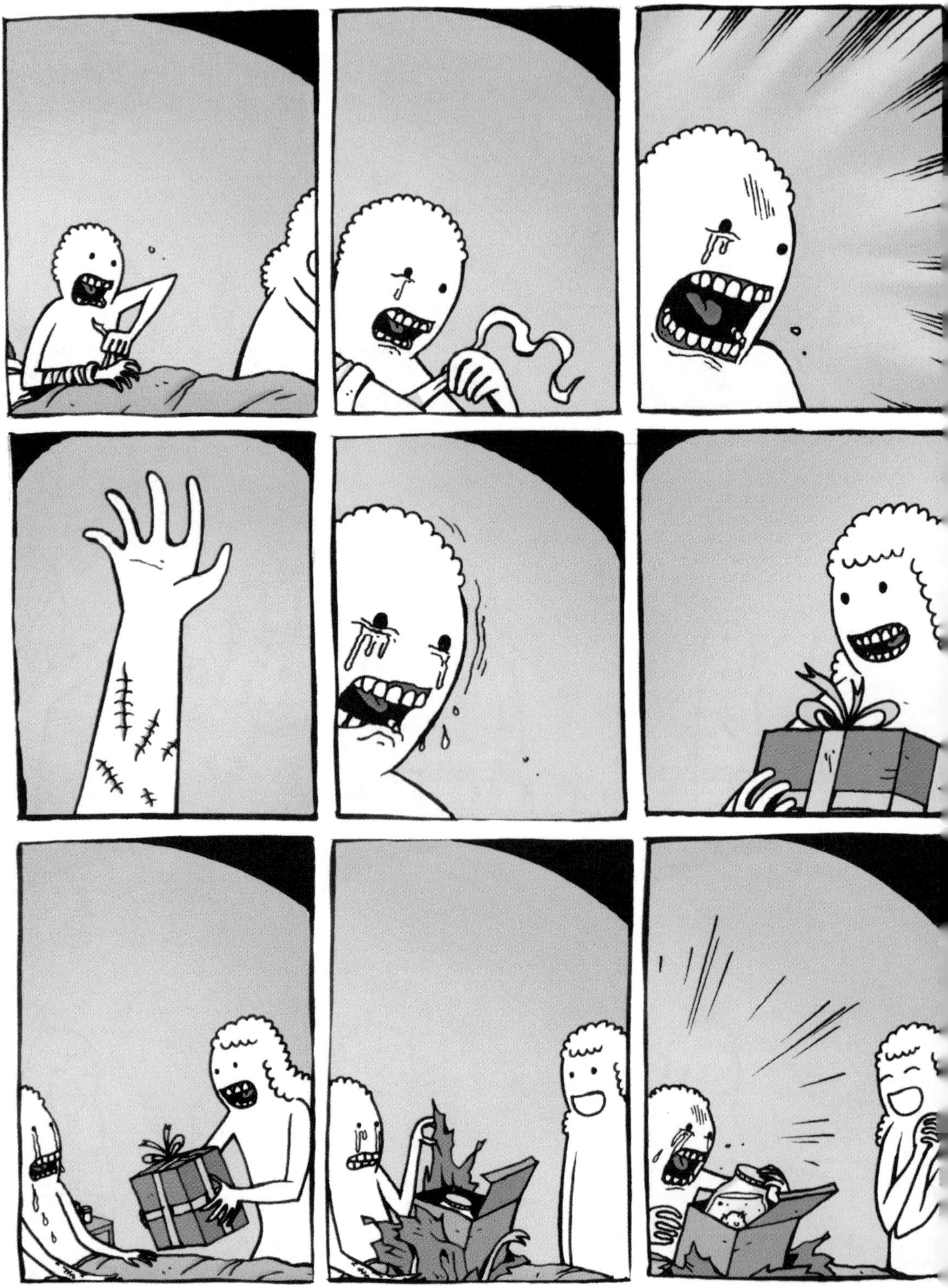

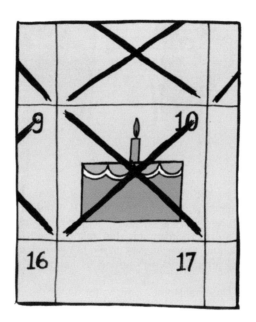

About the Author

Growing up, Manix Abrera loved to watch his father draw editorial cartoons and comics for the Philippine Daily Inquirer. In 2001, while Manix was still a Fine Arts student at the University of the Philippines, he landed a gig in the same newspaper and started contributing his daily strips, Kikomachine Komix. Since then, he has produced over twenty comic book compilations, including two wordless graphic novels entitled "12" and "14".

Manix is a three-time National Book Awardee for his works, "14", "News Hardcore", and "Kikomachine Komix Volume 14: Alaala ng Kinabukasan". He has mounted several solo exhibitions at Galerie Stephanie and Vargas Museum. Some of his works were also staged in a group exhibition at the Metropolitan Museum of Manila.

Manix loves to ride his bike, hike, swim, and dive. He lives in Manila, Philippines with his family.

manixabrera.com

@ kikomachinekomix

@ manix_abrera

@ manix_abrera